The Lightning Tree

EMILY WOOF

FABER & FABER

First published in 2015
by Faber & Faber Ltd
Bloomsbury House
74–77 Great Russell Street
London WC1B 3DA
This paperback edition published in 2016

Typeset by Faber & Faber Ltd
Printed and bound by CPI Group (UK) Ltd, Croydon CR0 4YY

The right of Emily Woof to be identified as author of this work
has been asserted in accordance with Section 77 of the
Copyright Designs and Patents Act 1988

Lyrics quoted on page 88 are from 'Jocko Homo' by Devo.
Lyrics by Mark Mothersbaugh. Reproduced with permission.

A CIP record for this book
is available from the British Library

ISBN 978-0-571-25402-6

FSC
www.fsc.org
MIX
Paper from
responsible sources
FSC® C101712

Born in Newcastle upon Tyne, Emily Woof has written for stage, film and radio. She has also worked as a trapeze artist and actor. Her first novel, *The Whole Wide Beauty*, was published to great acclaim in 2010. She lives in London with her husband and two children.

Further praise for *The Lightning Tree*:

'Woof's lyrical storytelling moves effectively through time and place [and] the result is transcendent. What unfolds is a story not just of young love but of how to cope when it is lost and shattered.' *Financial Times*

'An unusual but convincing love story that charts the often-distant lives of her two distinctive and appealing characters, written with wit and a lyrical flourish.' *Daily Mail*

'*The Lightning Tree* is a more ambitious book than *One Day*, moving away from the relationship much of the time to focus on themes of class, family and religion. There are undertones of Jeffrey Eugenides' *The Marriage Plot*, which also sees its college-age protagonists wade through issues of love and spirituality while looking for answers.' *Irish Times*

'A love story at its heart, it also explores the many strange ways in which our lives branch out and intersect. Even more daringly, it captures those rare moments of transcendence that elude not just words but understanding, yet still have the power to shape a life. As such, Emily Woof could easily have fallen foul of feyness or whimsy, but in fact, as her time-lapse narrative spools out, there is not a page of this sympathetic novel that isn't illuminated by her verve and wit.' *The Lady*

―――――――――――

by the same author

THE WHOLE WIDE BEAUTY

To Hame, Samuel and Louis

I

Let us start right here, with a man and a woman in bed by the sea. The woman is Ursula. She and the man are gazing into each other's eyes, astonished by the love they feel, and as they move together, without speaking, everything around them dissolves; the thin yellow curtains of the bed and breakfast, the polyester sheets, the two white teacups and tiny kettle all fly away to nothing. Ursula sees only this man. She is grateful it is him after all this time, and as they crash on to the shore of each other they touch the earth, the moon and stars.

It is not possible for you to feel this. All this astonished gazing, sea gushing and planetary union is too much, too intimate, too soon! – but I long to communicate love to you. These pages are so dry, the flat of your reading device so cold! If I could I'd jump out, strike you with the full weight of my arm, make your heart pound, tickle you, caress you, do anything in my power to make you feel it. I want to reveal love in all its forms, in a girl skipping, a boy reading; in a time before Ursula, with a laundry worker singing at her tub, or a woman alone on a hill, where a tree rears up, its roots alive, its branches stripped bare like a claw raking the sky, and in a single moment, she is hollowed to nothing by a blast so bright the world will ever after seem dark to her. I want to show you all this, and more, even the great failure of love, so this is a 'poor do' as Mary would say, and we must begin again, not with lovers by the sea, but at the root of the thing, in another time, or perhaps the same one, when Ursula is at the very beginning of herself, under the ash tree in the garden of 35 Eslington Road, Newcastle. She is only six months old, but already she has done much to be here; existing for billions of years in secret codes, imprinting herself on her infinite family, generation to generation, mud-crawler to bushbaby, hominid warrior all the way to Hubert Tate of Tate's Laundry, Padiham, waiting until her own double helix clicks into place making all her pasts present. Then the inevitable begins, cells slipping, splitting, silently dividing in the warm darkness, heart pulsing within membrane, the sudden bloom of liver, kidneys, lungs, soft sponges of blood, the astonishing hardening of bone, the skin clouding round, the wild free-fall into senses, briny sweetness, murmurs, muted fireworks, and pushing through unyielding skeleton to the shocking air, into the feel of skin, the smell of milk, and Ursula is suddenly material.

She inherits her pram, a wondrous vessel, in which she now lies, oblivious to all that's gone before, gazing up at branches veining the sky like spilt ink. Her blankets are wrapped tightly around her. She strains against the wool, her torso rolling this way and that until, with a surge of force, she reaches out for the black lines of the branches with their black buds swelling from their twigs. She knows them, reaches out to guide them inside her, but the wind blows them away. She gurgles, a light easy splash. They are playing with her! She'll get them next time. She reaches out

4

again but cannot touch them. Sadness mists her and is gone as quickly as it came. She gurgles happily as the branches thin into whiteness, and she senses distance for the first time, the deep wonder of it, the space between things.

Her mother is apart from Ursula, in the basement kitchen, putting an elastic band around a stack of CND leaflets, Save Our Future: Stop The Madness! This is Joyce. Her mind is always busy with the future. She intends to save the world from nuclear attack, singlehandedly if she has to, but she is also thinking about the children's supper, Peter's meeting, and the best six arguments for non-proliferation. Bethany (seven) and Jonathan (four) are at her feet playing with dolls and saucepans, busy at their tasks, as Joyce tips peelings, plum stones and burnt toast on to newspaper and folds it into a parcel. She opens the back door and puts it outside. There's an old veg box there already with another parcel in, ready to take down to the bins. She looks over at the pram beneath the ash tree, as big as a boat in a bay. She puts baby Ursula out in the garden every day. The fresh air helps her sleep, and if she's inside Jonathan can't be trusted not to reach in and hit her. It's best to keep the children separate; Bethany with her dolls, Jonathan by the radiator with his pans, Ursula outside under the tree.

Inside, she starts a list at the table: Osborne Road, Tankerville, Holland Road, Oak Lane, the route she will take with the leaflets. The children can help put them through the doors, and on the way back they might stop at the park for half an hour. If it wasn't for the baby, she could take them further afield, Heaton, Byker, Wallsend perhaps. Joyce is anxious to raise people's consciousness. Raise them up! Everyone in the city must know about the CND. Campaign for Nuclear

5

Disarmament. *Seee Unnnn Deee*. Even baby Ursula knows this sound. Joyce talks of little else; the Aldermaston March, Maralinga 1956, Monte Bello Island, Christmas Island where the servicemen were told they could simply wash the radiation off with soap.

In her pram in the garden Ursula follows the black lines of the tree. They are nothing more than herself, broadening and hardening, stretching outwards. She hears the sweet shushing sibilance of the wind. She is creating it all, blowing through her lips, making the wind blow, the clouds scud, the branches sway. The ash tree loves her and she loves it. She hears the click-shush of the back door. Her lips start to open and close, making plosives, suckings, kisses, coaxing the kitchen faces closer. She senses life, pans, intentions, voices, and her mother soft in woollen green with brown moons and milky skin. She wants her to come. No one comes. Great howls rise from inside her. She has heard them before. They come from deep within. She is a wonderful siren. She cannot stop the cries. They leap out of her, twisting her body, contorting it, searching for certainty. She reaches her arms high towards the branches. They are widening cracks in the sky. Something is changing. The branches are spreading. The branches fatten and flap, cawing and shrieking.

Mummy! Look! shouts Bethany, looking up from her dolls.

Jonathan pulls at Joyce's skirt at the window, Birsss! Birsss!

Joyce looks out into the garden. The hood of Ursula's pram is blown out of shape, jagged like a broken umbrella. Shreds of black stick out, jostling. A crow is on the baby. Joyce's body moves before her mind, up the steps and down

6

the path. The crow is pecking, flapping, positioning itself. She runs, arms waving, her screams as primitive as the bird's.

Aaaaaaaaagh. God . . .! Shoooooooo!

The bird lifts into the air, pumping oily wings. Others wheel down from the branches, and they fly off screeching across the Town Moor. Joyce clutches the baby to her, half expecting the woollen bundle to burst with blood. The bird has killed her. Joyce's heart pounds as she runs back to the house. Jonathan stumbles to meet her, watching, frightened by her mask of horror. She looks like the women on the statue on the walk home from Fenwick's, he thinks, frozen in black bronze, wailing for their dead. He starts to cry.

It's alright, my darling . . . It's alright.

She pushes past him down the steps. Under the orange lamp, she uncurls her arms. Ursula stares up at her, her mouth shut tight, a short straight line.

There there . . . they've gone now, Joyce rocks her.

Is she dead? says Bethany.

She will make a bottle and comfort her. Thank God. No harm done. She'll put the pram nearer the back door next time.

Bethany leans in close.

Caw caw! she croons.

Ursula is stiff as a corn dolly.

There there . . . says Joyce, and starts to sing, Ride a cock-horse to Banbury Cross, to see a fine lady upon a white horse, rings on her fingers and . . .

As she holds Ursula close, her voice is high and soft. She puts milk into a pan. Strands of hair fall on to her face and she pushes them away. She lays Ursula gently on the draining board, and cuts thick slices of bread. She gets butter,

7

breaks two eggs into a saucepan, puts a match to the grill, lowers the hissing blue jets.

It won't be long, not long, she sings, sliding the slices under the grill. This is the way we make the toast, make the toast . . .

She pours warm milk into Ursula's bottle, turns on the radio, serves the eggs to Jonathan and Bethany, sits in the armchair, and in one arm Ursula nestles, her little fingers gripping the bottle as she sucks. *Listen with Mother* begins. Ursula's eyes start to close. The wildness of the crows dims in her and she sleeps.

The attack by the crows is Ursula's first experience of the world as utterly separate. You might think it will stay with her, haunt her as she grows up; that some irreparable damage has been done to her that will influence her life and how she lives it, but the truth is she will remember nothing of it. She will grow up in what you might call a reasonably ordinary way. Far bigger birds will come for her in time; one greater than the rest, it will carry her clean away, and strip her of everything. This bird will be far harder to survive, but for now Ursula is sleeping, and the telephone is ringing in Eslington Road, and Joyce is answering it, Ursula still held in her arms . . .

Joyce . . .? Oh Joyce! Oh . . . the voice is desperate.

Mum, what is it?

They're here again . . . They're in again. I daren't go downstairs. Oh Joyce.

Call the police, Mum!

Oh God . . .! I can't . . . I . . .

I'll call them.

Joyce . . .

I'll call them, Mum. I'll tell them to come. I'm putting the phone down now . . .

Hurry, says Mary as she sinks back down into her bed. She cannot move. The eiderdown is pulled up to her nose. Her round face stares up at the ceiling, searching for help in the cracked plaster. This is Joyce's mother, Ursula's grandmother, two hundred miles away in Padiham, Lancashire, with unknown men downstairs. They have put her under their spell, robbed her of movement. If she moves the ceiling will crash down, the floor open up, she'll be dragged under Pendle Hill itself and sucked into the bowels of the earth. Their noise entered her dreams, woke her, in the early morning. She heard them downstairs prising open chests and cupboards. She's been lying there ever since. Last time they broke down the back door. Dennis and Iris from next door had called the police. Dennis and Iris had moved since, left their house unoccupied, retired to a bungalow in Morecambe, damn them. The sea air was good for Dennis's respiration, Iris had said. The way she said it, pompous. Curse them. Curse his bloody resp-ir-a-tion. Without them, she's easy pickings.

She longs for sleep, to stop what is happening happening, to let the past flow through her, so wonderfully light, while her body lies heavy in the hollow made in the mattress, fifty years her burrow. She can't tell if they are still down there, poking about, opening the walnut chest, rummaging amongst bags, touching her china. A church bell peals feebly in the distance, barely penetrating the thick velvet curtains at the window. Damn God. He's not coming for her. She moans aloud. Joyce said she'd call the police. She must get up, do her hair. She heaves herself to sitting, swings her legs to the floor, and shuffles along the worn path to the dressing table. She opens the curtains a crack. The sunlight is a blasted reminder of her darkness. The church steeple postures like a witch's hat against the sky. She lets the curtain fall, slumps to the velvet-covered stool, and feels for her ivory comb in the gloom. She parts her hair, scoring a line down the back of her head. Her thoughts prick as she starts to plait, her fingers snappy like knitting needles. What have they taken? The Chinese vases? The glass pictures? The ornate Chinese dogs? All her beautiful things. She is afraid to think of it. As she plaits, her thoughts turn in on themselves, repetitive and entangled as her braids. Nothing has ever been right. The man from the corner shop didn't give her a bag for her chocolate yesterday, Dennis and Iris had taken the magnolia tree with them when they left, dug it out of the ground and put it on a truck though she'd begged them not to, done it to spite her, she's sure, to rob her of its brief, astonishing flowers, and Wally, blast him, dead twenty years, never had ambition, never gave her more than the housekeeping, never paid for the luxuries she craved. All her craving had been for nothing; it's why she started the shop but nothing sold, Padiham folk had no taste. It's why her house was so stuffed with beautiful things, they were all from the shop, the remainders; filled her heart they did, and now the robbers were taking them, sadness and anger fold into her like the outer strands of the plait returning to the centre, the raw hurt of her. Life is unfair. Joyce is to blame. She should have stayed at home with her, her own mother, but she ran away, married a runt, spawned a brood, and lives like a slave looking after them and her no-good husband, wasting her time with politics. What's it to her?! When will it all end?

Her twisting fingers reach the bottom of her hair. The plait reaches to her waist; she secures it in her left hand, unwinds a length of cotton with her right, pinches the thread tight against the hair, wraps it five times fast around the plait and bites off the cotton with her teeth. The police will be here. She coils the two plaits carefully and pins them into buns.

Next the hat: secured with the pewter pin. Not her best silver one with the gemstone head, that's in the lacquer box in the front room wrapped in tissue paper with an elastic band round it waiting for things to be different.

The doorbell rings. She opens the bedroom door, hair done, hat on, still in her vest and bloomers. The air is cold. The front door is open wide, her house exposed, violated. She grips the banister and shuffles downstairs. She can see an empty space where the ornate dogs stood. The drawer in the sideboard's open. The hall cupboard has gone. The whole thing. Good God, they've taken furniture. Huge pieces, spirited away. Two policemen appear in the open doorway. Mrs Paige from the paper shop is behind them, her sweet face appalled. Oh Mrs Morely! Oh what have they done? A face of hypocrisy and contempt. Mary can't stand her.

My beautiful things! Oh . . .

Tell us what has happened, Mrs Morely.

They must have had a bloody lorry. What is to become of me? All my bags!

She's kept all of them over the years, in drawers, stockpiling them as though they were pound notes, little green ones from Grainger's, white paper ones from the corner shop, brown from the fruit shop, plastic from Benham's. She likes to lay one out on her knee, iron it flat with the palm of her hand, fold it neatly and return it to a drawer. Bags have comforted her over the years, but now the robbers have got them all. The policemen take her into the kitchen. Her chair and table are still there as they were, covered in newspaper. Mary never wipes a surface. It is a low slavish task. Her resolve never to engage in domestic cleaning is integral to her. She lays down newspaper to cover any mess. Her living space in the house has dwindled to worn pathways from bedroom to bathroom, kitchen to front corridor. She opens the drawer in the newspaper table and rummages inside.

My father's watch! His pocket watch! Gone! Gone . . .! Oh . . .

One of the policemen crouches next to her.

Now, now, Mrs Morely. Let's go through everything slowly.

The policemen make notes as Mary lists everything that's been taken in exact detail – the Peking China dogs on either side of the fireplace, the magazine rack of carved walnut, the Poole pottery filled with roses made of stiffened silk, so lifelike, the brass monkeys with the Indian faces, the Wedgwood clock, the glass paintings from Holland, the chaise longue, the glass lamp, all thick with dust but the robbers knew what they were doing, the lacquer box with the gold sovereigns, the Chinese fan, the German chest, her corn plasters! She cries out, thinking of them. They were unused. She left the rings of pink lint on the handle of the walnut cupboard. The bloody thieves'll have their hands on them now.

The policemen exchange glances. They're not sure whether to call for an ambulance. That glazed look. They've seen it before.

Why have they done this to me? What did I do to deserve this?

The church bells ring out in mockery. Mary hears the voice of her mother in them. You deserve what you get, Mary. You were not put on this earth to be happy. The sound blows her backwards through the years. She sees her mother's face, the deep lines carved out of something sterner than flesh, her grey disapproving eyes, Annie Tate, fierce and furious in her sudden hatred; her dreadful love of God.

Mrs Morely, says the older policeman, you can't stay here any more.

She's a daughter in Newcastle, says Mrs Paige, her number's in the table drawer.

May I use your telephone to ring your daughter, Mrs Morely?

Mary is coming crashing into Ursula's story. What has this old bird to do with love? With anything? Ursula doesn't want her; she doesn't need a bitter grandmother in a mushroom hat, with her bitter chocolates, and her bitter past. If she could she would unclasp herself from her mother, step down from her lap, take the train across the Pennines and give those police a piece of her mind. No! You can't ring anyone! Stop! Don't send her to me! This fearsome old vulture will corrupt and poison me. Keep her in her broken house of knick-knacks. Nail her in! She will crush me. She will suffocate me. The slim strands of Ursula's beginnings have survived the crows but may not withstand this. But no one can stop Mary, not Ursula, not even Joyce. She is

13

coming. She is storming into Newcastle like a dark cloud, making the sky spit with rain.

Ursula is in the garden of Eslington Road when she arrives. Five painted beads are tied to either side of her push-chair. Purple, yellow, pink, green and blue. Ursula watches them, all at peace. Purple and yellow fall against each other, green and pink fall against each other. Blue is separate. She moves it to join green and pink. It drags against the string. She shunts purple and yellow along to make a tight row, a caterpillar, five painted knuckles. She slides the blue away, and moves it back. Away and back. Sometimes it seems like the head of the caterpillar, sometimes the tail. Sometimes all the beads seem joined together even when they are separate. Sometimes beads, string, pram, and her own hands all seem joined as one.

Her mother's voice is coming closer.

Ursula, say hello to Ganny Mary.

Bulging eyes, bulbous nose, loose and sagging cheeks push into the pushchair. A smell of sweet caramel and face powder. A voice coos softly.

What a chicken . . .!

Mary pops something dark into her mouth. Ursula stares up, watching her chew and suck.

What a little chicken!

Mary places a small dark rectangle in Ursula's mouth. A black, intense secret. Ursula is astonished.

Bournville, whispers Mary, and starts to cry.

Ursula cries too. The darkness of this secret is dreadful. She tries to get it out of her mouth with her fingers.

There, there, says Mary, something sweet, for a sweet girl.

Skip! Jump! Land! Turn! Ursula is eight now, in a windswept playground in a grey corner of Newcastle. A loop of elastic is strung around the ankles of her friends, Ashley Freckles and Jeanette Pug-nose, making two parallel lines for Ursula Moon-head, to negotiate with a complex sequence of jumps, pings, and two-foot and one-foot landings. She is wild with enthusiasm. Higher, higher! Her jumps are impossible. No run-up, a standing start, hoisting her legs up into a tuck, just enough to clear the elastic. Higher! she cries. Inch by inch, centimetre by centimetre (Ursula's world is on the cusp of metric), the elastic moves up Ashley's and Jeanette's legs, up to the thighs. Thighs thighs! Thighs high skies!

Wooooeee! She does it!

The bell rings for the end of playtime. Children funnel towards the classrooms. Jeanette and Ashley run off to join a last-minute game of tag around the prefab building. A teacher bellows from the doors. Two boys, Howard and Daniel, in anoraks, skulk at the edge of the playground, watching Ursula as she gathers up her elastic. It's a new one and she winds it carefully round her hand. She's wishing she'd stayed with Jeanette and Ashley. She doesn't want to walk in with Howard, no matter how coincidentally.

Not that she is in love with him. Love is far from Ursula's mind. When it does come it will be with a different boy. Her discomfort about Howard is that his home, like hers, bears the special and confusing sign in the front window: a friendly, flowery sun that politely warns of total annihilation. Nuclear Power, it smiles; No Thanks. Howard makes Ursula think about the nuclear holocaust. He attends CND rallies with his mother like she does. Ursula thinks Howard's mother looks somehow smudged like a painting in the rain, but does not know why. She cannot know that his mother has acute depression and will one day take her own life on the Newcastle-to-Edinburgh line. All Ursula knows is Howard reminds her of things she prefers not to think about.

He's coming towards her across the playground, carrying conkers on strings. She is afraid he might want to talk about the exact position of the nuclear missiles in Russia and how long it will take for them to reach Newcastle. Once he told her radiation would cook her from the inside. To silence him she gives him her special slanted look. It says, what we know is secret, stupid. Don't talk about it.

Hello, Ursula, he says. His voice seems to resonate with the whole nuclear issue.

Hello, Howard, she replies quietly.

She gives him another look, then turns and walks quickly away, satisfied she has averted disaster.

Ursula is constantly developing new tactics for keeping at bay the things that trouble her. Not just the nuclear threat but more private tensions at home. Toast is one of her tactics. Buttered, it comforts most ills. Another is television.

Here she is on an ordinary Saturday, a seed of herself

in the dark house, invisible to the outside world, eating toast and watching Saturday-morning TV. It is the seventies, more or less, a time in the history of humans when an eight-year-old girl can watch the fluttering box in a darkened room, all on her own, for hours, without her parents knowing or caring. Ursula is neither happy nor unhappy. She is in her favourite position, in a headstand on the sofa, her legs stretching up the wall between the frilly-edged mirror and one of her mother's CND posters. The top of her head presses into the bright cushions, their floral pattern so close its tulips splash and blur before her eyes. She adjusts her gaze to follow them as they continue up along the sofa – red, blue, orange – red, blue, orange – until a seam interrupts the sequence and rides roughshod through the blooms, cutting their hearts in two.

On the television a man is standing in a muddy field holding a cow on a rope. Ursula has been here for hours like this, losing track of time, moving on and off the sofa, in and out of different inverted positions. She gazes around the room, imagining that she is the right way up in an upside-down world. She pictures the floor as the ceiling, the patch of sky outside as the ground, but she's unconvinced: the windows are too high up on the wall, and if the room were really upside down her feet would be on the ceiling but they don't reach that far. The mantelpiece, the TV and mirrors stubbornly remain unchanged in their correct place, telling Ursula that it is she who is upside down in a perfectly normal sitting room, until suddenly it comes, as it sometimes does, like a miracle; something slips, her mind gives up, and there it is, a whole new world where everything is brilliantly topsy-turvy. It makes her laugh. It had been there all along! The knowledge delights her, and instantly cancels out the topsy-turvy tensions at home, not least that of the mirrors.

Four years ago when Ganny Mary – Bethany's attempt to say Granny that stuck – finally accepted that she could never go back to Padiham and sold her house, the mirrors followed her to Newcastle. All forty-three of them. Ganny Mary has told Ursula a hundred times why she has so many. Wally's wet batteries wouldn't provide her with the income she deserved, so she continued with her half of the shop selling antiques and laces. One side of the counter for wet batteries for the factories, the other for 'beautiful things'. At first she had dreamed of customers in fur coats coming and going, ladies of the county, sophisticates from Manchester who knew quality when they saw it, but they never came. Padiham people had no money for luxuries. The shop was badly situated on the edge of the town, just where the traffic picked up speed heading into Burnley.

They were bankrupt, and forced to close. Mary couldn't bear to be parted from all her beautiful stock – the ornate dogs, the Chinese vases, the Indian lace, the lacquered cabinets. Her biggest passion, the lovely mirrors, gilt-edged, mahogany-framed, ivory-backed, were brought back to her house to gather dust. Burglars took most of them over the years, but Mary had kept forty-three hidden in the attic, and now Ursula's dark house glints with them from top to bottom. They are in the bedrooms, the sitting room, the toilet, on the backs of doors, along the corridors. In the bathroom alone there are seven. Even now from her headstand on the sofa Ursula can see at least two. There's one above the mantelpiece in which she can see her feet up the wall and one tucked into the bookshelf in which she can see the CND poster of a woman in front of a mushroom cloud screaming tell us the truth!

The mirrors often show things Ursula does not want to see, like this distressed woman. They also show her Ursula herself. There is no avoiding her face and body in them. She sees herself leaving the house in the vestibule mirror, senses her movement in the front hall. In the kitchen she sees the crown of her head, her waist, her feet from three differing heights. An arched mirror like a church window with a golden frame stands at the top of the stairs to the basement. There is a mirror on every landing and half-landing. On a trip from the basement kitchen to her bedroom at the top of the house she sees herself a total of twenty-seven times. It is hardly surprising she has developed a habit of looking for herself, for anticipating Ursula-ness. Here she comes, there she goes, arriving, leaving, standing, sitting. Ursula with sly look, Ursula with a swish. She is not alone in this; everyone in the house has developed a unique relationship to the mirrors. For Ganny Mary the mirrors represent beauty and the possibility of happiness. For Joyce the mirrors are a reminder of Wally, her mild-mannered father. He used to enlist her help to paint their chipped gilt edges. They'd work silently together on them with a pot of gold varnish. Even Mary had smiled to see them. For Peter mirrors are a reflection of the bourgeois obsession with the self. He wants them taken down. It is bad enough having to live with his mother-in-law without having to have her dusty things. Joyce wants them kept up and wins the argument. They live in a dark north-facing house, she says. Jonathan, at age ten, good at maths and science, works out that 43 mirrors =

1067 cubic feet of much-needed reflected light.

On the TV John Craven is riding a bicycle. Ursula is still upside down. The blood in her head is pulsing. Her legs fall akimbo on the wall. She doesn't like programmes in which real people talk about real things. They make her feel stupid, like when she hears her mother and father say important things like *foreign policy*, *unilateral*, *non-proliferation*, or *annihilation*. She likes cartoons, though she can never admit this to her mother. She can hear Joyce now, speaking on the telephone, using her serious nuclear voice.

If Sarah and Chris agree, Ernst, we can get this through at national level . . .

Ursula is surprised to hear her mother. She thought she was out at a meeting. She lets her body slide down from the sofa on to the floor, lies horizontal with her face against the carpet, and looks through the door. In a series of reflections in three mirrors, she sees her there, legs crossed, head cocked to the receiver, chewing a pencil, notebook in hand.

They have to understand, she says. They have to! . . . The Americans are going ahead no matter what . . . I'll talk with Sarah and Chris . . .

Sarah and Chris are her mother's CND friends. They are married but look like brother and sister. Ursula is wary of them because when they come to the house, her mother often looks worried after they have gone, and says things to her father like 'it's going to be tricky now'. It upsets Ursula that her mother is trying to save the world, and people like Sarah and Chris are getting in her way.

Over the past eight years her mother's CND activities have intensified. She is no longer a humble volunteer posting leaflets, but a prominent local figure, addressing rallies,

20

organising marches, and attending something called strategy meetings. She often meets with anti-nuclear colleagues like Jane, Ernst, Chris and Sarah in the front room. Ursula can hear the urgency in their voices as they discuss how long it will be before the inevitable happens. From hiding behind the sofa Ursula knows exactly where the SS-22 missiles are stationed in Russia, and how long they will take to fly to England. She assumes one is aiming directly at Newcastle, or her mother wouldn't be so worried. Howard once told her that it would only take an SS-98 missile twenty-seven minutes to arrive in the town centre from Minsk and that it would incinerate the entire city as far as Wallsend in exactly five seconds.

The rest of Ursula's knowledge is patchy. She knows a pasty-faced man called Callaghan, prime minister of England, Pershings. The Americans are behind it all apparently so Ursula hates them most of all. They are all men, her mother says, bad men, provoking attack. Callaghan might as well have put a target over the country.

She often accompanies her mother on marches to stop the madness. The last time she made a nuclear missile by painting a carpet roll, and they carried it on their shoulders wearing boilersuits and skull masks. Howard was there with his mother. She was still looking smudged, wearing a poncho, black eyeliner running, smoking a roll-up. Joyce addressed the crowd from a podium. We are not a peace movement, she said. We believe in armed struggle when it is needed, we understand the need to defend ourselves, but the threat of total annihilation is wrong. As right-thinking people I urge you all to rise up and be heard, to tell our government it must forgo!

Ursula is so proud of her mother's crusade for survival, but her nights are often filled with nightmares. She has the same one over and over again. A bomb is dropped in the centre of Newcastle. She and her mother are trying to leave along the Great North Road to Morpeth when Ursula loses hold of her mother's hand and wanders on to the wide empty coast of Northumberland. The death powder from the bomb is coming for her, airborne, and inescapable. She must find her mother before it's too late. Deep down Ursula knows that her mother is already dead. She wakes up shaking and silent, but never allows herself to cry. Her mother says crying is for spilt milk.

She is still upside down. *John Craven's Newsround* is still on. John Craven is a talking puppet. Once he mentioned Pershing missiles in his bland voice. Ursula does not trust John Craven. There is nothing bland about Pershing. She launches into a back somersault. Her head narrowly misses the floor and she lands on her coccyx with a thud.

Who's that? Who is it?

It is Ganny Mary shouting.

Ursula lies motionless, waiting for the pain to subside.

Joyce? Is that you?

Ursula jumps to her feet. She's upright for the first time in hours. The room swims. She runs into the corridor, expecting to see her mum there on the phone, but there is only her own reflection in the hall mirror. It is often like this. Her mum comes and goes without warning. There is no sign of Jonathan or Bethany either. It is hard to pin anyone down in the house. The only person Ursula can be sure of is Ganny Mary, who is always there.

She runs downstairs, three at a time, veers round the

newel post, skips along the back corridor and there in the toilet, on the seat, like an old toad, is Ganny Mary, a tear of paper in hand, grunting gently. Ursula steps back, disgusted. Ganny Mary never closes the toilet door. Ursula retreats into the kitchen and quickly flips upside down, her feet against the crockery cupboard. She watches the mirror on the back of the kitchen door for signs of her grandmother, hears a flush, and Ganny Mary emerges, buttoning up her fawn skirt, pulling down the brown housecoat.

Who's there? she says crossly.

Me, shouts Ursula. This me of Ursula has learned that her grandmother's past, with all its great failures, means toffees.

Ganny Mary sits back down at her place at the end of the long table. Apart from trips to the toilet, she is glued to this spot all day in all her brownness, like a swollen teabag, stewing in her misery. Her big hat provides a perfect circle of gloom from which she glowers at the world.

Where is your mother? It's not right! Good God! she sighs.

She looks at Ursula in her handstand against the wall, an upside-down slither of a girl.

It's all wrong, she says reaching into her cow-hide bag for a paper bag. Ursula kicks down, and walks forward with her mouth open.

What is all wrong? says Ursula, as a toffee is popped in, knowing what will follow, and how to play the game. Ganny Mary's outpourings can take her into the jaws of death: sometimes to places so deep and wretched with anger that Ursula's shocked to the core. She enjoys feeling breathless with injustice at Ganny Mary's stories of betrayal, while anticipating the next toffee.

Is it the robbers? says Ursula, unlocking her grand-mother's bitter box.

Oh Ursy, I still think of that green bucket, cries Ganny Mary. What could they want with it? They took my life away. Oh it should never have happened! I should never have been left like this. Families should stay together. Your mother should be with me, she should never have left. Oh the things I've lost, the bird pictures, the Chinese silks from Manchester, my daddy's watch . . .!

Never mind, says Ursula, in her best comforting voice. Her toffee is diminishing rapidly in her mouth and she wants another. I'm here, Ganny Mary . . . never mind!

Ganny Mary is reaching into the toffees again. Ursula steps forward with her mouth open. The old woman strokes her face, and pops another one in.

And the photographs, Ganny Mary! says Ursula, prompting, her mouth full.

All gone, Ursy. All the people from the laundry. They were all that was left of them. What could they mean to anyone else?

Ursula watches her grandmother's tears, amazed at the sheer wetness of her face.

The frames were worth money too . . . and oh my father . . .

Ganny Mary can see the space on the sideboard in the Padiham kitchen where the photographs sat accumulating dust and grease until it was impossible to see the frames were silver. Her father. Her mother. Wally, her husband. All gone. She feels her own death, the sadness of a life without sufficient joy.

What did they want with those things? Ursula chimes in.

Those robbers must be . . . she tries to find a word powerful enough for the utter perplexity of it all . . .

. . . mad! she concludes.

Ganny Mary has described the photographs so many times and in such detail that Ursula feels she knows each of her dead relations personally. Her great-grandmother, Annie, stern in her starched blouse, a woman of great religious devotion, full of fire and brimstone. Her great-grandfather, Hubert, loving and kind, everything a man should be, the foundation of all good things, who started the laundry from nothing, who wore the gold watch, and whose blue eyes sparkled with Lancashire sunlight.

Ganny Mary sighs.

Oh my daddy . . .! He was a man.

Ursula knows the doorsteps of Padiham gleamed like rows of bright teeth because of Hubert Tate. From the age of sixteen, he sold donkey stones door to door for the housewives to whiten them. He would offer to do the polishing himself, drop on to his knees in front of them with all the swagger of a musketeer. He was born with the power to transform, Ganny Mary told her; he changed the look of the very streets around him. It was his way, to brighten things, make them better. He'd saved fifty pounds by the time he proposed to Annie Featherly, the prettiest girl in Padiham, and he used it to build a laundry by the river.

He knew about progress, says Ganny Mary.

He brought in the labour-saving machines! rejoins Ursula. The iron warmer, the flat press . . .!

He was handsome too. And tall.

And he was the first man in Padiham to have an upstairs bathroom with a flushing toilet!

My mother was the prettiest woman in the town too. Until God made a hatchet of her face.

Aunt Sissy's doing, says Ursula, repeating what she's heard Ganny Mary say. She was a wrong 'un.

Obsessed she was. With bloody religion. She influenced my mother.

She made your mother hard. That's the trouble with religion! says Ursula, shaking her head and pouting slightly.

Oh Mary, says Ganny Mary putting on a high supercilious voice to mimic her mother. Cry if you must. Cry child, cry! You'll pee the less!

Ursula is captivated. She loves it when Ganny Mary puts on voices. Her language becomes strange and bristles with a kind of rudeness.

Your mother wouldn't let you have toys, would she, Ganny Mary? she says, stoking her fire. She wouldn't let you go to dances, not even when you were older.

Nothing gay or giddy, that's what my mother used to say.

Not for Mary! says Ursula, taking over the posh Lancashire voice, full of airs and graces. She jumps on to a stool, gesticulating theatrically. You are on this earth to suffer, child! Suffer!!

The toffee is sticking to the roof of her mouth. She waits for Ganny Mary to stand up and join in, to become her mother Annie again, to pound the table with her fist, and shriek Ursula's favourite line, 'Go to your room until the Lord comes for you! Begone child! Begone!' but Ganny Mary bows her head. Ursula knows she has gone to a place where she cannot follow. Disappointed, she jumps off the stool, and quickly puts a slice of bread in the toaster. She flips upside down again, hands on the floor, legs up the wall above the radiator as Mary fractures with memories, seeing the laundry photograph in her mind. Her father stands proudly in front of twelve laundrywomen in white aprons, the delivery boy at the end, his white terrier by his side. How fine he is with his thick moustache. A beacon of hope. Her mother, Annie, stands next to him, her arm through his, also smiling, and in between them is Mary, her little head poking out with a cheeky smile. She remembers how she wasn't to be in the photograph. It was official, for the laundry, her father had said, but she'd snuck in nevertheless; the laundry, her father's great enterprise, was everything to Mary. She intended to help him with the ledgers, understand the machines as she got older. She believed her parents were schooling her to work alongside them. Those were the good days, each one bringing happiness, whether learning numbers with her father in the laundry office, or walking with her mother to Tythe Farm for eggs and milk. Everything changed after. Her mother went up Pendle and lay down, and when she came back she was different. The women in the laundry whispered. Mary's home was shattered . . .

The toast pops up. Toast! Quick Ursula take it. Action! Don't get sucked into the cycles of Mary's past. Agh! It burns her fingers. She drops it.

Bloody hell! What are you doing there? snaps Ganny Mary, glaring at the fallen toast as though it might answer.

Nothing, says Ursula.

Mary groans, wrenched back from the storm of childhood, just as she was on the brink of being swept away, taking everything along with her. She looks around, registering the disappointing fact of her life now, in Eslington Road.

Where's your mother? she exhales reproachfully.

This is the question that nags Ganny Mary night and day. Where has her daughter Joyce gone? Ursula rarely knows the answer. Her mother's whereabouts are the great unanswerable question. Even her father seems mystified by it. Ursula picks up the toast, butters it, and bites into it with relish. Making toast, like going upside down, alleviates worries such as not knowing where her mother is, or the violence of Ganny Mary's temper. The taste of the buttered toast is utterly delicious, and always will be. Ursula will outgrow television and going upside down, but her love of toast will stay with her for ever. In her teenage years with Jerry, she will discover the art of combining toppings: Marmite and peanut butter and jam, processed cheese and tomatoes and ham, marmalade and Marmite. During her ghostly twenties, toast will be her staple, eaten fast, on the go.

Bugger you all! shouts Ganny Mary, suddenly banging the table, which rocks on its uneven legs. Bugger you! Ursula's heard it all before, and it's time to go. She wolfs down the toast, and flees into the TV room, flips upside down against the big mirror behind the door, and hangs there, the toast and toffees making her momentarily nauseous. An idea of an exciting challenge slips into her like a breeze. Could she get from the bottom of the house all the way to her bedroom at the top without turning upright? She's about to try when the front door opens.

I'm back!

It's Joyce. She *was* out. She had been in earlier, but she must have gone out again. Now she is back again. Ursula can hear her with her brother Jonathan. He's got a friend with him. She wonders where they have all been, and feels a prickle of emptiness, aware how long she has been alone. An upside-down version of them is reflected in a series of mirrors. Her mother in solid walking shoes, wearing a long cardigan over a brown-and-yellow-checked skirt. Jonathan with his friend Ian Poole are standing in front of her, grinning. They both wear anoraks, and carry small HMV bags. They rush past her, crashing down the stairs, as Ursula's father calls from upstairs. Joyce?

I popped out, she calls up, to chat through the vote with Sarah and Chris! It's going to be tricky . . .!

Mum? Mum, I really need some money . . .!

Bethany is calling from somewhere upstairs. Ursula hadn't known she was in. She rarely sees her sister. She knows very little about her, or what she does with her time, just glimpses her going up the stairs. Long hair, embroidered sheepskin, platform shoes, a flash of eyeshadow.

Have you got someone up there, Bethany? calls Joyce with disapproval in her voice.

Only Jack, says Bethany. Her door closes.

Jack is Bethany's friend, a denim presence glimpsed occasionally, carrying cider.

What can we do about Jack? says Joyce to Peter as he joins her outside the TV room.

Not much I expect, he says.

And I just caught Jonathan with Ian Poole, smoking, says Joyce.

She puts her hand on his arm. Ursula wonders if they will hug. Sometimes in one of the plethora of mirrors, she catches sight of them in an embrace, whispering to each other. Ursula imagines they are speaking about the nuclear threat, anxious to hide it from the children.

Marijuana, whispers Joyce. It'll ruin his brain.

They are only experimenting, says Peter, kissing his wife on the cheek.

Ursula's head is filling up with blood, and her arms are aching. She buckles and falls against the TV-room door, making it bang against the wall.

Ursula! What are you doing? says Joyce brusquely.

A handstand, says Ursula.

Have you been watching cartoons?

Ursula looks down.

You know when you're on your deathbed you won't wish you'd watched more cartoons, says Joyce with a funny sort of smile. Ursula knows she is letting her parents down. She cannot admit how much she loves cartoons. She has gorged herself all day on *Hong Kong Phooey* and *Yogi Bear*. Her favourite is *Top Cat*. She wants to share with her mother how hilarious the last episode was, how Benny, one of Top Cat's deputies, didn't want to tell his mother that he was just an alley cat, so he boasted to her that he was the mayor of New York – but then she came to visit from out of town so the gang had to make it seem he really was the mayor. Ursula loves their voices, the upward inflections, the mischief, the way that audience always laughs on cue. At the end of each episode, no matter what happens, the gang ends up back in the alley, without money or food, but together, like a big happy family.

Her mother looks at her watch, and moves on down the hall. Ursula has missed her chance to say anything at all.

Let's make something to eat, she says, starting down the stairs. Come along . . .

Ursula squeezes past her, leaping downstairs four steps at

a time, pitching wildly over the banister at the bottom and landing hard on her knees. In the kitchen Ganny Mary is giving toffees to Jonathan and Ian Poole. They are giggling in a strange sort of way.

Mum! Don't give them sweets, says Joyce, putting her briefcase on the bench. It'll rot your teeth, boys.

Sorry, Jonathan's Mam, mutters Ian Poole in his thick Geordie accent, his mouth full of toffee. Jonathan smirks and leads him away into the gloomy dining room, tugging his shirt. Ursula watches them through the open doorway as they hover over the record player tittering and snorting. What they are doing is not funny but their hysteria is contagious and she can't help but grin.

Oh Joyce, where've you been? cries Ganny Mary. When will it end?

I can't talk to you now, says Joyce breezily, getting a pan, chopping carrots. I've got a big meeting this evening.

You've just *been* at a bloody meeting!

No, I just popped out. I did tell you that you'd have to fend for yourselves today.

You say that every bloody day. Bloody hell. I wish I'd never come . . .

There's stew in the oven. The carrots are going on now.

It's not right. You should be here, with me. When is it going to end?

The kitchen door opens, and Peter creeps in. Ursula stands behind the chair, knowing it will end badly. Her father shouldn't come in now. Ganny Mary tuts loudly in his direction. Ursula feels tempted to go upside down. Her father takes two wine glasses from the high cupboard and carefully places them on the kitchen table. Two glasses, not three. Joyce's mouth tightens into a thin line. The boys chortle in the dining room. Joyce flicks a wall switch. Five strip lights flicker and hum, flooding the room with brightness.

Jonathan, you and Ian should do your homework, says Joyce, looking into the dining room.

It's Saturday, Jonathan's Mam, says Ian Poole. We've not got none.

Ursula's father quietly opens a bottle of wine. Ganny Mary turns the page of the newspaper noisily and glares at him. The table rocks on its legs.

This bloody table! she cries. Bloody hell!

The table is another daily reminder for Ganny Mary of how life has gone against her. When I think of that mahogany table! The beauty of it! she says.

Ursula's heard it many times, how Ganny Mary offered her parents the mahogany dining table from Padiham. Joyce had rejected it, telling her they didn't want it, Peter had salvaged a single piece of sycamore from a skip, and commissioned a welder to make a frame and legs for it. It was a table of their own, she'd said. The mahogany table with its shapely legs had been sacrificed and sent to auction. Ganny Mary can't forget and will never forgive.

Bloody man! says Ganny Mary, turning to Joyce as though he was not in the room. You were normal before you met him, Joyce.

Ursula feels tension flooding her body. Ganny Mary is contravening the universal law that fathers and grandmothers should never speak of each other while in each other's presence. If they are to be in the same room, they must, at all cost, ignore each other.

Joyce, says her father, holding out a glass of wine to her.

32

Oh I can't drink now, Pete, she says quietly.

Of course you can't. For God's sake. What's the matter with the man? says Ganny Mary.

Stop it, Mum, says Joyce.

But Ganny Mary is just warming up.

He's ruined you. Look at you! You are harassed to death. This house! This bloody house. He put a motorway next to your own home! People must laugh at you!

According to Ganny Mary, Ursula's father is bad through and through. He not only stole her daughter, and nurtured in her an obsession with politics and CND, things that really shouldn't concern a girl who might have stayed in Lancashire and become a respectable teacher at the grammar school, but he brought her to this north-facing house in godforsaken Newcastle. Then, as town councillor, he encouraged the building of an urban motorway right on their own doorstep. He's not only bad, he's stupid.

Joyce takes the glass of wine from the table and sips it, preternaturally calm. Ursula is panicking. There are too many ambivalences, and hidden anxieties. The Cold War is taking place in her own house. One wrong move could mean utter devastation.

The man is a runt! says Ganny Mary.

That's enough, says Peter, smiling in a fierce way, and looking directly at Ganny Mary.

Mum . . . whispers Ursula.

She must say something, do something, step in to stop what is happening. Her father is directly addressing Ganny Mary. They are actually looking at each other. Ursula must do something to defuse the tension before it tears them all to pieces.

Mum . . .! says Ursula more loudly. Mum! MUM!

She knows not to distract her mum from saving the world but what else can she do?

I want pocket money! Bethany has it! And Jonathan has it, Mum! Why can't I have pocket money too?

All the significant adults in her life turn to look at her.

Ursula, says Joyce sternly. This is not the time!

Ursula's blood rushes to her cheeks in shame. She hangs her head, but her heroic gesture has worked. Ganny Mary goes back to the small ads. The tension dissipates. Her father shakes his head at his daughter slowly, gives her a strange crooked smile, and slopes from the room. Ursula once saw a cartoon on TV about a yeti. The creature had the same heaviness she notices occasionally in her father. If he had hair growing all over his body he too would be an abominable snowman.

Sound explodes into the room, a new sound, raw and violent and ugly, chords like fists to the face, smashing the world as it is, calling to destroy, an anti-christ screams anarchy.

In the dining room, the boys stand mesmerised by a vinyl single on a turntable. They start shaking their heads, a revving energy in their bodies.

Too loud, Jonathan! calls Joyce. I have to go. I'll be back later. Lunch will be ready in half an hour. Ursula, no more cartoons! Peter, are you there . . .?

She goes out. Ursula hears the door slam.

Her father, the great mystery, has gone too, absorbed back into the rest of the house. Or perhaps he has gone out with her mother. Ursula is not sure. It is hard to find the centre of things. On the kitchen table a paper bag. Inside a copy of *Bunty*, and a new skipping rope. Her mother must have bought them for her. She takes them out. A feeling like love fills her.

She had no business getting involved with that bloody man! spits Ganny Mary. She's a sponge in water!

Ever since she was a baby, Ursula has heard these words about her mother, and tried to fathom their meaning.

She's not a sponge! She's saving us from nuclear attack, Ursula says fiercely.

Mary looks at her. She hates the child, all that stupid innocence.

Bloody hell! When will it end? she cries.

It won't, says Ursula defiantly, not quite knowing what she is saying. It won't ever end! So there!

She married a runt, says Ganny Mary, pounding her fists on the table. Your mother is a skivvy and a slave. She's harassed to death. You are all wrong. It's all wrong. You . . .

Ursula steps forward, bravery shining in her eyes, Shut up! Shut up shut up shut up shut up!

Ganny Mary turns on her.

You little bugger! You harass your mother to death! You ruined her life! You should never have been born!

Her poisoned arrows land deep in the small of Ursula but she does not fall. Instead, hot indignation lifts her up.

I should have been born. I am born! I'm standing right here in the kitchen! If I hadn't been born I'd have kicked and kicked until I was!

She dances from toe to toe.

And if you'd tried to stop me I'd have kicked you into outer space! And when the nuclear bomb gets dropped, you'll be right in the middle and you'll be incinerated and

35

turn purple and evaporate into radioactive dust!

Pow pow pow! She's cowboy Ursula, *Hong Kong Phooey*, firing on all cylinders, blasting her grandmother to kingdom come. That'll see her run out of town!

Ganny Mary groans and turns away, her appetite for a fight gone. She looks back at her paper as though Ursula is no longer in the room, losing herself again, the cracks in her widening, like dried mud before the tide.

Ursula feels suddenly sorry that she might have hurt Ganny Mary. Her frustration exploded before she could stop it. She doesn't know where these feelings come from. She runs up the stairs, passing her siblings' rooms – incense from Bethany's room, dank mushiness from Jonathan's – to her bedroom at the top of the house, and closes the door behind her. She stands on her head with her feet against it. Her blood rushes into her skull, forced through her capillaries, making her eardrums fill with soundless hush. Things make more sense upside down. It's calmer, and the upset swims through her and subsides.

The moon is on the floor as she stares out at the upside-down night. The traffic roars on the new road. Ursula blinks: she does not know it yet but she is searching for love. A boy is not far away, but she knows nothing of him; Jerry with the soft sudden smile, like her, is barely formed. He's eight years old, at home inside the Byker Wall. It is not a real wall but the idealistic vision of the architect Ralph Erskine who was employed by the Labour Council to clear the slums in the Byker district of Newcastle and replace them with compact social housing. He built a wall, a long unbroken block of 620 council flats. Rows of back-to-back houses were torn down to make way for it. One was Jerry's home. The family was rehoused in a brand new flat on the sixteenth floor of the groundbreaking Byker Wall. When it was done, the people of Newcastle said it could be seen from the moon.

He sits on the small balcony now, wrapped in his duvet, doing a drawing for a school project. Draw a picture of your own home, Miss Summers has asked. Her pupils do so every spring term. Over the years she's seen hundreds of pictures of the Byker Wall, but none quite like Jerry's. He looks out, surveying the banks of windows, jutting balconies, all set in concrete, and thinks about how all the little units are filled with people. He thinks about how each person is filled with dreams. He does not draw a building, but a landscape of minds, each different from the other. He draws people's thoughts. When he hands it to Miss Summers at school, he will say, It is a time collage, Miss.

What do you mean, Jerry?

Just because a picture is flat, he will say, it doesn't mean it can hold only one moment in time. The Wall contains a million lives, so all these are millions of experiences at the same moment in time.

I like it, Jerry, Miss Summers will say.

So do I, Jerry will say, smiling suddenly. It's why I drew it.

Jerry and Ursula leap together through time, along parallel lines. Days sweep through them, then months and years; now they are eleven, and it's the summer before secondary school, another long hot holiday. The weeks stretch out, a sea of unremembered days. Jerry researches topics that interest him, the causes of World War I, the history of the blues from the Mississippi Delta, and the solar system; he goes on adventures round Byker with his best friend Mackie, and sometimes he just sits in his room, thinking, waiting for the world to grab him. Ursula kicks around in Eslington Road, hot and bored. Her mother and father are in their own worlds. Her friends are away, Ashley on Guide camp, Jeanette with her dad on the Costa Brava. Bethany has bought herself a Eurorail card, and gone to possibly France, possibly Spain, possibly to pick fruit. Occasionally Jonathan lets Ursula play table tennis at the church hall with him. She makes shows in which she plays all the parts, and writes a letter to a newspaper about saving the whale. Mainly she is Ganny Mary's little companion in the downstairs kitchen.

Today is a special day for Ursula. It will make an impression on her that stays in the memory for ever, cherished and indelible. Ganny Mary is taking her on a trip to Padiham. It happens also to be the day when the paths of Jerry and Ursula will cross each other for the first time.

Mary has spoken about going back to Padiham to visit her father's gravestone ever since she left. Joyce promises to accompany her, like old times, but year after year she finds excuses not to, and so her granddaughter must do. Ursula is only too happy to oblige. Having barely ever left Jesmond, she is keen to experience the places further afield, so here she is, boarding a green double-decker at Burnley Station for the final leg of the journey.

The engine rumbles on the forecourt, belching diesel, in no hurry to depart. In her hat and coat, Ganny Mary seems immediately stolid and immovable, like a giant toadstool growing on the seat. She has been asleep most of the train journey from Newcastle, waking only for squares of dark chocolate, but now she's more alert.

The bus zigzags through the country lanes. At every turn it seems to Ursula it will veer into the hedges. She looks at the fields and farms whizzing by the window, thrilled at the scale of the world.

Look, Ganny Mary, she says, pointing at a field outside. Pasture.

It's a word she's proud of. She learned it from the Heidi books, stories of adventures and happy endings, unfolding in perfect days. Mary presses the request button and the bus veers and brakes hard at a single metal pole. She had planned to go straight to Padiham, to show Ursula her old house, the site of the laundry, Patty Henshley's sweetshop, the steps her father had whitened, but the girl is right, it is beautiful pasture. There is sunshine on the fields and the rich slopes

39

of the hill, so much greener than the dreary North East. The most perfect spot on earth, her mother, Annie, used to say. Yes, they'll stop here and walk up the way she used to through dappled woods, and lilac tops. Mrs Littlewood will be at Tythe Farm, the greatest buttery in Lancashire. There is always a cake on the go.

They step from the bus. Mary walks unevenly in her court shoes along the hedgerows, to a stile. Ursula is amazed to see her lift her skirt, and skip lightly from one side of it to the other into an oak wood.

Where are we going? she says.

Pendle Hill, says Mary, her mind on cake.

They walk under the trees over fresh acorns towards the open green of the hill. Mary stops to take off her shoes. Her bunions bulge like onions. Ursula skips ahead opening her coat like wings, leaning into the wind. With Ganny Mary there is always plenty of time. With her mother there is always something to do, somewhere to get to. On family walks in Northumberland, Joyce brings guides by the Ramblers' Association, and bribes the children with Mars bars. Just one more horizon, just to the top of the spinney, just till we see the view. They march after her through farms, bogs and thickets, with scratched legs and stung hands. Her mother is always on a mission.

They reach the green slopes and Ursula runs across the grass, which is dotted with yellow flowers. She spots an orange stone, lying beside the track.

Look Ganny Mary! she cries, picking it up. It's full of holes, like a brain.

It's an old brick, says Mary. Very distinctive. Bricks are made in Lancashire.

For the rockery, says Ursula.

On their outings to Long Sands in Tynemouth, they bring home 'nice stones' from the beach. Ganny Mary is making a rockery in the garden at Eslington Road, her little bit of beauty among the rot.

We'll fetch it on our way down.

Someone might take it. I'll hide it, says Ursula. She runs to a clump of grass and buries it carefully in the centre. Mary watches, touched for a moment by her granddaughter's innocence. They climb on. The ground becomes rougher, the slope steeper. They reach the edge of the grey slate. A blasted tree stands on the edge of the scree. An astonishing sight, its branches fracturing the sky. It is full of a wild energy, frozen into an eternal stillness.

It's like lightning! shouts Ursula, running towards it.

She turns to Ganny Mary and shoots her arms up to the sky in a jagged shape imitating the tree, holding the pose.

I'm going to climb it!

No! shouts Ganny Mary.

I won't fall, Ganny, protests Ursula.

She hangs on to one of the branches and swings up her legs.

Come down! We've come the wrong way!

Ursula jumps down, and runs up the path to the left of the tree.

Is it this way? she shouts, looking up at the swathes of heather.

Bloody hell! Come back! Oh me nerves! Me nerves! Mary snaps, her voice hard and high.

Ursula stops and looks back as she slumps on to a stone. She has heard this talk of 'nerves' before. She is not sure exactly how they function; at school she is told they are everywhere, even in your toes. Ganny Mary's make life difficult for her. Even something as simple as a tree on a hill can be difficult for her if her nerves have gone. Ursula runs back down to her.

My mother went that way . . . Mary starts to say.

Ursula's all ears. She thought she'd heard all of Ganny Mary's stories, a thousand times each one, but she hasn't heard this one.

She came for milk and butter from the farm, didn't she? Ganny Mary?

Mary looks away from the tree. It frightens her, half living, half dead, its spiking branches stripped bare like bones. Their stark ugliness hurts her.

What happened, Ganny Mary? Did something dreadful happen here? says Ursula eagerly.

The mystery of what happened to Mary's mother is compacted and tight inside her. Her eyes fill with tears. She stands up and starts walking down the path.

Ursula watches her, perplexed. She feels suddenly ashamed.

How about a cup of tea? she says, catching up, adopting her grown-up voice to protect herself from Ganny Mary's nerves. Where's that place you mentioned previously?

Aye, tea, says Mary, rallying. Tea, yes, that's what we need . . . and cake.

She sets off round a small knoll where the slope flattens towards Tythe Farm, with one thing on her mind, cake. As they reach a plateau, the wind dies away, and the hill itself seems to settle. The air becomes softer. A stream widens across the green expanse of the fell, curling through a field of cows. They cross it on stepping stones as it roars, filled with pebbles, the water rushing over them, and come to a hilltop farm. In front of it is a child's swing on a free-standing frame.

Someone's garden, whispers Ursula.

There is a climbing rose around the door. Mary smiles; it has always been this way. She swims in memories, the times before Annie hardened, how she and her mother came for eggs and butter, and brought them home for her father. She remembers Mrs Littlewood's mother, long dead now, but how nice and right her daughter took over the farm, learned to tend the animals and the garden, and bake as her mother had done. Mary remembers thick slices of fruit cake. What will she have today? A scone? A piece of tart? They'll sit in the back garden and chat. Mrs Littlewood is not sophisticated, of course, never came to Mary's shop; French mahogany and Chinese inlay meant nothing to her, but a good woman nevertheless.

Is this where you used to get eggs during the war? says Ursula, skipping after her, delighted to be seeing the places she's heard so much about, hoping they won't set Ganny Mary's nerves off again.

The front door of the farmhouse opens straight on to the land like a welcome. Mary goes in without knocking. Ursula hangs back, too shy to follow, and runs to the swing. The earth is bare under it, kicked and scraped. It's cold against her legs as she pushes forwards and back, strong as a piston, climbing high into the sky. At the top of her swing, she can see the ridge of Pendle Hill. It seems to move as she flies through the air, not just the million shapes and colours of its trees and plants, but the whole mass of it, alive.

*

Jerry isn't on a hill, he's with his dad at the quayside market buying school shirts. There's still five weeks before term starts but his dad wants everything ready for the first day of secondary school. The wind blows hard off the North Sea, but even this cannot cool the hot summer sun. They browse the canopied stalls next to the oily river.

Quality, these, says Mike, holding up a clutch of light blue shirts.

They look about right, says Jerry, squinting at them.

You'll knock 'em dead in these! grins Mike.

Jerry suspects he's referring to girls again. He's not interested in knocking anyone dead, least of all girls. Jerry is more interested in facts. His current favourites are:

1. Plato was sold into slavery by Dionysus (Greek Tyrant).
2. Elvis Presley was brought up in social housing.
3. There are more than a million colours in a rainbow, not seven.
4. The final chord in the Beatles song 'A Day in the Life' was played on three pianos, and multitracked four times, making it the sound equivalent to twelve pianos.

The Tyne Bridge arches above them, surreal and magnificent, the green copper girders plunging into the buildings on the north bank. It reminds Jerry of the futuristic cities in *Flash Gordon*. A fact he likes about the bridge is that it was the prototype for the Sydney Harbour Bridge in Australia. He loves this, the idea the whole world can be connected through a single engineering project, from one side to the other. Knowledge like this makes him feel solid and fearless. Newcastle to Australia in one curving hoop. The entire universe can be shaped and held together by his thoughts, like a massive dot-to-dot. His ambition is to join all the dots of civilisation together in one great evolutionary march.

I'll take ten for a tenner, says his dad to the street vendor.

Dad . . .! I cannot wear ten shirts in a month of Sundays!

His dad loves to bargain. He's always warning Jerry about market vendors, how they hike the prices as the summer goes on.

Least you'll not run out, says his dad ruefully.

Jerry's parents are always worried about things running out: time, jobs, money, health. They leave the market with ten nylon shirts in a polythene bag, and pass next to the floating nightclub, the *Tuxedo Princess*. The gangplank rattles in the wind, its strings of lights unlit, the life gone out of it. His sister Andie and her friends speak about it in hushed tones. At night it shines and pulses. Every weekend Andie boards it and sails off into the arms of another. The wind gusts as they turn the corner onto Neville Street. Jerry's dad stops to do up his leather bomber jacket. He hands the plastic bag to his son, holds down the ends of the zip, pulls upwards in two sharp tugs.

Mind, this weather's not funny, he says.

Jerry sees a small plaque in front of him, on a stone-fronted building.

What's that, Dad? he says.

His father shrugs, grimacing into the wind.

The Literary and Philosophical Society, reads Jerry. Can we go in?

His father looks up at the building, the carved frontage,

45

the statue of a man in a robe. The high windows. Like a church, he thinks. Like law courts.

We're not allowed, he says, but Jerry is already through the entrance, walking up the stairs.

Jerry! Jesus, man! It's private . . . Jerry?

It's alright, Dad, says Jerry.

No, son! What d'you wanna gang in here for?

Literature and philosophy, he deadpans, and opens a heavy door.

Jerry steps into the reading room. It is a cathedral of books, stretching from floor to the arched ceiling, a hundred feet above him. Ladders lead to a high walkway that encircles the entire space.

His father lets out a slow whistle.

It's like the Tardis, man. You'd never know from outside, there was all this . . . !

Jerry's heart is beating fast. He stands like a child looking up at a sky full of stars in wonder. He sees desks, round-backed chairs, a small hatch where tea is served. A grey-haired man wearing glasses reads, a pile of books beside him, a young man in a T-shirt, his face deep in concentration, a cup of tea next to him, gone cold. The great matter of learning is happening in front of Jerry's eyes. This is where he will forge the links in his chain of ideas.

Come on, son, says his dad, edging back out of the door, there's nothing for us here, but Jerry is at one of the shelves, taking down a book.

Mike shakes his head; his son has always been different, and obstinate with it, like Kath. Christ! he mutters. Literature and Philosophy. It's beyond him. He has long given up trying to get Jerry interested in having a trade. It used to

46

grieve him when he saw other dads taking their sons out on jobs. Jerry knows all about Greeks, Romans, Tudors, the Reformation, the battle for independence in the colonies, planets, saints, composers, but sod all about water pressure. Cocky is what his sister calls him. She has lots of names for him, egghead, bookworm, weirdo, div. His teacher Miss Summers calls him the Wizard. Mike remains unsure. Sometimes he calls him soft, but he cannot help feeling that his son is special.

Jerry walks over to the librarian behind a high wooden counter, thumbing through index cards, and smiles.

I want to join, he says.

She looks at him, frowning.

How old are you? she asks.

I'm his dad, says Mike, stepping forward, ready for the worst. I'm sorry, miss, he's only eleven.

The librarian smiles. She rustles in a drawer and hands Jerry a form.

You'll be our youngest ever member, she says.

Ursula slams her feet down on the dusty ground, and jumps off the swing. Pendle Hill sways for a moment and then comes to rest. Ganny Mary has not re-emerged from Tythe Farm. The sun burns down, and everything is eerily quiet and still.

Ursula walks around the side of the farmhouse, avoiding cowpats, and finds herself at the threshold of a large kitchen garden. Only a wire fence keeps it separate from the hill. She climbs over, walks down a path. It is like Mr McGregor's garden, with rows of lettuce, radishes, poles for beans, and raspberry nets.

A young man is kneeling on the soil. He looks up at her without surprise. His eyes are as brown as the cows in the field. He holds out a pea pod to her, and opens it. Inside she sees a row of five perfect green peas, strung like a bracelet. She grabs it, and runs off through the rows of plants. Ganny Mary is on the far side of the house, sitting on a crate, watching Mrs Littlewood dig up potatoes, warming to her favourite tales of woe.

There's nothing nice about Newcastle, I can tell you that! And Joyce's house is dark, north-facing you know, but what can I do . . .?

Who's this? says Mrs Littlewood, looking up at Ursula.

Mrs Littlewood is old like Ganny Mary but her eyes shine like the pebbles in the stream.

I'm Ursula.

Joyce's daughter, says Mary.

It's a shame my granddaughter Lottie isn't here, says Mrs Littlewood. She must be about your age.

The gardener gave me peas, says Ursula, holding out the green pod.

He's one of the guests staying with the sisters, says Mrs Littlewood.

She plunges her hands into the dark soil and pulls out a white round potato.

Help me get these up, she says, handing Ursula a basket.

Ursula crouches down. She thrusts her hands into the soft black earth. Her fingers feel a potato. She lifts it out, a perfect treasure, round, clean and white.

Life is a poor do, Mrs Littlewood, a poor do, says Mary,

resuming her tales of sorrow. Joyce is a slave, and the children a burden, and that husband of hers, well he's no good. No there's nothing nice about Newcastle. It's a dreary city, without charm, not handsome like Padiham used to be, mind that's changed too . . .

The pea man passes, walking slowly between the bean-poles, heading towards a building, some way off, on the far side of the garden. It is Victorian, made of red Lancashire brick. Ursula wonders if it is a school. There are green lawns in front of it, dotted with the ruins of an older building, low crumbling walls, the remains of an arching doorway. The pea man disappears inside. Ursula looks back and sees a worm in the soil, pink and glistening.

How about a piece of cake? says Mrs Littlewood, getting to her feet. Let's see what we've got. The back door is open, and they go inside. There is the smell of butter and sugar. Herbs hang from the ceiling in thick bunches. On the huge wooden table there is a home-made cake with swirls of lilac-coloured icing. Ursula looks at it in amazement; a purple cake. Mrs Littlewood cuts a slice for her, then one for Mary. She sits on the floor, and takes a bite. It is as sweet as honey and perfumed like a flower. She lets out a sigh of pleasure.

Lavender cake, says Mrs Littlewood. We'll take the rest over for the sisters.

Can I stay with your sisters too? Like the man? says Ursula thinking about the cake, the lovely garden, about Lottie, and the swing.

They're not my sisters! Mrs Littlewood laughs. They're nuns from St Agnes' Priory. They're mainly all old now, like me. Sometimes they take people in, you know, like that man, if they need to come.

Why do people need to come?

Usually they're looking for something.

What are they looking for? asks Ursula. Peas . . .? Or cake?

It's a wonder they indulge in cake, says Mary, biting into a second slice. You don't expect religious folk to like cake! Not in my experience, any road. Religion did me in! It'll do anyone in. Look at my mother!

I remember her fondly, says Mrs Littlewood, unflustered by Mary's outburst. She used to walk up here with you ever such a lot when we were little.

That was before, says Mary, darkly.

Come, Ursula, we'll take the cake over for the sisters, says Mrs Littlewood. You can see the Abbey ruins, and we'll fetch butter and eggs . . .

It's late afternoon before it's time to go home. As Mary and Ursula leave, Mrs Littlewood gives them a brown pot with butter in it. Ursula looks inside. It is yellow like the sun, and solid as candle wax; a little pot of gold. Mary thanks Mrs Littlewood with tears in her eyes. Like my dear father always said, she says, butter never spoils anything.

Ursula is glowing with it all as they make their way back to Newcastle. Her first experience of travelling in the big wide world brought her to somewhere quite magical.

Jerry's full of wonder too. As the clock ticks slowly in the Literary and Philosophical Society, and his dad drinks tea from the serving hatch, Jerry reads. He's in a landscape he never dreamed of; the shelves of books are like cliffs for him to scale. When the reading room closes, he staggers out on to Neville Street with his dad, clutching a bag full of books, feeling the joy of newness, while, around the corner, Ursula and Ganny Mary, weary from the long day, come out of the Central Station. Ursula sees three big kittens outside the newsagent's. A notice on them says help the blind. The trip to Pendle is changing her. She thinks of the blind man with a sticky-out tummy who taps along Eslington Road with his white stick, and his shoelaces undone, and runs back to the kittens. She makes a wish, puts three pounds twenty into the slots, all her pocket money, enjoying the sweet fit of the coins, the sense of giving, the clink as they fall.

As they walk down Neville Street, Ganny Mary is too tired to carry the orange stone for the rockery. Ursula takes it and runs ahead, knocking it against a lamp post.

Bless you! she cries, smiling back at Ganny Mary.

It's the game they played when Ursula was younger, while bringing stones back from their trips to the beach at Tyne-mouth. The lamp posts had colds and needed tapping to cure them.

Oh dear this one has got an awful cold, she says. Bless you! . . . Bless you!

Jerry is with his dad walking towards her on the same pavement. A boy with his books, a girl with a stone, hitting lamp posts.

What's she doing? says his dad as they pass.

No idea, whispers Jerry, smiling, but she'll have her reasons.

*

Joyce is out when Ursula and Mary arrive home. Muffled music comes from Bethany's bedroom. Jonathan is reading *MAD* in the dining room. They go out into the garden. The moon is above them as they place the stone on the rockery.

Ganny Mary loves you, says Ganny Mary. The words feel foreign to her. She moves her hand slowly over Ursula's head, smoothing her hair towards the nape of her neck. A warm coconut. Her little companion by the rockery. Her little island of beauty among the rot.

Cars are nose to tail, billowing exhaust among the red brakelights, indicators ticking. Something is going to happen on Oak Road today. On this wintry afternoon, love will be set in motion. Ursula will make it happen. She is walking along the thin corridor of pavement between the jammed cars and bright shopfronts. She no longer lives with unthinking lightness but one step ahead, always slightly in the future. It is a future full of boys.

The feelings have been getting more and more intense over the past few months. She's been watching fifth-formers on the football field behind the science block. One in particular draws her; something in the way he moves, his agility. She wonders how she can get near to him, have something to do with him. She's entirely focused on this problem. She imagines kissing him like she's seen on TV. She wants to let the boy know about her but also to keep her feelings hidden.

Last week, she heard a girl in the sixth form say that she was going to the Carriage, a pub in Heaton. Ursula knows this girl is part of a group of friends that includes this boy. They are what Ursula longs to be part of: a scene. She is convinced her destiny will unfold in the Carriage. The thought tickles. She feels the sensation reach to her unknown places, fizzing lines running up and down her legs – as though her French skipping is inside her now, moving around, as she imagines the boy, his face so handsome, turning to notice her across the crowded bar. Warmth stirs in her, like frying potatoes; she's hot and buttery with anticipation. The boy motivates everything she does. She is driven to get close to him, to be held in some kind of womb-hug, to somehow unlock the utter greatness of herself. This is why she is walking down Oak Road wearing her new jacket, of fake silver leather, wholly ineffective against the cold, but making a wondrous *shushing* noise, as she heads for Annabel's, the local stylist, to add the final touch: Ursula will have a perm.

A sign in the window, Training Night: Models Wanted. No Appointment Necessary. Wednesdays. A bottle-blond girl is reading a magazine in front of the mirrors. Ursula opens the door. '99 Red Balloons' by Nena fills the room.

Yes, pet?

I'd like to be a model.

How old are you? There is laughter in her voice.

Fourteen.

You're too young, says the girl, licking a finger, flicking a page.

Ursula will not let love fall at the first hurdle. She has seen the photo in Annabel's window, the goddess with the flawless skin, the half-moons of pink on her eyelids, white liner on the rims, curls cascading around her face, the faraway look in her eyes. For weeks she has scrutinised her on the way back from school, convinced she is a mirror of her future self. Ursula will transform from flat-head into curly-head; her dreams of womb-hugs and utter greatness will be realised.

You local? says the girl.

Are you? says Ursula innocently.

Nah man. I'm from Byker.

The Wall. There are kids in her class at school who live in Byker. Ursula tries not to be afraid of them. There is hardness in their faces. They speak like they are talking backwards, their accent angling the words, shunting them into each other, crushing and winding them. There is no warmth in their voices yet they are full of jokes, sharp as knives.

You'll have to get yer mam to come in.

Please . . . says Ursula, reddening, seeing the Byker Wall rise up in front of her to block her path to happiness.

My mother says it's fine, says Ursula as coolly as she can. She has not of course mentioned her plan to Joyce, who she knows would only deride it as vanity and sigh with disappointment. You used to be a serious little girl. Have you become frivolous? she'd asked recently. Ursula had not wanted to accompany her to an Amnesty International lecture at the Civic Centre. It's aimed at young people, Joyce had said, but these days even the threat of nuclear annihilation does not motivate Ursula as much as curls.

I booked, says Ursula defiantly.

Julie! shouts the girl from Byker.

A woman with pink pearly lips shuffles in from the back of the shop.

This lass is here for Training Night, says the girl.

Have you got something particular in mind, pet? she says.

Ursula points to the photo in the window.

A perm? That's a big move.

One of her teeth is dead, grey among the perfect whites.

Why not, pet? she says, smiling. Curls will suit you.

Ursula is going to be transformed. She sits in the chair, and wills the women to use their powers. She will be a new Ursula. Ursula Deluxe. Ursula of Him.

Andie, why don't you take over? she says to the girl.

Andie. The girl from Byker with a boy's name frowns.

Don't worry, pet. You know what you're doing. I'll be supervising any road, says Julie. It'll look gorgeous. Right, let's get going, shall we? Relax.

She picks up a strand of Ursula's hair with a *Mmmmmm*. Ursula tries to relax. She has never been to a hairdresser's salon before. Usually her mother cuts her hair, just as she cuts her own. The problem with having a mum who is busy saving the planet is she does not look like the other mums who wear jeans and tight T-shirts, and have their hair in *layers* like Lady Di. Her mother doesn't have time to look like a woman.

The women work around her. Despite her surliness Andie has deft, quick fingers, lifting Ursula's hair in long wet ribbons, scooping it into pink curlers, pushing in the loose strands with the end of a comb and winding it quickly until it sits on Ursula's head like a brandy snap.

That's coming on lovely, says the older woman. It's John's birthday. I've promised him. I'll leave you to it, Andie. Lock up, will you?

Nay bother, says Andie.

Ursula notices herself in the mirror, suddenly anxious.

Don't worry pet, says Julie. You're in safe hands.

Ursula makes herself smile. Julie puts on her coat, and leaves.

Andie picks something like a sauce bottle in a cafe from a shelf and holds it over Ursula's head. Ursula imagines watery ketchup farting and squelching on to her, and Andie laughing. It must be a joke, of course! Ursula can't have a perm! She can't be a model on Training Night, can't be the woman with curls in the photo, can't ever discover the truth about love. She's just Ursula. Andie squeezes the bottle. Nothing comes out.

Dozy cow, says Andie to herself. Left the lid on, didn't I?

Ursula watches as she twists the nozzle, and thin perming solution trickles coldly over her scalp.

All done, says Andie. Let it cook.

Andie disappears into the back room. Ursula looks at herself. How is this trickle going to do anything? She had imagined a huge machine, one of those helmets, some kind of electromagnetic current that would zap her follicles. A Permanator.

She hears Andie on the phone in the back.

Greg . . . howhey . . . I'm knackered, man. I've got a perm to finish . . . You dirty bastard. You will not! Be here in fifteen. I'm dying for a drink.

The shop door opens. A thin boy walks in. Andie pops her head round from the back.

Look what the cat brought in!

Look what you brought in, says the boy, as though it has great meaning.

Piss off, Jerry.

Very polite, he says.

Ursula adjusts her head so she can see him. He stares back at her.

What d'you want, Jerry? asks Andie.

What do you want? That's the question.

He stares at Ursula in the mirror.

Mam says don't not forget to call her, or forget to not call her, he says.

Talk proper, Jerry. What for? says Andie.

For a laugh, he says, smiling at Ursula.

Are you trying to impress someone? says Andie, mocking, glancing at Ursula as she brushes her cheeks with blusher. Because you're not impressing anyone.

She snaps the make-up into a purse, and leads Ursula to the leather chair at the sink.

Let's get these rinsed. Lean back.

The porcelain edge hurts Ursula's neck.

Where d'you live? asks Andie, making conversation, the way she's learned from Julie.

The water from the shower scalds Ursula's scalp as Andie eases the curlers from her hair. Ursula doesn't answer. The boy makes her feel self-conscious. She'll be discovered. Jesmond girls are possibly weird, possibly too posh for a perm, but surely it is too late, it's nearly done, nearly hers.

Where? repeats Andie as she lifts up Ursula's head, wraps a towel round like a parcel. Jesmond?

Yeah, mutters Ursula.

She feels her head is quite separate from her body. As she is led back to her seat, she smells chemical jasmine. The boy is standing by the door, staring at her. Andie removes the towel. In the mirror, Ursula sees a golliwog. The word is not allowed. Her mother removed all the golliwog jam from the house but that is what she sees. Her head is an orb of tight whorls. Her eyes prickle with tears. The boy smiles at her.

I'm not in the zoo, she says, turning sharply to him. She should be. Or a circus. She looks like a light bulb with poodle locks. The thought makes her hot with indignation.

Jerry watches her, a girl with crazy curls, a blushing clown.

Andie turns away to hide her panic. She glances out of the window, wanting Greg to come. She needs a drink.

It'll be fine. I'll get the tongs, she says. It'll relax. They're always like this at first . . .

Ursula puts her hand to her head and starts to cry.

It'll settle down, says Andie, stretching out some of the curls with the tongs but they spring back into a ball. A car pulls up outside.

It's Greg! says Andie, as though he will save them all from the dreadful situation. She sees the tears welling in Ursula's eyes.

Don't cry, pet. Greg will drive you home. What's your name? She really needs a drink now. She can feel the first taste of it in her mouth already, nothing like it, the strength of it, the day falling away, laughing about the perm that went wrong.

I said, what's your name?

Ursula, says Ursula fighting back tears.

Urs–u–la, repeats Jerry quietly.

For fuck's sake, Jerry. Go and wait in the car! snaps Andie.

She takes a hairbrush to Ursula's hair and pulls at it sharply to no effect. I think it looks nice, she says in a kind voice, and Ursula's worst fears are confirmed.

In Greg's car Ursula is numb. She sits in the back next to Jerry with her face turned away. He can't see what the problem is. He likes her hair. It looks odd in a good way, possibly Irish.

Where does she live? Greg asks Andie as though Ursula isn't there. She doesn't want to be there. Or anywhere. She wants to die.

Jerry watches the tears roll down Ursula's cheek.

Andie turns to her with her best smile and singsong voice. What's your address, pet?

Eslington Road.

Ask her what number, says Greg.

I want to get out, Ursula says.

I don't want you walking home alone. You're shocked, says Andie, soft and motherly now she's close to getting rid of the girl. Jerry sees Ursula's anger behind the tears. It strikes him that he might have an interesting conversation with her. They turn down a street of tall terraced houses.

Stop, says Ursula.

Greg brakes, and Ursula gets out and runs into one of the front gardens. Andie follows her in her long boots, white coat with fake-fur trim. Jerry opens the car door.

Jerry, fuck off! Wait in the car.

He lingers on the front path. His sister shoots him an angry look. Ursula is ringing the doorbell. No one answers.

He feels impulsively nervous for Ursula. It surprises him to feel this empathy over which he has no control; most things in his life can be rationalised but something about the girl unsettles him. He watches her reach up to her hair. There is a sign in the front window: Nuclear Power No Thanks. He imagines the family inside, united in social conscience. Nuclear weapons are never mentioned in his home, except when his dad makes jokes about the lesbians at Greenham Common. Jerry looks in the bay window. There are bookcases and hanging lamps, a chandelier in the centre. Paintings on the walls. High ceilings. No one in the rooms. In Byker Wall everyone lives on top of each other. Even when you go out, you're not alone, you'll meet your mother, your mother's friend, your dad's mate, your sister's friends, the lads who make Jerry nervous, unless he's with Mackie. No one comes to the door.

Is this your house? says Andie.

Jerry watches Ursula's embarrassment. She rings the bell again.

A voice comes behind the door.

Who is it? Who's there?

It's me! says Ursula loudly, wishing the ordeal over. Let me in!

The door opens. It's Ganny Mary in her brown house-coat, and mushroom hat.

We've just give her a lift home, says Andie, glad to unburden herself. She was upset by her hair, but I've told her it'll relax. It really will.

Mary looks at Andie, vague and cross.

Her mother's not in, she says.

Ursula pushes her way into the house and is swallowed up by the dark interior. Jerry tries to peer after her.

What the fuck did you do to that poor lass's hair? says Greg, leaning on the bonnet, smoking a cigarette.

Shhh! Let's go! Fuck, I don't know! I've never seen anything like it! She was weird though, weird hair maybes. Her hair reacted. Ah man, her shoes didn't go with her trousers, and her jacket . . .! Oh my God, did you see it? She was trying too hard! Give us that tab. Oh God I feel bad! Really bad.

She looked nicer than a lot of people, says Jerry. Nicer than Greg. And definitely far nicer than me.

Andie smiles at Jerry as she blows out smoke. Daft bugger, she says.

Despite everything she's grateful for her brother's words. He starts to walk off.

Where are you going? she says. It's freezing. Don't you want a lift?

He doesn't turn back. He wants freedom, to swing his arms, to walk the whole way back to Byker, feel the distance. He doesn't care about the cold. He walks down Osborne Road towards Heaton, the big houses shrinking to tight terraces. A group of men fall out of a pub in black-and-white scarves, complaining about the cold, the score. On Shields Road he walks fast, head down until finally the colossal Wall looms above him. The streets segue into a series of walkways and underpasses. He breaks into a run, winds round the bends, reaches the north entrance, slows in the tunnel under the Wall feeling the weight of a thousand flats above him and runs past the children's playground into Stairwell B. The lift is stuck as usual so he runs up the stairs, passes Mackie's door. He won't call in now. He wants time to himself, to feel what's inside him.

The front door is open. He can smell polish and air freshener. His mother has been 'blitzing'. He can hear *Blankety Blank* on the TV in the sitting room, his mam's and dad's favourite programme, and a cause of heated debate: his mam preferred Terry Wogan, his dad enjoys the ribaldry of Les Dawson.

I've left something on the table, calls his mother.

In the kitchen, her sense of order and cleanliness is fanatical. Everything is white. All around the walls are thin shelves his dad made, full of her porcelain shepherds and shepherdesses, arranged neatly in rows. On the white table, there is white food, two triangles of cheese spread, two

slices of buttered bread, and a bowl of Hula Hoops. A *Daily
Mail* lies on a plate. Her Tory rag, Jerry calls it. It is her joke
to leave it for him. She scours it cover to cover every day,
taunts him with Margaret Thatcher's triumphs.

Where've you been? calls his mother. Andie said she left
you hours ago!

Walking, he calls back.

He's not hungry. He closes the door of his bedroom,
relieved to be in the cluttered haven of his books and magazines. He puts Rickie Lee Jones on the turntable and listens
to 'We Belong Together'. He sings along, reaching the high
notes with unabashed tenderness. He loves the words she
uses, how they conjure an America inside him. Cunt-fingered
Louis. There is beauty and revolution in the words. He
imagines what kinds of words Ursula likes. Urs–u–la. Urs
Ooooo Laa.

Jerry's in the Literary and Philosophical Society. It's four years since he joined, but it is still his favourite haunt. His taste in books is eclectic. He's undaunted by the densest of reads, philosophy, politics. Today it's the past. Spread out on the table in front of him: *English History 1914–1945* by A. J. P. Taylor, *The Native American Land Struggle* by Professor Johnson, *Myths of the North East* by Dennis Butcher, *The Complete Works of Shakespeare*, Marx's *Grundrisse*. A scuffling beneath him. Someone grabs his feet and starts to drag him from his seat. He kicks out hard but can't free himself.

Fuck off, Mackie!

They're under the table. Mackie is on all fours, facing him, grinning wickedly.

Dost thou banter with me?

I defy thee to banter!

Thou arst a twat!

Twattest me, thou cock?

I twattest thou to fuckest off.

Mackie is Jerry's best friend. Mackie Mackenzie. Small and tight. Lives next door in the Byker Wall. Mackie who is mental. Mental Mackie. Everyone in Byker says so. To Jerry he's a philosopher, a scurrilous wit and anarchist. He

64

goes everywhere with him. On their trips to the Literary and Philosophical Society, Mackie reads comics if he can find one, or books about Arthurian legend. Mainly he just likes to be there. Once he climbed up on top of the stacks, hopped from one to another, like a monkey, leapt on to the walkway. Sometimes he brings books from the shelves for Jerry to read. Right now, Mackie is dusting himself down after his attack on Jerry, and making his way to the tea hatch to see Iris the tea lady, Jewish, thin-boned and pale. She has a soft spot for him, and lets him into the kitchen.

How much do you earn, Iris? asks Mackie, leaning into the hatch.

Not answering that one, says Iris, pouring a pan of water into the urn.

Have you got a husband? What do you think of popular top programmes like *Top of the Pops*, Iris?

He stands there with his head on one side, smiling, waiting for answers.

Where's your friend? she says, offering him a slice of buttered malt loaf.

The god head? says Mackie, biting into the sticky bread, or is he the dog head?

Iris likes the boys' banter. Jerry's cleverness reminds her of her older brother, a scholar and teacher in Israel. Jerry rarely comes into the kitchen. He's too busy with his books, making an encyclopedia of his mind, she says. Mackie's not a learner. She always feels an empathy for him, lets him open the biscuits, put them on the plates. He blows her a kiss and takes a handful back to Jerry.

Fancy a walk to Jesmond? says Jerry, suddenly grabbing a biscuit.

Walk? I cannot even wakkk!

I'm going, says Jerry.

Then I'm coming, says Mackie. Karen Grey! Let's go round to her house. She is most enlightened.

Mrs Grey lives in Jesmond, and is Mackie's favourite teacher.

She'll never let you in.

She will. If I pay her.

They set off along the river. The Tyne Bridge is lit up above them, a shining portal to the sky. They walk past the shipyards, cut up by the Ouseburn, cross the road bridge into Sandyford. Jerry keeps his thoughts to himself; he's not ready to tell Mackie about Ursula.

You are an anti-establishmentarian of the first order, Mackie, he says, in fact you are fat.

I am. And you are lush.

Luscious.

A dog.

I am the dog of a dog, says Jerry.

I'm hungry, says Mackie.

Jerry leads them to Eslington Road. There is a black Victorian church on one end. Beyond a playing field lies the road, and the Town Moor stretching out to nothing.

I'm waiting here, says Jerry.

What for? says Mackie.

For nothing to happen.

Mackie climbs on the church wall.

What about Karen Grey?

See you later, says Jerry.

Mackie walks backwards along the wall, teetering on purpose as he goes. For the first time in their lives, something

66

stands between them and their playfulness.

Aye, says Mackie, unsurely. Aye.

He jumps off the wall, and walks away. Jerry is about to call after him when he sees a light go on in 35 Eslington Road. Mackie disappears round the corner. Neither Mackie nor Jerry knows that this moment is the germ of their growing apart. In time sadness will develop in Mackie. When he is older, in his shop on the Shields Road, he will realise that when they were growing up Jerry was always improving himself while he was tagging along, playing the fool. He will feel a small sense of betrayal.

Jerry steps into the front garden of number 35. Behind the dense privet hedge, under the darkness of a beech tree, he stands on thick layers of uncleared leaves, and looks through the basement bay window.

Inside, he sees the CND posters on the walls, the mahogany bookcases, a bead door, tied back on one side, the deep-red Persian rugs. He sees mirrors and marble mantelpieces; an Aladdin's cave. There is a clutter of books in a pile, a modernist painting of a farm, a red-and-silver Chinese vase, bronze statuettes, a row of brown and gilt-edged cups, patterned plates, and lamps glowing under different-coloured shades.

In the kitchen a boy is playing a guitar. A woman is sitting at a long table in a big hat. Jerry cannot see Ursula. He pulls himself up on to a branch of the beech tree and looks into the floor above. A woman is writing at a desk. A girl with long hair, older than Ursula, talks with a man, raising an eyebrow ironically. It seems to Jerry they are aware of how they appear. They seem to have a kind of knowingness. There is no sign of Ursula.

He cannot know it but she's not there. Half an hour earlier she'd opened the front door and said, 'Going out,' and tottered down the front steps to meet Jeanette and Ashley, friends from school. Right now they are standing together in the underpass near St Anne's Church in the cold darkness. They wear short skirts, their legs are bare, feet crammed into stilettos. They stamp them like colts to keep warm. Ursula is wearing a black beret to flatten her perm.

It's nice, says Jeanette. My mam had a perm.

Let's go, says Ursula. She will not talk about her hair.

They totter through the underpass, arms linked to steady themselves, heels clattering in the tunnel. Ursula has a small bottle of rum in her bag; she took it from the cooking cupboard. She takes a sip and offers it round. The girls sip in turn and gasp, feeling the burn of the alcohol.

Where did you say you were going? says Jeanette.

I told my mam I was going to yours, says Ashley.

Eee, I did that too! says Jeanette, laughing.

Me too! says Ursula. She hasn't told anyone anything. As she'd left the house her father looked up from his papers and asked in a perplexed tone if she was wearing a wig. It had prompted her decision to wear the beret.

Jeanette takes out a lip gloss, puts some on, sliding her lips together, hands it to Ursula.

Cherry, she says.

Ursula puts some on and passes it on to Ashley.

How much have you got?

Six pounds.

I've got eight.

Eight pound fifty.

Their lips shine in the street light. As they emerge from the underpass, the blue star of the Carriage looms ahead of them. Ursula licks her lips, tastes the bittersweet of the gloss. They step inside and push through the crush of bodies to a small copper-topped table next to the one-armed bandit. They sit on the cushioned stools, bags on their knees, affecting the studied nonchalance of grown-up women.

They daren't go to the bar, and sip surreptitiously from the rum bottle. Ursula looks around for The Boy. She recognises no one except Howard, her old CND counterpart, with his friend Tommy Gaughan. They are standing in the corner in long black coats that are too big for them. Their presence is embarrassing to Ursula. They do not seem from the same species as The Boy.

Pathetic, says Ashley, nodding at them, and pursing her lips. Ursula looks away in case Howard catches her eye. He and Tommy look so young and awkward. They could ruin everything.

Fucking hell! He fancies you, says Jeanette to Ursula.

Howard? says Ursula, feeling despair.

No. Him! says Jeanette.

She points to the bar towards an older boy. He's red-haired, smiling. Perhaps he's a man. He winks at Ursula.

He's coming over, says Ashley.

Ursula feels scared. At the same time she recognises that she has been chosen. How lovely she must look, with her painted face and her eyes spidery with mascara. How wise she was to get the perm. She might not have Ashley's smile or Jeanette's bust, but she has curls.

The ginger-haired male looms over her.

I've seen you before, haven't I? he says. Can I buy you a drink?

Half a lager, she says quickly.

He cocks his head on one side in a cheery smile.

Howhey, come on then!

He sets off to the bar. His voice is higher than she'd expected.

Don't go, says Ashley, urgently. You don't know him.

He's left school, says Jeanette. He's working I think. He's called Craggy, or Cracky or something . . .

He must be nineteen, maybe even twenty . . .! says Ashley.

Twenty-one! says Ursula, squeezing Jeanette's arm with excitement. She stands up and pushes through the crowd towards him.

Are you Craggy?

Caggy.

His face is piggish. There is something almost rubbery about his skin.

I've seen you before, says Ursula.

That's my line, he says.

It's mine now, says Ursula, touching her curls.

Caggy laughs. His eyes sparkle. Ursula knows she is making them do so, and it makes her bold and exhilarated. He gives her a cigarette and she drags the smoke down deep into her chest. He puts his arm around her, and she smells the aftershave. He likes her hat, and asks if she is French. She laughs and says, *oui*.

Later, outside, he presses into her against a wall, breathes into her neck and kisses her ear, warm and wet. He puts his hand between her legs. This is what she's been waiting for. Somehow he's found his way to her heart, the most tender, ineffable place inside her. Her body responds with waves of pleasure, pulsing from her like rays from a lighthouse. Her tongue is in his mouth and Ursula disappears. The troubled world of Sandyford, Heaton, Byker and Jesmond floats away, and with it all the tensions of her life, nuclear annihilation, the unfathomable nature of mothers, grandmothers, the mysteries of hairdressing, all disappear as pure pleasure floods through her, and Ursula and Caggy gasp together in the cold Newcastle air.

For an hour or more Jerry has been walking up and down Jesmond streets looking in at the houses. Some are dark, their Victorian frontages imposing like stone gods; others glow, their bay windows bright displays of lives within. Jerry imagines professors, teachers, artists, politicians. He is about to leave when he can't resist going down Eslington Road one more time. She's there on the doorstep, ringing the bell, wearing a hat. He stands on the pavement looking at her. If she looks round she will see him. He does not try to hide. He wills her to turn. If she does so, he will know what to say. But she is oblivious, leaning her head against the door.

Ursula is thinking about Caggy. When her brother Jonathan finally lets her in she runs past him downstairs without saying a word, goes into the dark dining room and turns upside down. The blood falls into her head. She stares into the bay window gleaming with reflections of the room like a mirror, a jumble of furniture, and bright spots of light bulbs below skirt shades. In the background, Ganny Mary is muttering to herself at the table. Beyond the reflections, there is the real darkness of the night. The lustre of Caggy is fading. Ursula is all questions; doubts begin to crowd her. Was this the wonderful beginning she'd imagined? The handsome boy from school had turned into Caggy. He was sweet, wasn't he? But what had happened? Has she discovered herself? Is love so brief? She feels again the moment he touched her. In the darkness outside, something moves. It is the shape of a boy. She drops to her feet and runs to the window, cups her hands against the glass. There is no one. Even the bushes are boys now.

Mary sees her granddaughter at the window, but she is oblivious to her trembling sense of the future. She is lost in the past, rocking with memory now, *Too loo la bumbity ay. Too loo la bumbity ay* . . . she sings quietly.

As the owner's daughter, she is superior to the laundry-women, but it doesn't stop her listening eagerly as they sing the songs they've heard at Padiham Picture Palace the night before. She tries to catch the tune. Their voices rise over the noise of the stirring tubs and boiling pans, the slopping and the sloshing, the squeaking of the mangles as their great cogs grind, and the flat irons hiss as they hit the wet cloth.

Too loo la bumbity ay. They sing freely. *Too loo la bumpity ay. Too loo la bumpity ay, Too roo roo bumpty ay!*

Her father, Hubert, is sitting at his desk with the accounts. He looks over at Mary, raises an eyebrow, and tuts loudly.

Go down there, Mary, and stop their singing, he says in a severe voice.

Daddy, she says, it's important to let the women sing. They must sing.

He laughs out loud to hear her parrot his words. Hubert prides himself on his understanding of human needs and impulses. He stands up and looks out from the open door of his office, raised from floor level on railway sleepers.

That's right, he says, putting his arm round her. They work hard. They must take their pleasure where they can.

For Mary, the laundry is a place of progress and renewal – dirty items are made clean, folded into neat piles, loaded on to the carts for delivery. It is an enterprise of importance. Her father has a high reputation in Padiham. His laundry takes the linen for Gawthorpe Hall, and Huntroyde. The song finishes, and a new one starts. Mary watches her father's face light up as he hears it. Harriet Peters, his oldest washerwoman, steaming handkerchiefs, one after another, sings out, rich and passionate.

> *As I walked out one midsummer's morning*
> *For to view the fields and the flowers so gay,*
> *Down on the banks of the sweet primroses*
> *I beheld a most pleasant maid.*
>
> *I said, 'Fair maid, what makes you wander?*
> *What has caused all your grief and pain?*
> *I will make you as happy as any fair lady*
> *If you will grant me one small wish.'*

The women respond in unison. The young ones laugh in mockery at the song, but the older ones savour each word of indignation.

> *'Stand up young man! And don't be so deceitful!*
> *It is you have caused all my grief and pain.*
> *It is you that caused my poor heart to wander*
> *To give me comfort lies in vain.'*

Mary joins in; a sad small voice. Hubert smiles at her as her eyes become mournful and she holds her hand to her heart.

> *Oh I will go down to some lonely valley*
> *Where no man on earth shall e'er me find*
> *Where the pretty little small birds do change their*
> *   voices,*
> *And every moment blows blusterous wind . . .*

When the women have finished, he strides on to the laundry floor, Mary at his heels.

In fine voice today, Harriet, he says.

Thank you, Hubert.

How's the new starch from Manchester? he says.

Better than the old.

That's good, isn't it? he says to Mary, squeezing her hand.

Less time in the tub, Daddy, she says confidently.

Harriet laughs, and Hubert does too. Mary smiles broadly.

Her mother Annie comes in and waves to them from the open door, sunshine flooding in behind her.

Come, Mary, she says.

Where are you off to, your majesty? Hubert asks his wife playfully.

I'm going up Pendle. Come, Mary. We'll get butter at Tythe Farm.

I can't, Mummy. I've to fill out the order, says Mary. I am

so good with numbers and writing now.

Go on, Mary, says her father.

It'll do us good to feel the wind, says Annie, smiling at her daughter.

He watches them go. The daughter running to catch the mother who strides with a freedom in her steps. Annie, the woman he loves, full of astonishing forces, unmanageable as clouds. He thinks of how she gives herself to him in the intimate hours, and his joy in her release. She lets him take her to the edges of herself and hold her there until they are open to each other, like the sea and the shore. In those precious moments, all his worries vanish; he is no longer Hubert Tate, founder of Padiham Laundry. Annie makes him innocent again. When they walk to church on a Sunday morning, arm in arm, Mr and Mrs Tate once more, for Hubert, their secret knowledge of each other is his calm beneath the sky.

The Newcastle Civic Centre, modernist tower of white concrete and glass, gleams in the bright North East sunshine. It is crowned with a dozen green sea horses that jut up into the sky like gargoyles. Poseidon hangs upside down on one side of the building, water cascading from his long hair into an ornamental basin.

Time has moved on and Ursula has a new number for her age: sixteen. It is a good number on a good day. Saturday 12 May. The first ever CND women's fun day in the North East. Newcastle Civic Centre. For women only!

Joyce is delighted it is being held here in such a prominent location. She's spent months organising it. Peter pulled a few strings for her in the Council so they could use the Civic Centre gardens. Stalls are being set up, selling badges, T-shirts, leaflets. There is a sense of celebration among the women; everyone enjoying the sun, happy the rain kept away. Joyce's friends from Greenham Common have travelled up to gather support in the North East. Ursula stands slightly apart from everyone, thinking about her boyfriend, Tony. She can't wait to show him her new hair. Today it is orange; short and tufty, like a carpet sample glued to her scalp. She cut it herself the night before, standing in front of the mirror in her bedroom with a pair of scissors. She used peroxide to incinerate all natural colour then pasted on manure-like henna that she'd mixed up in a teacup, all the while listening to Radio One, *Fame, I'm gonna live forever!* and thinking, catchy commercial shit but listening anyway, while the wet dung steamed on her head, *I'm gonna learn how to fly. High!* Afterwards she looked in the mirror, saw her hair the colour of washed carrots, her skin all weird and pasty-looking, and smiled with satisfaction, lush!

Her mother has dragged her along today, despite her protestations about band practice with Tony. She doesn't really have band practice; she and Tony currently are embarked on a sexual adventure which is nothing if not addictive, but Joyce's involvement in CND has intensified again, and she didn't take Ursula's no for an answer. A journalist is coming, and there will be a photo opportunity. Ursula must be there to show that young people are involved in the campaign. Joyce had her eyes opened to the power of the media by the protests of the Greenham Common women. She spent last Christmas at the camp. It was more important that her children had a planet to live on than presents to unwrap, she'd told Peter. Besides, the family was barely at home any more: Bethany at university, Jonathan in Fenham, playing in his band, permanently stoned, only coming home to pick up clothes. Ursula is the only one left.

The women gather at the war memorial, the bronze women, their counterparts, behind them, wailing for the dead. They wear ghoulish costumes, and carry home-made warheads and painted banners. A woman with a headscarf has a huge Tupperware tub filled with cupcakes. Joyce hands out xeroxed copies of the government's public information leaflet: *How to*

Protect and Survive in the Event of a Nuclear Attack.

Hide under a table?! laughs one of the women. Take a door off its hinges, lean it against the wall, make a lean-to shelter. Good God! We've nothing to worry about, then!

Ursula is hoping Tony won't go out before she can escape and join him. Underneath Poseidon, other protestors are putting on skull masks. One wears a long cloak, and carries a cardboard sickle. It's Howard's mum. Her face is ashen, her eye-liner smudged. Ursula's heard from someone at school that Howard's mother had a nervous breakdown. She walks next to a blood-stained nuclear missile. Trainers and jeans poke out the bottom of it. Ursula wonders if Howard might be inside, smuggled into the women-only event in case his mum breaks down again.

How about this? cries Sarah Thornton, one of Joyce's compatriots on the Jesmond committee, reading the xerox to the assembled women. 'If you live in a flat, start negotiating with the neighbours on lower floors now – so that if a warning comes you can shelter in their place.' Bloody politicians! What do they care?! They're hiding in their bunkers!

The skulls chuckle in agreement.

Joyce sees Ursula through the crowd.

Get inside the warhead, Ursula! The journalist will be here soon. He's going to take a picture for the *Journal*. And chant!

Do I have to? says Ursula.

Yes darling, and later you can get your face painted.

I'm too old, Mum.

Don't be so po-faced! says Joyce brightly. We're celebrating!

Joyce's nervousness is making her infuriatingly cheerful.

78

Ursula knows why. There are a lot of women from different factions and all of them want to be in charge. It is hard for Joyce to find her place.

If the police move in, let's all chant! cries Joyce, turning to the skulls. Joan and Sylvie, new friends from Greenham Common, are arriving, dressed like ghosts. Joyce calls out to them, Girls! You look fabulous! Just in time! Oh good, here's the journalist!

A man with a camera approaches tentatively, shows his press card.

Hi. I'm from the *Journal* . . .

Time for the photo everyone! cries Joyce, smiling at the journalist. She gives Ursula her pleading look. Ursula sighs and gets into the nuclear warhead.

Nearby in some shrubs, their feet sinking into the loose soil, Jerry and Mackie peek over the top of the foliage. Jerry pulls two crumpled skirts out of his pockets, one red Lycra, one beige wool.

An old lady died in this, man, says Mackie, taking the beige one.

Best top quality, says Jerry. Ten pence. Charity shop.

They step into the skirts, fumble with the fastenings, secure them around their waists.

Trousers?

Off, says Jerry.

They wriggle out of their jeans and stand laughing at each other.

Man, you're a fucking fright!

Sexy!

Sexy as my dad's hairy arse.

They squint into the sun as they step out of the bushes.

Across the gardens, the photographer is trying to position the women on the memorial in front of his tripod, but they are in no mood to be marshalled by anyone, least of all a man.

Please ladies . . . costumes at the front . . .

Mackie and Jerry saunter over nonchalantly.

Jesus! Who's this? cries one of the women pointing at them.

Will they cut me balls off? whispers Mackie, tying a blue headscarf under his chin.

Indubitably, says Jerry. Smile.

Ursula watches the two odd-looking girls approaching. One of them, in a tight red mini-skirt, is smiling directly at her.

Who do you think you are?! shouts Sarah Thornton. It's not the bloody pantomime!

We are lesbians! Let us in! cries Mackie putting his hand on his hip.

The women burst out laughing.

That's it, everyone smile . . .! If you can see my lens I can see you . . . shouts the photographer, rushing back to his tripod.

Jerry makes his way towards Joyce.

Hi, says Jerry, charmingly. We want to join in.

You can't, says a woman in tie-dye. You are male.

I beg to differ, says Jerry. I am neither male nor female. None of us are. We are only gendered by our cultural conditioning.

Boys, says Joyce, I'm going to have to ask you to go.

We want to join CND. We are studying politics at school, says Jerry quickly. Mackie here is writing an essay on whether nuclear weapons herald the inevitable end of capitalism. His thesis is that Marx himself would have very much thought along these lines.

Aye, says Mackie, grinning.

What school do you go to? says Joyce, not sure whether to be charmed or annoyed.

The illustrious Byker Comprehensive, says Jerry.

Ill being the operative part of the word, miss, says Mackie, instinctively addressing her like a teacher.

Ill-mannered, says Jerry.

Ill-equipped . . .

Ursula watches them from inside the carpet-roll warhead, stifling her laughter.

This is brilliant, says the journalist, this is a great angle! This'll get on the front page!

Will it? Yes! cries Joyce, seeing an opportunity. Of course they can join us. All group together. Ursula! Girls. Come on. Boys, whatever you are! Hold up your banners! All together, say, 'CND!'

They all smile, previous tensions loosened, Ursula in the warhead, the skulls, the Greenham women. Mackie shows his leg, Jerry winks at Ursula, the bronze women of the statue behind them, forever weeping. The journalist's camera flashes.

Perfect! he shouts.

The women break into small groups, and start to set up stalls.

Hi, says Jerry to Ursula.

Hello, she says, instantly tongue-tied. She looks down at his hairy legs beneath his tight skirt, covered in goose bumps.

Let's go, he says. Let's just go.

81

Where? she laughs.

I dunno. We'll get food. Cake. Chips.

He looks at her with the same openness she remembers from the hairdresser's.

OK. Chips, she says.

Mackie runs up to them. His skirt is starting to slip, and he holds it up with one hand. Finally, man! I know who I am! I'm a lesbian! Through and through. A big fat lesbian!

He roars with laughter. Ursula and Jerry hold each other's gaze.

Hello? What's going on here? says Mackie, clocking the look between them.

Nothing, says Jerry.

Are you his minder? says Ursula, too quickly.

Aye, sister, says Mackie. We are umbilically joined. By a joiner. I can thoroughly recommend him . . .

. . . for all your joining needs, says Jerry, unable to stop himself. Joined-up writing, aching joints, smoking joints.

Ursula tries to wriggle out of the warhead. As she lifts it over her head, her T-shirt rises up, revealing her bra. She quickly pulls it down.

Don't be shy! says Mackie. Look at me. I'm a jelly. Wibble wobble.

He lets his skirt fall and lifts up his top, shaking his belly.

A god amongst men! laughs Jerry.

What's your name? says Mackie.

Ursula, says Jerry for her.

Your hair is not a natural colour, I believe, Miss Ursula, says Mackie.

I've got to go, she says.

Where? asks Jerry.

I'm meeting my boyfriend.

Come on now, be fair, says Mackie. He's not really a boyfriend, is he? He's more of a gibbon.

See you, says Ursula, walking away.

Jerry blocks her path.

Don't go, he says, smiling. We've only just begun.

I'm late, she says, hesitating.

You do everything in your life to please men, he says and looks at her. Just looks and looks. She wants to move away, but can't. What right does he have to say that? What right does he have to judge her? What does he know about anything?

What's he called then, this gibbon boy? asks Mackie.

None of your business, says Ursula.

None of your business, echoes Mackie mocking her voice. Mental name!

It is you, I believe, who is mental, retorts Ursula, regaining her composure. Technically speaking, I do believe that you are what is known as a right mental case.

She turns on her heel. As she goes Jerry feels an unnameable excitement. It is both an incredible lightness, and intense desire. He watches her disappear behind St Thomas's Church, and a desperate longing takes hold of him, to cling to her for dear life, to run freely with her, to lift into the sky with this Ursula and fly away, like two balloons.

Danny Dovedale stands on the stage in assembly in front of a sea of fifth-formers. The local television station has come to recruit kids for a new discussion programme about Issues That Really Matter. Danny Dovedale wants to meet Real Kids.

Hi guys! he says, throwing wide his arms. Who here wants to represent their generation on television?

Two hundred teenagers in black school sweaters, grey shirts and blouses studiously ignore him. They sit on black plastic chairs in messy rows, like a catch of grey mullet dumped in a trawler. Dusty shafts of sunshine play through the windows on to the wood panels of the hall, sparkling on ear-rings and carefully careless hairstyles.

OK. So, I'm hosting a new exciting TV show for Tyne Tees Television, says Danny undaunted. By the kids, and for the kids!

A scuffle breaks out among the mullet as a girl's pencil case is snatched. It is a sign of love. Boys unzip it, gut it. Pink stickers, pink pencils with pink feathers, and a pink notebook fall to the floor.

I'm gonna kill you! Kill you. Kill you! the girl screams angrily, bustling through the rows, thrilled to be loved. The boys huddle together, and throw the notebook into the air. Its pink petal pages fly into the air.

Cheryl fancies Carl but so do I . . . reads one of the boys.

I'm gonna fucking kill you. Give that back, you fucking little shit.

Mr Hendry, Hender the Bender, wades in, a violent dog.

Settle down! he barks. Pay attention! Or detention!

Everyone looks begrudgingly at Danny Dovedale. Ursula is thinking about Tony. She's going round to his bedsit as usual after school. They've got band practice.

OK. Hi. OK. OK. Kids, I want to say some words to you. Religion. S. E. X. Sex. Yes, I said it. Sex. Money. School. Family. Sex.

Danny Dovedale grins, breathing fast. Ursula thinks there is something of a thirsty whippet about him.

Who wants to talk about these things on TV? Who's got something to say to the world?! Six programmes over six weeks! Live television! Let your opinions be heard!

The fifth-formers glare at him. It is summer. Exams are finished. They are on the verge of impossible newness. The doors are about to open and release them into a long hot summer they will remember for the rest of their lives. They do not care about Things That Really Matter.

It could be you on the TV, says Danny Dovedale, a little desperate. He was warned about Kempton Comprehensive. Not a good school. The teachers more apathetic than the children. The buildings are in the shape of the infamous prison H-blocks in Ireland. It is the fourth school he has visited this week. He's got Byker next, toughest of all, God help him.

A boy puts up his hand. Ursula winces. Sainty always

85

puts up his hand. She knows what he will say. Everybody does. He never says anything else.

We have a brave volunteer, beams Danny Dovedale. Great!

Please sir, can I go to the toilet, says Sainty.

The hall erupts with laughter. The toilet is Sainty's only line, his only joke. He once defecated on someone out of a tree. He squatted on a branch by the front gates with his trousers down, and waited for Mr Jordon, the hated metalwork teacher, to walk beneath him. Danny Dovedale laughs too, loud and nervous.

Right right. So . . .? Yeah. Does anyone have any questions? he says, hopefully.

Can I go to the toilet too? another boy shouts.

Hender the Bender stands up.

Year Five. Detention!

There are groans and more laughing.

Keep your mouths shut and sit on your chairs!!

The grey mass shuffles and murmurs. Danny Dovedale crouches down at the front of the stage, and switches to his quiet, intense voice.

I'm looking for kids who want to make a difference, for young people who care, who have something to say. Come on, people, say yes!

Ursula raises her hand.

Yes, she says.

She is not sure why. It is just one of those times when she says yes. There will be other moments in her life like this. Yes, without thinking. Yes; she will make a difference. Perhaps there is something familiar in the way Danny Dovedale appealed for help; something of her mother. She's heard her do it so many times: we've got to get together, to make a difference. Who'll join me? Together we cannot be outdone!

She walks home through the Dene, a wooded ravine, moving in and out of sunshine and shade, feeling the temperature rise and drop, mulling on what she's done; Danny Dovedale; Television. She's a Real Kid. She'll make a difference.

She crosses under the Armstrong Bridge to the allotments and walks through Sandyford. Tony's bedsit is a single room on the second floor of a mid-terraced house. The door to the corridor is wide open. Tony is sitting at the open window, tanning himself in a pool of sunlight. 'The Passenger', by Iggy Pop, blares from the speaker.

Ursula's been seeing Tony for four months. He's older than her, studies part-time at college, claims dole, and plays in a band. She made a list about him once on the back of her English file.

Good Things About Tony

He has his own bedsit.
I get to play in his band.
He is sexually experienced.

Ursula particularly likes to 69. Tony has taught her this. She likes the way he lets out great sighs of satisfaction when he is enjoying her soft pink vulva.

There is barely any furniture in the bedsit – purpose-built

shelves, a bed, a kettle and cassette player on the floor. Ursula puts down her school bag and lies down.

Band practice is cancelled, he says.

Shall we 69? she says.

I thought you'd never ask! he says.

He takes off his clothes, and lies next to her. Licking, dabbing, scooping, squeezing, spit polishing, rubbing, mindless comfort, endless titillation, multiple orgasms, lost hours.

Ah man! cries Tony eventually. Ah man!

Ursula is always dumbfounded when her throat is filled with the thick salty liquid. She doesn't mind, but sometimes a slight, unfathomable loss enters her, and she feels distant from everything. Sometimes Tony's exuberance thrills her. I have a fantastic cock! he exhales. And you, Ursula, have a fantastic cunt. A match made in heaven! He ejaculates into the air, his penis straight up like a rocket launcher. He watches his semen shoot up in a spurt. It makes him roar with laughter. Look at that! he cries. Mental!

She wraps the duvet round her, leans over to the tape recorder, turns over the cassette.

Are you going then? she asks.

You bet! he says. I'm starving!

He returns with two newspaper parcels as big as bricks. Cross-legged on the bed, two layers of newsprint, two of white paper. Piles of steaming chips and gravy.

Ursula savours the salt and vinegar, the hot of the chips. Devo thumps out from the tape recorder. *Are we not men? We are DEVO! D–E–V–O.*

This is what life is all about! says Tony.

Yes, life is all about chips, says Ursula smiling.

OK! Hey, so, I want this to be real, says Danny Dovedale.

Ursula is at the first recording of *Let's Talk* at Tyne Tees Television studios with twenty-six other Real Kids from across the North East.

Spontaneity is the name of the game, cries Danny as they are funnelled into the studio through double doors. No rehearsal or prep! Just go for it!

Jerry is arriving too. He's late, wearing a pale-green T-shirt. He is coming along the corridor, joining her at the end of the line.

Weird, he says, looking straight at her. I didn't know you were representative of the nation's youth.

Danny Dovedale visited Jerry's sixth-form college after Ursula's school. There was little enthusiasm among the pupils, but Jerry's history teacher is a personal friend of Danny Dovedale and persuaded him to sign up. He would be a credit to his school, he said. It was touch-and-go whether Jerry would show up. He told his sister Andie it would be a pretentious charade, a piece of piss. She told him he'd fit right in. Mackie said he'd go instead. When Jerry arrived at Tyne Tees Television studios, Mackie was at reception in a Batman costume claiming to be Jerry, demanding to be heard by the nation. Jerry had to persuade him to go home before the woman on the desk called security. So here is Jerry now, following Ursula into the studio, following her beacon of red-and-newly-blue hair, on to the set for *Let's Talk*.

There are semi-circular rows of cushions in parrot colours. Cameras glide slowly like floor polishers, finding angles. The teenagers squint anxiously in the glare of the lights.

Anyone bring sunglasses? says someone, and everyone titters nervously. Danny Dovedale sits on an orange pouffe at the front to host the event; in front of him is a coffee table with magazines and a bowl of fruit. Ursula looks at Jerry across the semicircle. She catches his eye and looks away.

Don't worry if you don't get a chance to speak, barks Danny with forced hilarity. We'll be filming drop-ins. OK, kids. Relax! Let's rock and roll!

OK, five four three two one . . . says an assistant, and Danny Dovedale shines towards the camera.

Welcome to *Let's Talk*. This programme is by you, for you . . .

A camera glides towards Ursula as though expecting something of her. She nods sagely at Danny's words, worried her nerves are making her lips curl.

Over the next six weeks we're going to be talking about things that bother you, that make you curious, that get you into trouble, says Danny to camera, things you can't talk about. Tonight we're going to start with two of those subjects – sex and religion! I want to know whether you can discuss these things with your parents? Can you? Do you?

Suddenly everything is happening fast. People talking, raising their hands. Two cameras waltz across the floor.

A girl with thick black hair is holding forth. The cameras zoom in on her.

To be quite honest, there's a lot of fuss made about sex, she says.

Go on, Joanne, says Danny.

Look at the media. Just look at the media. Joanne smiles and shakes her head to show just how exhausting and incomprehensible it all is. Girls dress up, go out on the Bigg Market, and they're under pressure to get off with a lad. It's like a badge.

A ginger-haired boy raises his hand and the cameras veer towards him. It's the same for lads, he says nervously.

Right, says Danny, good point. Advertising. Peer pressure. Mmmmm . . .

Ursula looks at the bowl of fruit. It is out of reach, even to Danny Dovedale. The fruit will never be eaten, the magazines never read. Nothing is real, except the cameras. Danny Dovedale is asking for another perspective but Joanne is still holding forth.

There's more to life than snogging, says Joanne.

Is there? says someone, and the studio erupts with laughter.

Of course there is, she says, tossing her hair. I'm a Christian and, in my book, sex should be in the sight of God.

Ursula feels a prickle of anger, and opens her mouth to say something. A camera hovers near her in what seems like anticipation, ready to catch every word and expression. She feels overwhelmed, and nothing comes.

Why are we even talking about sex? says someone else. I agree with Joanne. We are obsessed with it in our society. There is so much more to life than sex.

It's a girl with long straight hair, pale skin, older, her voice quiet and serious.

OK, Zoe, says Danny Dovedale. Go on . . .

As a Christian, interrupts Joanne, I believe we should live our lives, not for sex, but for God.

Living is our humanity, says Zoe quietly. It has nothing to do with Christianity, or sex. What you do with your life matters. It has nothing to do with God.

Her accent is foreign, perhaps she is American, or Australian, or Danish.

You're wrong, says Joanne.

I want to do something useful with my life. To help people, to make a difference.

Really? Like what? asks Joanne.

I've spent time in India. My father works there as a doctor, helping children with cerebral palsy, says Zoe. I just want to help in any way that I can.

Everything is God's will in the end, says Joanne insistently. You can't help people because you want to. It's up to God. You should do it for God. I'm a Christian, and the idea that you can make a difference is wrong. Only God can make a difference. That's what the Bible says.

That's . . . blurts Ursula, unable to stop herself.

What? says Danny. Go on, Ursula.

A camera moves in on her, its red eye flashing. Ursula suddenly feels unaccountably angry.

You want everyone to believe in a Christian God, she says to Joanne, to take them away from their own feelings, from who they are. That's fascist.

I can assure you I am not a fascist! says Joanne indignantly. You obviously don't have faith.

Faith is just what you've learned in a church. It's nothing to do with anything that is actually real!

Are you saying hundreds of generations of believers are wrong?

Yes I am! shouts Ursula, violence rising in her.

Why are you so angry? says Joanne.

I am not fucking angry! shouts Ursula. Why are you saying that God exists? How dare you?

I feel God everywhere, says Joanne evenly, smiling patiently.

No, you don't. You just feel yourself. You can't own mine or anyone's experience. You've got a stupid horrible face. You are fucking ridiculous!

Ursula stops, shocked at herself, breathing hard. There is silence in the studio. Everyone stares at her. The girl with the red-and-blue hair has gone mental. Joanne has tears in her eyes. No one knows where to look but Jerry does. He looks straight at Ursula with pure, unadulterated, golden, gargantuan godly, ungodly love.

Cut! says Danny Dovedale. Cut! Brilliant! Let's take a break.

At the post-show party, Ursula stands apart at a table of sandwiches and crisps. Danny Dovedale is talking consolingly with Joanne. They glance at her and she looks away, picks at some crisps, glugs a shandy, desperate to leave. She crouches down and feels under the table for her coat. When she stands up, Zoe is beside her.

Hi, says Ursula. I liked what you said about India.

You should come, she says. The children are amazing. India is incredible.

Is it? says Ursula.

Yes! And it's a good feeling, helping people.

Ursula nods. She'd like to talk longer with Zoe but she's already moving off.

Can I take your number? says Ursula.

Sure, says Zoe, writing it on a napkin. Call me any time if you want to know more.

Ursula takes the napkin, and folds it into her coat pocket. Zoe is gone, and Jerry is there.

There's not much green in here, says Jerry, for a green room.

There is a plant in the window, she says, without friend-liness. Why are you here?

I'm just here for the crisps, he says, taking a handful, and offering her the bowl.

I've got to go, she says.

She zips up her coat and turns to go.

You certainly made an impression, he says.

Impression? she mutters. Depression.

Concussion.

Confusion.

Confession, he says, following her to the door.

What impression are you trying to make? She turns to him sharply.

A ridiculous one, he grins. Fucking ridiculous.

She frowns. It's what she said to Joanne during the pro-gramme.

I was the ridiculous one. I went mental. Everyone hated me. I don't know what happened.

94

A blush creeps down her neck. Her discomfort touches him.

You were lush, he says matter-of-factly. Who wants to be in this piece of piss anyway?

Ursula looks at him. This is it! The moment Ursula looks and sees Jerry the rational materialist, objectivist, too clever to care, and sees more than that, senses the anarchy in him. He is still holding the crisp bowl. She takes one. His hair is longer than she remembered.

Long hair, she says.

Long head, he says. Going to meet your boyfriend, are you?

He's in hospital having his nose broken by the doctors.

His doctors are out of control! he says, laughing.

Don't laugh at the afflicted, she says. He has a sinus problem.

Let's go, he says. Come on!

She hesitates.

Me or old gibbon no-nose? . . . What's it to be?

They walk out of the TV studios and on to the quayside. The Tyne shines with the promise they feel.

Are yous famous then? a voice calls from the darkness. Mackie is lurking in the forecourt of a closed garage among the dark pumps, robot-like, standing in formation. He bounds across the road towards them in his Batman suit. Ursula falters.

Am I scaring you? says Mackie. Is it my disguise? Are you weird? Weird like not weird at all?

Goodbye, says Ursula.

She turns and walks towards the Barley Mow, disco lights flashing in the windows.

Fuck off, Mackie! says Jerry. Blunt as a punch. Mackie spits hard on the ground. Jerry won't let Ursula go again. To hell with Mackie. He sprints after her.

You forgot something, he says catching her by the Egypt Cottage.

What did I forget?

His smile is easy.

Me, he says.

They walk through streets to the west end of the city, and the Town Moor. The Hoppings fair is at one edge of it, in the distance; a million dancing lights; its outline like an ocean liner in the darkness. They don't speak much, just walk together as though they know exactly where they are going.

I feel bad about Tony, Ursula says.

You really do do everything in your life to please men? he says, challenge in his eyes.

Of course, she says lightly, although to be honest I'm only agreeing with you because you are a man.

It will go on like this, their jousting, their opinions. It's a conversation they can't stop, a conversation without end. Their battles might destroy them over time, in the time-honoured fashion of men and women, or perhaps they will be together for ever, held by their love for each other, and somehow survive. It is unknowable, too early, but as they reach the edge of the Hoppings, feel the bass throb, the generators roar, the people screaming as rides wheel and circle, they feel it beginning between them. They stop by the side of Northumberland Road.

Ever climbed on a roof? she says.

I'm trying to cut down on it to be honest, he smiles.

They walk through the gates into the Royal Victoria Infirmary, moving through shadows until they find a fire escape. Ursula leads the way up the side of the hospital building. At the top, they reach a barbed-wire roll and, breathless with daring, they clamber over it on to the huge flat roof. It's a new world. They run zigzag through the cooling towers, and lie side by side on the asphalt, the pale moon high above them.

It's the sea, says Ursula looking up at the sky. We are lying at the bottom of the ocean.

A torn cloud passes across the moon, just for them. They smile at it.

It's smiling, says Ursula.

Laughing, says Jerry.

Its mouth is open . . .

A laughing cloud! They see it, and it sees them.

Ursula turns to Jerry. The clouds are alive!

You're beautiful, he says.

You are, she says.

It's all beautiful . . . and they are kissing.

I want to 69, Ursula says.

What? OK, says Jerry, astonished.

And then 82! And then 58, 102, and 5,063, and 4,886,640! They make love as it rains, open-mouthed, cloud-drinking. Unflinching they dive into each other, sparking atoms whizzing in thin membranes, some breaking out, wildly free, becoming new, like billions of years ago, the first chemical spark, when alkali and acid came from the mouths of underwater vents, connecting for the first time, they make the zing of life, feel it now there's no turning back. Here is a schedule of events.

7 September

Ursula visits her boyfriend Tony in hospital. The procedure to improve his sinus has gone well. He is sitting up in bed with a black-and-green bruise across the bridge of his nose, cotton wool protruding from his nostrils.

Tony, I have something to say. I have met someone else, says Ursula gently. I am sorry this comes at such a difficult time with your nose and everything. I am grateful for the time we have had, and for how you have loved me but now I love another. I honour the connection we have had, and let it go.

Of course she doesn't say this! She is Ursula – the great mess of her! She looks away and mumbles, Can I have my Cure LP back?

What?

Can you drop it at my house?

Why?

I . . . want to finish.

He groans. She can't bear to look at his nose.

I'm sorry, she says. You can keep it.

20 September

At Jerry's invitation, Ursula joins the Literary and Philosophical Society. He picks out Simone de Beauvoir for her. They go through the text, reading it aloud to each other in urgent whispers. Jerry is pleased when Ursula is filled with righteous indignation. They move on to feminist theory, and soon she is awash with *écriture* and all sorts of hegemonies.

29 September

They decide to eschew all conventional behaviour and expectations. Jerry wears a dress to the Guildhall Bar to feel what it is like to be a woman in a phallocentric world. They decide that in future they will dress as badly as they can to make a stand against the oppression of women in general and the poor in particular.

15 October

They celebrate Jerry's seventeenth birthday by joining the Revolutionary Communist Party in a small community centre in Wallsend. They are the youngest people there. They attend two further meetings, but soon tire of what Jerry calls the parochial attitudes, and decide to create their own political party. Ursula writes the manifesto, which demands a complete and utter dedication to chips, toast, and 69-ing.

31 October

Jerry and Ursula discuss their future.
 I'm not going to university, says Jerry, it's a construct.
 Yeah, says Ursula.
 They decide to be autodidacts; they will learn all they need to learn at the Literary and Philosophical Society.

10 November

In between reading bouts at the Literary and Philosophical Society, they make love in the ladies' toilet.

I'm going to come, she says, a diver trembling on the board above the sea of ecstasy.

Wait . . . he gasps, longing for the death pounce of a tiger.

They experiment with staying on the verge of orgasm for as long as they can.

This is tantric, says Jerry solemnly.

I need chips! cries Ursula, releasing herself into waves of ecstasy. Iris puts a lock on the ladies' door.

25 November

Apart from Ganny Mary, Ursula and Jerry have the whole house to themselves. Joyce is away at a CND conference and Peter is in London addressing the Parliamentary Committee on Transport.

They spend five days in bed.

Capitalism's destiny is utter collapse, says Jerry.

He loves to read post-Marxist theory, and analyse their relationship in terms of economics, while his body tessellates with Ursula's. She reads about economics and learns that the most direct approach for calculating GDP is the product approach which sums the outputs of every class of enterprise to arrive at the total. The expenditure approach works on the principle that all of the product must be bought by somebody, so the value of the total product must be equal to the people's total expenditure in buying things. She has to read this bit ten times.

30 November

Jerry and Ursula are still in bed. There is a scream from downstairs. Ursula runs down to the kitchen as fast as she can. Ganny Mary is lying on the linoleum crying. She has fallen and bruised her head. Ursula tends to her, gently holding her head in her hands. Jerry watches from the door.

When they go back upstairs, Jerry feels relieved to feel the thinness of their bodies together in bed again.

'What made her fall?' he asks.

'The weight of the past,' says Ursula lightly, climbing on top of him.

16 December

Ursula is worried about all this reading she is doing. Isn't she meant to be active? How is she to become the magnanimous creature she hopes to be? How can she feel the rich realms of life she intuitively senses to be there?

1 January

Ursula and Jerry discuss freedom. Jerry says there can't be any while they are living in Western white male hegemony.

Let's go somewhere else, says Ursula. Italy, Africa, India.

Too far, says Jerry.

Ursula accuses him of preferring to read about foreign places than visit them. They have their first fight.

2 February

Ursula and Jerry march against apartheid in London.

Ursula joins in with gusto. Pigs! Pigs! she shouts at the

police. She joins the crowd pushing over metal barriers. Jerry asks her what on earth she is doing. She says she is angry about apartheid, angry about injustice in general, and basically just angry. Jerry tells her she is a sheep following the flock. There is no point directing anger against a few policemen. They are just working men like any other working men in a corrupt system that relies on force to maintain it, he says.

She tells him he's just scared of being arrested.

He tells her she is asinine.

You are phallocentric! she shouts.

Any man who is a feminist is equally oppressed, he shouts back.

Crap! You have a phallus!

I have, he shouts, but it all depends on what I do with it!

21 *February*

Ursula has a nightmare. There has been a nuclear blast in Newcastle. She and Jerry are leaving the city along the road near her house – the motorway that never ceases. She has lost her mother in the blast. She and Jerry walk all the way to Scotland. Then Jerry has gone and she is alone walking in hills in silence. When she wakes up, she longs for these hills, and the silence. She doesn't tell Jerry about her dream in case he mocks her.

13 *March*

A friend of Joyce's lends Jerry and Ursula a cottage. It is in Fairleigh in Lancashire between the sea and the Lancashire hills, not far from where Joyce was brought up in Padiham.

The cottage is cosy beneath vast skies bruised with rain clouds. They buy tins of tuna and pasta from the village shop, and sit wrapped in blankets, reading books. Jerry tells her they will live a life of the mind, and make love every day. At night they sleep curled around each other.

On the sixth day, a gash of sunshine cuts through the clouds.

I'm going for a walk, says Ursula.

She walks along a road shimmering with the night's rain. She strikes up a slope on one side of the road, mulling over various feminist theories. She thinks about the phallus; tries to see it as dominating. She was flashed at once as a girl on the way to school. The man's phallus had hung from his trousers like a long white toadstool. She'd run all the way to school dumbfounded, and hadn't told anyone. She thinks about Jerry's penis. It seems benign and lovely. She tries to see it as her oppressor, but keeps remembering how it felt that morning, warm and soft against her.

She reasons that a phallocentric phallus is not a real penis. It is, of course, an idea, a symbol – of power, of straightness, of penetration – and this is bad, most definitely. Why is it bad? It is bad because . . . women are treated as second-class citizens. Their ideas are not heard. They cannot contribute to society in equal measure to men. They are discounted. Men keep thrusting their penises into women's lives and keeping them down . . . Ursula reaches the top of the brow. The sight of the pebble shore and the shining sea sweeps her thoughts away. A container ship edges slowly along the horizon. The vast empty space is a blast of wonder.

When she gets back to the cottage, it is dark.

I was about to send out the search party, says Jerry.

I found the sea, Jerry. Let's go. It's not far.

He's cooked sardines on toast, made tomato salad.

It'll wait, she says, come on. The moon is out.

Tomorrow, he says. There's something I want to read.

You don't want to come because it is my idea, she says.

He puts on his long coat, wraps a scarf round his neck.

They trudge along the road in the dark in silence. Ursula has to guess the place where she cut up the slope to the sea. They follow the sound of the waves until the ground starts to descend and becomes soft and sandy, and stand together, the moon above them, its tail glittering on the black water.

Let's never get married, Ursula says.

Never trap each other, says Jerry.

I want to see places, experience things. I want to understand how the world turns!

Me too. I want to spend my life reading books under palm trees and being happy.

She kisses him.

Can I kiss your eyeball? he asks.

No, she says, laughing. Yuck!

I read about it, he says. We should try everything.

She keeps her eyes open as he licks into the corner. She wants to flinch and blink.

It's like a cat licking me.

I love you, he says, laughing. I'll always love you.

12 May

Jerry and Ursula are having a drink in the Archer. Unusually for them it is the first time they have seen each other in a week.

I've been offered a place at Oxford University, says Jerry.

Great, says Ursula.

I'm not remotely interested in Oxford, an institution for over-privileged bastards who should be lined up against the wall and shot, says Jerry. I only agreed to take the exam to prove what a piece of piss it is.

Talking of the future, says Ursula lightly. I'm going to India.

India? When?

Don't know yet, but . . .

When did you decide this?

I want to teach handicapped children.

Handicapped children? What are you going to teach them?

Music, lots of things. Zoe's helping me find somewhere. Zoe from the TV thing. I just need the air fare.

I think they can probably manage very well on their own without you coming all the way from Newcastle and getting under their feet.

I want to help, to get away from . . .

Me . . .?

Of course not.

You don't have to go halfway round the world to do that!

This has nothing to do with you.

He starts to laugh.

I can see that!

Possessiveness is phallocentric, says Ursula.

4 *June*

Why do we fight? says Jerry.

105

Jerry and Ursula are fighting. Fisticuffs, tantrums, almost every day. Jerry is confused by the instability of their relationship. It makes his heart pump and his blood race. His mind scrambles to stay in control in the face of Ursula's emotions. He is forced to sense new emotions of his own tumbling and battering as they break over the stones of himself.

2 *July*

Ursula books a flight to Madras, using £300 donated by a local newspaper for her humanitarian mission (there is a picture of her in the *Journal*, posing next to an atlas, looking purposeful) plus money she has saved from income support and housing benefit falsely claimed with the help of her brother, Jonathan.

3 *July*

After months of indecision Jerry decides to accept his full scholarship to Magdalen College, Oxford. He accepts the place in order to highlight the absurdity of privilege.

24 *September*

Joyce and Peter say goodbye to their youngest daughter, wishing she wasn't going quite so far, advising her to be careful. They give her Traveller's Cheques and a brand new backpack. When it's time to leave, Ganny Mary stands on the doorstep of Eslington Road and watches Ursula and Jerry set off together. Jerry with his plastic bag of books, Ursula with her backpack. They wave goodbye to her, to the house, and their childhoods, about to enter new and distant worlds. Ursula runs back and hugs her. See you Ganny Mary, she says, and is gone.

25 September

Ursula and Jerry say their goodbyes at Heathrow Airport. As she flies over the Gulf, he steps into the quad at Magdalen College, Oxford. Mary sits at the kitchen table in Newcastle, thinking about them, thinking how easily they left each other, and how foolish they are to believe nothing will change.

She knows better. Life is delightful one moment, broken the next. She sits in the quiet of the kitchen in Eslington Road. It is lonely in the house now. Jonathan and Bethany left years ago to do bemusing things in the world like psychology degrees and part-time business studies, and now Ursula, her little companion, has gone too. To the subcontinent of all places, while Mary stays put, never roaming, except backwards in her mind, reliving the shocks of her life. One in particular comes back and back. She sees her father at the sink, washing, his chest bare. Her mother is still not returned from Pendle Hill. They'll have tea when she gets home. Maybe she'll bring some of Mrs Littlewood's cake. Mary smiles; there's still time for a game of snatch-the-watch. She tiptoes up behind her father, knowing he knows she is there. He hums a ditty as he lathers the soap. Deftly, she reaches under the shirt towards his trouser pocket, feels the watch chain, gently tugs.

Who's there? he bellows, turning quickly with soapy hands.

She scuttles behind the table, splashes of water landing on her face, refusing to let one giggle escape.

No one, he says, bemused, and turns back to the sink.

He lathers up and resumes his singing, more loudly than before. Mary creeps over to him again, and slowly, very slowly, reaches to the lip of his pocket. He swivels fast and grabs her.

Caught you! he says, tossing her up into the air. She giggles uncontrollably, breathless, squirming in his wet hands.

You're a thief, Mary! A pirate!

I'll have that watch, Daddy! she cries, breaking free. She runs round the table. Her father does not follow her. Her mother is standing in the doorway. An apparition, her clothes unbuttoned, her face streaked with mud, her mouth open without sound.

Mary and her father stare at her. There is something wrong. This is not her mother. This is a woman, floating. She is soaking wet, and her clothes are torn. Her dress is ripped at the neck, and she is shining. There is ecstasy in her eyes. Mary runs to her father, but he pushes her away.

Go upstairs, he says quietly.

She holds him tighter.

Go on Mary, he says, eyes on Annie.

She runs from the room but listens, and watches through the hinges of the door. Hubert goes to Annie, takes her in his arms. What happened, Annie? he says. Who has done this to you? Mary doesn't speak. She is passive in his arms, trembling. He tries to hold her, but she is no longer his. She is wild, utterly beyond him, and her words are strange.

Mary watches her mother closely over the next few weeks. She is in a heightened state, confused one moment, full of joyous energy the next. She takes Mary on long walks and runs laughing through the woods. Hubert finds her trembling at the sink, her hands in the water, seeing visions. She takes to holding Mary's head and crying. He finds her staring at a leaf with a look of pure joy. Her strangeness frightens him.

Mary hears the laundrywomen say her mother has lain with another on Pendle Hill and is now racked with guilt. She hears the word 'slut'. Hubert fears worse still, that Annie was taken by another man; that some dire brutality has occurred, robbing her of speech. Mary hears him remonstrate with her, begging her to explain to him, to please, please explain what happened! She hears Annie crying, I lay down . . . on the hill and I . . . something entered me. She hears her father slam his fist on the table, and her mother's sobs. Once she hears her mother shouting, Who are you, Hubert? Who are you?

Hubert is a man of logic; whatever happened to Annie has brought her into turmoil. It must be stopped, controlled, managed, like any other business. He turns to his elder sister, Sissy. She lives in Manchester. She is devout and without children. Hubert has always considered her a rock. Sissy hears the work of the devil in her sister-in-law, and arrives from Manchester to see what can be done. Hubert takes her into the parlour, and they discuss the situation. Mary listens with her ear to the door. She hears her father express his darkest fear; his wife is losing her mind.

The next morning Sissy takes Annie away for a few weeks to Manchester. It will do her good to have a change of scene, she says, someone to confide in. Hubert is grateful. Soon his wife will be herself again, his own Annie.

She will never be. Sissy is involved in the Plymouth Brethren. She spends every second of the day with Annie talking about God. She speaks of his power to punish, about how this world is not to be loved for itself, but as a gateway to the next. Annie, in her openness, does not resist. Slowly the words penetrate her. Sissy gives her a Bible, tells her to follow its every instruction. When Annie tries to speak of what happened on Pendle Hill, Sissy reads to her from the Book of Job.

Canst thou by searching find out God? Canst thou find out the Almighty unto perfection? It is as high as heaven; what canst thou do? deeper than hell; what canst thou know? The measure thereof is longer than the earth, and broader than the sea.

Annie smiles and laughs, it's true! Sissy's face sets; her sister-in-law is glorifying herself. It is a sin to do so. She reads from Timothy: *Let the woman learn in silence with all subjection. But I suffer not a woman to teach, nor to usurp authority over the man, but to be in silence.* She takes Annie to Brethren meetings on the Wigan Road in a starched blouse, her hair pinned tight. The wildness of the hill slowly fades in Annie, and the Brethren enter her heart. When she returns to Padiham six months later, Hubert is baffled by the change in her. She prays in her bedroom without cease. When he touches her, she pulls away.

In his bewilderment, he sees her on the hill in the arms of another. Mr Trent from Kelly Street perhaps, or a stranger from out of town. It is guilt turned Annie to religion. He waits patiently but the delight of their intimacy becomes only a memory. Her heart seems to be against everything he loves, his work, the laundry, his Mary.

You should be afraid, Hubert, she cries. All striving in the world is for nothing. The laundry, the machines, the pride you have in them is sinful. Her voice breaks with tears, I beg you, Hubert! Repent while there's still time. Let the Lord govern you!

Dear Ursula,

It is eight hours since you left. It was so hard to leave you. I was full of contradictions and desperate not to see you go. I've never felt as though I needed someone so much or that they loved me in return, but I want you to go and experience everything and have a good time. After I saw you off at Heathrow I got the tube back to Finsbury Park. It's been a whirlwind. I'm in Oxford now. I feel weird. I am worried about how your flight was. I will send this letter with a normal stamp and try to work out how long it takes for it to arrive in India. I'll see if it's worth spending the extra £1.50 for special delivery. I don't mind at all if it makes a difference.

Dear Jerry,

I am finally here. I haven't slept since those frantic hours with you. How long ago? Days and days. I write this lying on my bunk, a mosquito is trapped inside my net. What am I doing here? I wish you would walk in and climb into bed with me. The flat is above the main road in Vellore and the sound of beeping of horns incessant. I feel exuberant and numb.

I hated leaving you at Heathrow. I thought that moment's separation would kill me. Sorry I cried so much. I soaked your shirt. I had been so tense with all the preparations – packing, getting to London, our last orgasms together. I cried both for fear and relief but most of my tears were for you.

I have already been on four planes and two buses! Warsaw! Dubai! Delhi and finally Madras, and Vellore. Warsaw airport was a no-man's-land. I was given ration tokens for a dinner of rancid gravy in a plastic tray. Everyone got the same in true communist style. The Polish women wore ill-fitting coats and fur hats like dandelions. Dubai was sleek and shining and freezing with air-conditioning. When we landed at Delhi six Indian women, tall and slim, wearing bright saris, walked past my window in a perfect line. Each had a huge pyramid of twigs for a head.

I took my first steps on Indian soil. I had to find my way across Delhi for the flight to Madras. I was hit by a wall of heat and a swarm of beggars. Please lady lady please . . . one rupee one rupee. I only had Traveller's Cheques. I've never seen beggars before. A man pointed to a bus and told me to get on. It looked like it should be going for scrap. No windows, no paint, it was like it was from a war zone. I was the only passenger. I thought I was going to be kidnapped. I sat on the front seat with my rucksack and my guitar. As we drove, I stared out at squalid one-room huts and families sitting outside. Delhi seems makeshift, dusty, incomplete. People flock like starlings, millions in a glance.

My flight to Madras was delayed for twelve hours. I panicked. Someone from the school at Vellore was going to be meeting me. Would they wait twelve hours? I sat in the domestic airport surrounded by people I have never imagined. A man with a rounded stump, his hands just knuckles, a blind woman, solid white eyes in her walnut face, sweeping the floor.

Somehow I arrived in Madras. I suppose I must have slept on the plane, but I'm not sure. I was freaked out. Thank God Debbie was there! An English woman in a sari with a wide face, open as a field.

It was too late to take the bus to Vellore so we slept in the airport on the floor. Debbie has been in India for six months. She is much older than me. She just lay down on the hard ground and fell asleep like it was the most normal thing to do. I lay down next to her but my mind was racing in a kind of waking nightmare. I thought I was still on the aeroplane, with the Indian beggars on the seats next to me. I thought you were holding my hand. I could actually feel your fingers against mine. My dream lasted until we got up and had sweet tea and biscuits.

Debbie is training to be a physiotherapist. She's been at the school for six months. She talks too much, but is strong and sensible, and very conscientious. She is beautiful too. From Madras airport to the school in Vellore took five hours. The driver never stopped sounding the horn the entire way.

Dear Ursula,

I still haven't heard from you since you left. You promised to write. It's awful, not knowing if you're OK.

Everything is askew between us. I hope my letters are arriving. I've written every day. Sometimes twice. You would love it here in Oxford. I'm rehearsing a play. I have an idea about a non-existent boss who becomes synonymous with a machine and keeps order out of fear. There will be a huge machine on stage hanging over everyone, even the audience. It is potent. The set will be black and white and the actors made up in black and white, but the machine will be green with flashing lights. At the end, it breaks and kills the central character. I want it to be funny with people continually trying to mend the machine but never managing to do it.

Provisionally it's called 'The Day the Sun Stood Still' as a reference to those ridiculous thirties films like *Seven a.m. to Seven p.m.* which examined factories in wartime. What do you think? The panoptic idea is quite interesting in respect of the omniscient narrator in literature. The structure itself is powerful but does not substantiate its power because it is latent.

Yesterday I met up with Tam who I met at interviews and his friend Caroline. She is an anarcho-feminist and lush. You'd like her. We got stoned and played loads of music. I've been writing to famous people trying to get an interview for the college magazine.

I think of our night in London before you left and am riddled with sadness. It was one of the best nights in my life. I've never felt so much about someone ever, not anyone. These thousands of miles between us feel like nothing. I'm sure in a month I'll be going crazy missing you. Don't be surprised if I walk out of the Indian Ocean having swum all the way.

I've just been interrupted from writing this for three hours by Caroline and Tam. We had a magazine meeting. There is much to do. I've got a new typewriter. It's a Casio. I suggested you could write something for the magazine from India. Tam has some poems. If you could write some and send photos it would be great. Perhaps we could even pay for them. We have a budget.

I was going to go out tonight with my new friends but I can't be bothered. I have to read the instruction manual of my typewriter. Great fun! It snowed last night but nothing settles.

Dear Jerry,

I slept! Debbie gave me a shiatsu massage, and I lay on my bed. I love my mosquito net. It keeps out all the baffling madness of India – and of course the devil mosquitoes. In the morning she brought me a cup of rich aromatic Indian coffee and we ate honey, banana and lentils – a speciality in Kerala. I eat in the traditional style, my hand cupped like a little shovel. It is earthy. Toilet paper is unheard of. Left hand for washing your bum, right hand for eating. Life is not hard; there are no mud huts, no jungle fever. The weather is fine and the food good.

Debbie has curly hair, blue eyes and wide cheekbones. She is very serene. She laughs a lot and occasionally half shuts her eyes and tilts her head back and says something like 'you wouldn't believe it' or 'it was just so, so, so amazing . . .'

She is a yogi. Do you know what that is? Every morning

and night, she unravels her mat and stands on her head for ten minutes.

She says that travelling on your own here is the best way to travel. I am impatient to hit the road. It sounds so exciting, visiting the temples, meeting people, taking boat trips, still I like it here at the school. There is no backbiting and the teachers are cheerful. I am called Baby even though in a height contest I was actually the tallest. The other teachers laugh and run away from me, expecting to be chased. I never met grown women who want to play like this. They are lush.

I just got your letter! Joycilli, one of the teachers, just ran over with it for me! I was so happy I ran and hugged Rambubu. He's very lovely, very mental. Debbie says he is one of the most backward of all the children. He is sitting on my knee as I write grinning like mad, pointing and drawing his finger over the page.

Sorry I only write this in snatches. I had to take a speech class. I'm back at the flat now. There is a girl called Sujata who cannot move her body at all. She lies on a plank on wheels, that gets moved around. She has a wicked subversive sense of humour, and twists the rules in all the games I make them play.

I hope your plans for The Machine come off. I never thought of you doing plays! I like the panoptic idea but I can't get too involved in your activities in Oxford so please don't expect me to. In a way I would like to, but I just can't. I cannot write something for your magazine. Now that I have escaped Newcastle and England, I just want to be free.

I watch red-horned cows pulling tall hay carts and I can't believe I'm here. I listened to some of the tape you made for me but couldn't get through it. You sounded so miserable. I wish I was there just to hug you.

I hope I can believe the declarations of fidelity in your letter. On my side you need have no fears, although admittedly I find Indian men sexy. I look but without temptation. I am going to find out about dancing lessons – it's all stamping feet and pointy fingers. Who is Caroline?

Dear Ursula,

I just got your first letter! Oh God it was crazy! Loads of things didn't make sense at all. I hope you're OK. It all sounds so frightening. I don't know what I can tell you. I am a bit upset. It's awful. Not having you here. Please write all the time. I am missing you. It's like a permanent ache, after only two weeks! I will keep your letters in a special file. I hope you haven't become disillusioned with me. Last night I lay in bed and felt sick to the pit in my stomach. I love you so much.

Dear Jerry,

I just took the baby class. It consists of Rambubu, Lando, Sujata and Manu. We sang 'The cook found a lizard in her idli' which tells the tale of the misfortunes of the school cook who ends up being eaten by a huge policeman masquerading as a pig. One of my own, in case you hadn't guessed. The kids love it because it's got ridiculous actions and noises. I've also taught them 'Dance to your daddy' from *When the Boat Comes In*. The children even have a

Geordie lilt in their voices! They shorten my name to two syllables, just like they did at school. Urs-la.

When I first arrived I thought that the school was friendly but the oppressive treatment of the kids is becoming very apparent. It's all one big muddle really and when you think this is the best place for children with cerebral palsy in the whole of India it's maddening. I feel guilty about wanting to travel for my own enjoyment. Nelly, the head teacher, has put her trust in me, so I must stay here longer.

The kids have never had a chance to write stories or be creative. Joycilli, the so-called occupational therapist, who should encourage their imaginations, is anaemic and apathetic. She is always angry with poor Rambubu and keeps asking the manager of the school to send him home. I begged for him to be able to stay. If he was sent home, he'd be treated as a freak and an outcast and probably die. All the children are from extremely poor families. Most have to sell a cow or jewellery to send their child here.

By the sound of your full life in Oxford I suspect you won't be able to come out for Christmas.

I went into town on my own yesterday. My mission was to send this parcel to you. So here it is, stitched up in cotton, like a little pillowcase.

Dear Ursula,

Your letters are taking about a week to get here. I just read the latest one. After I'd worked through its labyrinthine design I felt exhausted and jealous. It's amazing, incoherent, but jammed with glorious vivid descriptions. You make it

119

sound so wonderful but don't ever forget the economic and political reality, and for God's sake be careful with yourself. I'm going to try to get some money for Christmas so I can come out and join you. I think the chances are highly unlikely. Unfortunately, some of us are poorer than others.

I am sad you don't want to write about India for me for the magazine. I just want a piece of the action. Your letters are amazing. Please, please, please keep writing. I am experiencing India through you. You are my ears and eyes out there.

It's so easy to get lost enjoying oneself doing drama and politics in Oxford. The kids you're working with will probably end up begging – that is the reality.

I dreamt about being in India. I was trying to find you. I can't remember much of it, but I thought you were dead. How do people see death in India? Is life less precious? I will die young. I know I will. I am too unhealthy but you can't worry, the aching will end and I will dissolve. Love and death are the same process. I have so much of you in me.

Dear Jerry,

You cannot die yet. I love you too much. I don't know how people regard death here, but it must be very different. I woke up crying last night, I had been dreaming about a nuclear attack, and it was my mother's funeral. I was the only person there.

We had a dreadful visit from American and English Church people. They say 'how cute', or 'I could cry'! 'Look at that one trying to clap his hands'! They were brought tea and biscuits and left with a look of self-satisfaction on their faces. One more step toward heaven! We have to put up with it because we are funded by their Church.

The children had to sit on mats while the dignitaries peered down at them with stupid smiles, delighted by the freak show. The sheer physical size of these huge Americans is staggering. I had to talk to one of them – a great tree of a bloke wearing a baseball cap. He was saturated with God and spoke to me as if I were a brainless piece of shit. What right do they have to be so patronising? To take up the children's time, to make them perform? Christianity is foul, as you know. I hate the do-gooding look they have on their faces, the smug fulfilment. They don't actually look at you, they are too concerned with the Lord. The Lord is really only their own ego. I'm going to make an effigy of the baseball-cap man and stick my sari pin in him. I am trying to read the book by Foucault you sent me but it is a struggle.

Dear Ursula,

My blood boils when you tell me about the crazy Christians and their Victorian attitudes. I feel like flying out to scream at them. Whatever you do don't let them drag you down. I love hearing about the kids.

Last night in the Junior Common Room there was a Blind Date show, in typical student style, with some prick dressed as Cilla Black. It was all supposed to be in good humour but when the girl and boy were paired off, the girl had to perform a forfeit. My friend Caroline was the unfortunate one who had to lick crisps off a rugby player's crotch. Everyone laughed but Caroline was upset. I was furious and walked out but no one else seemed offended. This place drives me mad and every time I get so lonely. I miss holding you and talking and laughing with you but we definitely needed this break. I sometimes feel as if you are at the end of the bed reading a book. Please, please be careful. Out of the four billion people in the world you are the only one I care about.

Dear Jerry,

Debbie has turned her back on Christianity. I have never thought of faith as a possibility for me. There is so much I have never explored. She gets up every morning at five for yoga. I have been observing some of Debbie's positions. Perhaps I will do yoga when I go on my travels! Stay at an ashram or something. You will think I've flipped.

Debbie also has a boyfriend in England, a P.E. teacher in Nottingham. We both dream of letters of airmail paper and penny-sized pictures of the Queen. Everyone knows about it. If we look sad, Jaykumar, one of the children, says 'no letters, auntie?' and tries to give me his banana.

I'll get some printed cards in assorted colours to tell you I love you. What do you think? I could send one a day. Bright colours when I'm feeling happy. Dull when I'm feeling sad.

P.S. I have got Indian ringworm. A weird round thing just below my jaw. A parasite is living in me. My own pet! Joycilli is treating it with medicine that smells of Bovril.

Dear Ursula,

Today I got up early and the porter handed me a missive direct from God, the fucking Dean. It said the head porter and domestic supervisor have told me 'you have a mattress in your room for guests to sleep on. If this is not removed by the end of the week it will be confiscated and you will incur storage costs.' I blew my lid, and wrote a vehement letter to my tutor. It must seem petty from India but it's ridiculous that they should try to stop you having things in your room.

I can't believe it's still so long before I see you. It will be a quarter of some people's married lives that I will be waiting. I can't wait to see you at the airport. I will kiss you from head to toe. Please get your ringworm seen to by someone proper before it gets worse. If you get really ill I will fly out. Good plan. I hope you do get really ill. I'm joking. Be careful. I miss being stupid and touching each other. Remember when we used to get stoned and be babies? It was lush.

Dear Ursula,

Still no letter from you. It is constantly snowing here. How much I would love to be in India. The mattress saga trundles on. Got hauled in to see the Dean. He was conciliatory and said he would give me seven days to get rid of it.

There were demonstrations today. The government is chopping departments off universities like fingers.

I can't be bothered with the Machine play. I started writing some poems, not good ones, but I'll send them when they're finished. What is an ashram? Isn't it a place where public-school hippies try to catch loose cosmic energy? Don't go there!

I'm sorry I am feeling really miserable. I am green with envy and annoyed and tetchy because of the privilege this place exists on. I don't know whether the fault is mine or whether it is healthy to think like this.

The whole fucking place drives me to tears. I am almost at the point of glassing people. God knows what's going on in my head. Your Indian hedonistic trip seems to make more and more sense. My enthusiasm for things always has long-term motives. I never do anything just for its own sake.

I only have two friends, Tam and of course Caroline. I told her how much I am missing you. I am jealous of you and I am in love with you. Thank you for the presents. Your little package finally arrived, the silk, the toe rings, and the shells.

Don't forget to convert the Christians to Marxist materialism. Encourage dialectic and then you'll be fine. I can't imagine the poverty which you must be seeing. Stay away from religion of all kinds, don't forget all temples were built by hungry men even if they were so holy they could fuck upside down.

I have to be honest and say I feel bitter. It's quite irrational and unwarranted, but I feel the distance between us symbolises that huge class divide I seem destined to straddle. It is always tearing us apart. I hope it won't destroy us.

Dear Jerry,

I went into my first Hindu temple and received holy ash. There is a tall sculptured gateway, then, inside, there is a series of courtyards. The first is full of men and boys chipping away at large stones to make heaps of tiny stones. It is strange to find a gravel industry in a place of worship. Everything is mixed up, the holy and the ordinary. In the second courtyard we found Shiva, Vishnu, Krishna and Kali.

I was so happy to receive your letter. But when I read it, I was really unhappy. I am glad you say how you feel about that huge class divide, because it would be hopeless to suppress it, but I cannot help being middle class. I come from Jesmond. You come from Byker. I feel guilty about having the freedom and money and I get muddled and don't think I can justify it. Your resentment is understandable though my parents didn't help me financially. I am envious of you too! Oxford sounds exciting and you have such power and command and respect and everything you do is a success – all your talents and ideas impress me and you are always getting so much done. I feel in awe of you. Everyone likes you and I love you.

Don't let class stand between us. If you really love me, don't torment me about who I am. I know that I need time away from you and from my family and I hope you understand this. It is different for a girl. There is something I have to prove to myself; independence, confidence, awareness. They are all taken for granted by a man. Don't you think? Please don't be unhappy. I'm thinking of you all the time.

I listened to your tape last night. It was like you were lying under the mosquito net with me, talking me to sleep, but when it stopped there was only the sound of dogs barking and I felt lonely.

Dear Ursula,

Your letter about the class divide has been worrying me all day. I think you misunderstood me. I felt terrible having made you feel guilty or even annoyed. You don't deserve it. What I meant to say in the letter was much broader than our personal relationship. I feel that university, home, my heart, all the things I find important and fulfilling, are caught in the schism between our two classes. I am no working-class hero. Our backgrounds are different but I don't care. I respect you and love you more than anyone else in my life. It'll sound ridiculous but I admire your bravery in being alone, finding your limitations, not accepting those others put on you. If you remember some of our arguments, I could see you weren't happy. More than anything I want you to be that. I want to make you happy. I know we said we never would, but will you marry me? Seriously. Will you?

Dear Jerry,

My husband! I accept. I will. Marry. You. I will buy a Hindu wedding sari, and a lungi for you. What do you think? They are splendid and very cheap compared to what you'd pay in England for a dress, about Rs.300 for a good silk one which is only £15. They are like peacock feathers, all blues and greens. I need your opinion – this must be a joint decision! Do you even know what a lungi is? It is a sheet that wraps round you like a skirt. Most of the men wear them here. I think they are very elegant. They show off a bloke's skinny bum which is easily the best bit and you always did like to wear a dress, didn't you?

It is so hot tonight. I am writing this by candlelight. The fan is on so that means there's not enough power for the light. Electricity is negligible, and we have to choose between heat or dark.

I will be travelling soon, around the South for about six weeks – then heading north to Nepal. I will return via Darjeeling to Delhi. If you decide to come I will meet you in Bombay. This would be best then perhaps we could both go to Nepal.

My husband! How does it feel? It's very strange to write it. I don't like it. Perhaps we should get divorced . . .

Thank you for your tape – Joan Armatrading in my ears. Thank you. Such a good choice. I love you my spouse! What a horrible word that is – spouse. I shall call you my love.

I cannot believe how hard women have to work here, in the fields or the building sites doing hard manual work. The men do nothing. Just sit around drinking tea.

Thank you for everything – tapes, earplugs, your existence. I feel thankful for everything. Now I feel like I should say one of those school prayers.

Thank you for the flowers, the sunlight and the trees.
Thank you for my life, my eyes, feet and knees.
Thank you for friendship, for love.
Thank you for my candle, for the starlight above.
Thank you to the postman who brings me my mail.
Thank you for the weathermen for wind, rain and hail.
Thank you for the beggars who sleep outside my door.
Thank you for the lepers that live below the law.
Thank you for the cripple that leans on the Lord's Prayer.
Thank you for the clubfoot that lives below the stair.

Thank you for the woman who might as well be dead.
Thank you for her baby with sores upon its head.
Thank you for the bricks that she shifts from here to there.
Thank you for her neck which will break from all this
wear.
Thank you for the shop and the house.

Dear Ursula,

It is cold here but at least the sun is shining. I can't imagine the hot summer you're having. You won't see the snow until next winter.

The female students here are going to demand a woman's officer on the student governing council. This may seem a pretty bland request, but it has caused a huge storm here. I will be there being obnoxious and self-righteous no doubt. There can be no objection, but inevitably the vote will not represent a rational perspective. This is Oxford and prejudice outweighs reason every time.

I have just read six hundred pages of *The History of the Labour Party* in twenty-four hours non-stop. It was ludicrous and consequently my time scheme is severely misaligned.

Andie, my sister, is here. She came down this morning. She says Mam and Dad are extremely worried about you, and send their love. Andie wouldn't mind if we get married. I'm worried about you. Some of your letters almost sound like you're tripping.

Oxford life is hurtling towards the end of term. I suddenly feel insanely jealous of you. I will call Mam and Dad and ask them if I can have £200 to come out to see you. Don't hold your breath.

Last night I got stoned with my friend Caroline. It was fun but I felt lonely and wanted to cuddle her, but I didn't because she would have taken it wrongly. I knew then what a huge commitment I've made to you. I have taken on a whole load of things which I hadn't realised. I am happy that I have. You mean so much to me, my wife!

Dear Jerry,

I am finally travelling. Debbie gave me some balloon trousers and a jade top. She says if I look respectable I will get less hassle and be treated better. I left the school at five this morning.

The bus to Mahabalipuram took three hours all along the coast, passing new luxury-hotel resorts among the villages, and shelter slums.

I miss sex so much I eat bananas all the time. Instead of being slim and tanned, I am red and rounded. I am thinking of sending you some bananas. I know you don't like them but you would love these. They are not like the ones in England. They are delicious cold puddings, each individually wrapped.

Write to the postes restantes in Mahabalipuram, Pondicherry, Kodaikanal, Auroville, Cochin, Bangalore. Promise. Your letters will be essential when I'm on the lonely trail.

Dear Ursula,

I won't be able to come to India. I don't have enough money. My grandma is holding tight on to Uncle Harry's money and it's too risky to take out a loan. It's the rag end of the year. The trees are empty and frayed and it's cold.

It will be the holidays soon. I'm going home to Newcastle. Write every day, at least three letters. Buy the wedding costumes. I hope you're serious about all this. I am absolutely devoted to you. I will finish my exams in the middle of June. I want to do well because my supervisor really likes my work.

Dear Jerry,

I have met some boys, Mani and Juddhur. They were fishing on the beach. I have just been out on their catamaran. They pushed it out through the waves to a moored trawler from where they dived and somersaulted into the sea. I joined in. They think it's strange a girl knows how to swim.

We played without words pushing each other in. It was a wonderful feeling. Grappling in the waves. I wish you had been here.

Afterwards I helped tie up the fishing nets. Mani is strong and lean. They have the most open smiles and their bodies – my God, they're like gods! We went to see a Tamil film in a great aeroplane hangar of a cinema. Afterwards we all went to Mani's house, a two-room hut. He lives with his mum and five sisters. I was given an enormous meal of fish and rice. They sang me Tamil songs. Mani has a beautiful voice.

He tilts his head back and sings out his heart. They have offered to take me out fishing again tomorrow.

Dear Ursula,

How are you? It sounds idyllic playing on a raft on a blue ocean under a big blue sky. The sky here is grey. I wish I was with you in paradise. I'm at home in the Byker Wall. Home drives me crazy. Mam and Dad have prosaic eyes. They are always constricting and condemning me. When you get back we'll go away to America, or China, anywhere. The sun is all we need. We'll get married and have kids and be happy.

I've been asked to go to Brussels to participate in a United Nations student conference. It is the most prestigious thing to do at Oxford, and all I want is to be with you. Please help me decide what we should do . . .

Dear Jerry,

I'm in Cochin. The fishing nets are impaled on sticks along the shore like massive daddy-long-legs, drooping and dead. A businessman called Altaf who lives in Bangalore has offered to put me up while I renew my visa. He bought me a coffee at his hotel and I swam in the hexagonal pool. He is an orphan-made-good from Bombay. He now lives in Chicago, but runs a string of cheap-labour computer factories all over India. I knew from the beginning that he only wanted to get me into bed, but don't worry I'm not interested. I have no qualms about using him if it can save me some money.

I got a letter from my mum. She said you came over and sat talking to my brother in the kitchen, a line of beers between you on the table. How cosy and domestic – talking to my mum and my brother! I can just see you all, putting the world to rights while Jonathan plays his music and Ganny Mary mopes about, reading her beloved small ads.

Dear Jerry,

I am in Bangalore at the house staying with friends of Altaf. There is a whole gang of them, Kabir, George, Rahul, all rich, middle class, and living the life of Riley. We went out on motorbikes. I was like a heavy-metal girl clinging on as we flew past the palms and paddy fields, scattering livestock, hay carts, bicycles. Lorries blared their horns at us. I reached around Kabir's body to hold the handlebars, and felt the vibration through the grips.

They have gone out to drink whisky. I am alone in their house. They took me to a nightclub last night. They flit from five-star hotel lounge to restaurant to nightclub and back again, ride through the slums, the 'low-income' areas, as they call them, with mindless speed. Beggars and children wait for rupees at the gates of the glorious hotels, while inside Altaf and his friends gorge themselves on Western food. My sense of reality has gone haywire. The children at the school in Vellore, the fishing boys, now I'm in a Martini advert! It is a status symbol for these boys to have a white girl around. They don't realise I am using them. I like Kabir despite the fact he stands for everything I detest.

Dear Jerry,

I am still waiting for my visa in Bangalore. After I get it, I will go to Varanasi and bathe in the sacred river.

I picked up your letter at the poste restante, and had a moment of self-disgust. I felt sick and wanted to be with you. Kabir kept telling me he had never met anyone so open. He likes how free I am, he said, compared to most Indian girls. He asked me to have sex with him, and I know you won't mind hearing that I said yes – but only because I need to stay here until I get my visa, and I'm running out of money, and they give me a nice clean room, and food and take me on trips, and of course I have no intention of having sex with him. I was just going to string him along and then hit the road, but last night his friends said they all wanted to have sex with me too. They laughed at me for being loose and I felt scared. One of them kept touching me. It was like they had lost all respect for me and hated me. They spoke in Hindi and laughed. I didn't know what they were saying. I should have kicked them in the balls and left, but there were so many of them and only one of me, so I just laughed along. I feel horrible now, I'm going to leave this afternoon.

Dear Jerry,

I've been covering vast distances. I had to get away from

Bangalore, as far as possible. I was thinking of getting a flight home but I met a travelling Zen monk. I told him I needed to purge my soul after the horrible experience with the men and the hedonism of Bangalore! I don't think he knew what I was talking about, but he seemed happy enough that I come along with him. He's taking me to a monastery. It might be interesting. I'll stay a few days then possibly take a two-day walk to the border of Tibet, and then head back to Delhi and fly home. I'll see you soon! Is there a general election?

Dear Ursula,

I have sent so many letters you will never get. There are bits of me lying all over India. I haven't had one from you for weeks. They used to come every few days, sometimes five at once, I hope you're OK. I feel ill, so excuse me if this letter becomes strained. I am missing you a lot but I don't know what it'll be like seeing you again.

I have decided to go to Brussels to be the mock-president of the Oxford contingent. I got it under hot competition. Everyone says it's a big deal, but I don't see what they are so excited about. It's only student politics. The upside is that I will get a free holiday in Belgium and some college money. I want you to come if you get back in time. It probably sounds like the worst thing in the world to you.

I can't bear to think of not loving you but I am resolved to accept you as you are when you return. I can't say more than that. I love you and have never stopped. I know how you feel about being trapped. We can't go back to having the same relationship as before. There's nothing more to say. I've worried about you and cried sometimes.

Just got a pile of letters from you. Five or six all come together. The men in Bangalore sound disgusting. You should have cut their balls off and burnt them in a sacred fucking pyre, and spat in their laughing faces. Please be careful.

Dear Jerry,

I'm in a monastery high in the Himalayas. It is like looking through a magnifying glass at the world. The stars are so close you can touch them. The monks are just starting a three-month silence. No one speaks English here so even if they did speak I wouldn't understand. We sit in meditation for ten hours a day. The monks have given me my own room.

I look at the orange sunset. Ascetics wear the colour orange to show their lack of worldliness. It is a beautiful colour, at the beginning and end of every day. There is no orange in between. It just happens to start and close the day. What is starting and closing? It's weird but I wonder if everything in the whole universe is this sunset. But I know that the sun will set and rise again, that time will move on, my feet will walk, crows will croak. Everything will seem to happen one after another, each different from the other. While my mind splits everything up it will never be at one with itself. But is there just the one guttural croak? This must sound mad!

Time here hardly exists. I feel happy, but my only worry is you. When I think of you I feel pain. I long for a letter from you. I know that I love you but I don't know if I want to be in love. I am in a state of freedom I fear I can never have with you. Sometimes I am no longer sure if I've understood anything you've ever said to me. Whenever I think about my life in Newcastle I feel afraid. I never want to be like that again. The potential of being alone here seems so exciting. The only thing I can be sure of is what I am thinking and feeling this exact minute. I feel a sorrow I can't place but I fear it is you. For the first time I realise how young I am – and how good it is to be young – there is so much to do, and discover.

Dear Jerry,

The monks accept me but I am often afraid and have no one to talk to. All my foundations are threatened. Much of the time, I just cry and cry. I feel I am being pulled somewhere, against my will, but I no longer know what my will is.

I had been meditating all day with the monks and then I came down by the dried-up lake. I was singing anything that came into my head, when my mouth lost all sensation and I couldn't feel my tongue or lips forming the words. The sounds and my head and face felt enormous. I can't explain it, my chin and mouth as big as the room and my back started folding out behind me. It felt like my whole body was distorting but at the same time I was not aware of my body at all, or my breathing and looking back I didn't even know where I was. I had been sitting there for at least an hour but it seemed like seconds.

Dear Jerry,

What I am going to tell you in this letter is very hard to put into words, but I am going to try. I want you to be patient with me, and curious, and not tell me that I'm mad. I was sitting outside looking over the hills, and I was aware of the seconds passing, and of the four perfect stars above me, of the rock I was sitting on, the hills across the valley, the sensation of my legs on the ground, and I don't know how long I had been sitting there, but suddenly a few words came into my head, and they said, I don't exist. And I just sat in the silence, and there were no more words, there was nothing, all of a sudden, it was mad, totally wild, mind-blowing. I can't explain it. It happened. This thing happened. I can't explain . . . the world shattered, the sky broke in two, and the hills filled with love. The hills flooded into me, the hills poured overwhelming peace into me, and I was the hills, the beautiful hills, and they were me, and there was no gap between us, and there never had been. I had no fear. I cried out, shouting and laughing, Oh God Oh God . . . I was shaking. I am still shaking as I write this. I cannot share this with anyone. There is nothing to share. I will not send this letter. There is nothing to send. Nothing to say. Ursula is only a dream, a shattered dream . . .

Dear Ursula,

I haven't heard from you for six weeks. Please write or phone me with details of when you will return. I will meet you anywhere, at any time. I miss you and love you more every day. Phone me. Leave a telephone number at the Porter's Lodge and I will call you back.

Dear Ursula,

I haven't heard from you for so long. Where are you? Have you met someone? I am sending this to Kathmandu poste restante, hoping it will find you. Yes there was a general election here. The Tories won again. So fucking depressing.

Dear Ursula,

Three months since I heard from you. Where are you?

Where has Ursula gone? Something has happened, sudden, and unfathomable, but what exactly? Has she been robbed and kidnapped, left for dead in the Indian sun, her poor body swept off by carrion crows? Or has she been recreated, the dandelion of herself opening for the very first time in true and delightful connection with the sun? I promised you connection, I promised love, but is Ursula any closer to it as she walks barefoot through the airport, rolling slowly heel to toe on the hard white floor? Something has happened. Terminal 3 fills her. She is the gleaming glass and the shining silver, the glass reflecting glass reflecting watches, bags, hats; she is a pile of plastic cups, people passing in black, and grey, in a million pairs of shoes. She is all the wonders of Heathrow as they roll out before her, and into which she is instantly woven, even the pale young man in a black coat waiting with a plastic bag, Jerry, a book open in his hand.

He looks up as she clears customs. A bone-thin girl in a green sari, hair cropped, eyes wide and staring, smiling at everything. She has no shoes.

Hi, he says.

Hello, Jerry.

He hugs her. She feels small, the bones of her like a bird.

He is aware of his coat, heavy against her. He opens it and hugs her again. He's dreamt of this moment for so long.

I bought you a cup of tea, he says pointing towards a cup of tea on a seat.

I'm OK, thank you. Would you like it?

I bought it for you, he says.

Why is she asking him if *he* wants it? He bought it for her. The cup sits in obedience behind them. Ursula smiles at it; a cup person.

Ursula! Ursula!

Her brother Jonathan calls across the concourse.

Ursula! Jesus, you look terrible, he says, striding towards them. Mum said I should meet you. She's sorry she couldn't come. She's still at Greenham Common.

Ursula feels the rhythm drumming away in him.

Hi Jerry, aren't you in Oxford? My God, Ursula. Mum's been worried. Christ, what happened? You look awful!

She's fine, says Jerry.

She doesn't look fine.

They look at Ursula. She looks back at them.

Look I can't stay long, says Jonathan, I promised Mum I'd come. What's your plan, Ursula? Do you need any money? A drink? A cup of tea or something?

She doesn't want tea, says Jerry.

How do you know?

I bought her some. She doesn't want it.

People surge past them. A group of tourists, ears glued to Walkmans, a Thai family wheeling cases bursting at the seams, an Indian woman pushing a pram . . .

We can't stand here, says Jonathan. Come on, Ursula. I'll carry your bag.

He picks up her bag and strides off across the concourse, Jerry at his side.

Still playing music, Jonathan? Jerry asks him, eyes on Ursula.

Real estate. It's crap, but fun to be in London. Sort of. Actually I'm thinking of moving to Brighton. He looks about him as they walk, as though constantly searching for something just out of sight. They reach the exits by a doughnut stall. Ursula stares at the perfect rows of sugary Os in delight.

Right, says Jonathan, turning to her. What are you going to do? I can give you a lift to the train station if you like.

They're beautiful, she says, looking at the doughnuts.

Jonathan sighs. For God's sake, Ursula! Where do you want to go? Newcastle? Oxford? You can crash at mine if you want . . .

I need to see a doctor, she says, simply. I'm sick.

What with? asks Jerry. Is it serious?

I don't know, says Ursula.

She should go home, says Jonathan. Ursula, go to Eslington Road, see Dr Tindal, get yourself sorted. I'll call my mum.

He seems pleased with his plan. It was his duty to come here and make sure she is OK, she's not OK, so he's taking appropriate action.

I'll give you some money for a ticket, he adds.

Ursula stands very still, looking at the doughnuts.

It's alright, Jonathan, says Jerry, picking up her bag. She's coming to Oxford with me.

*

On the train, he holds her hand. He wants to tell her that he loves her, but he is scared of her distance. He tells himself she's jet-lagged, exhausted. She needs time, that's all. As they walk up the Cowley Road in Oxford, he has to stop himself wanting to walk ahead of her.

Wouldn't you like to put your shoes on? he says.

Yes, she says, laughing, that's a good idea.

They stop by a petrol station. He opens her bag. There is nothing inside except for a sweater, some papers and a pair of flip-flops. He puts them down on the pavement in front of her. Slowly she slips her thin feet into them and smiles.

They feel good, she says.

When they arrive, the house is empty. Caroline and Tam are at the library writing essays. Jerry takes her upstairs. He's tidied his room for her; gathered the books into piles, emptied his bin, laid a spread borrowed from Caroline's room over the bed, bought a candle.

I like it, says Ursula. She sits on a chair by the window.

He's made a makeshift curtain from an orange blanket. One corner has fallen down, and the evening sun makes a triangle of light across her face.

There is so much to tell her, so much to ask her. He wants her to be curious about his new life, to engage with him, to hear her talk and laugh and question. He sits on the bed and watches her, the shape of her head, the curve of her neck, her shoulders. The old love swells for her.

Ursula, where have you been? Why didn't you write?

He wants her to come to him, but she sits mountain still.

You're angry, she says. I did write. Didn't you get my letters?

The last one was four months ago. You said you were coming home.

Jerry, I'm sick.

What's wrong? he says.

I don't know. I was really sick. The monks said I should come home.

The monks? What monks?

Can we talk later? she says. I need to sleep now.

In the corner shop he buys a bottle of Lucozade and six tins of beer. When he gets home Caroline and Tam are in the kitchen. They are excited about the trip to Brussels.

We're coming to give you moral support, and to drink Belgian beer, laughs Caroline.

And then fuck up the Tories, says Tam, rolling a spliff.

Jerry hopes Ursula can hear them, that she'll come downstairs and join in, be the Ursula he knew before she left. He's told them all about her. Caroline in particular has been looking forward to meeting her. He's imagined them being friends, Ursula moving in, all of them living together while he finishes his degree. Now she is here, he feels embarrassed by her, her sari, her silence, her maddening smile. Monks? What was she doing? The Ursula he knew didn't have a religious bone in her body. He tries to rationalise it; she's had a long flight, she's sick. Be patient, people don't really change. There is no sound from his room.

I bought you a secret weapon, says Caroline. To help you with your speech.

She hands him Neil Kinnock's book *How to Speak in Public*.

Not that you'll need it, she adds, smiling, kissing him lightly.

They drink until late. Jerry staggers up to his room in the early hours. Ursula is asleep on the floor next to his bed. When he wakes, the orange blanket has fallen down. Morning light floods the room, and Ursula is gone.

A white box room with a single bed. The faint smell of disinfectant. Ursula has been here for three weeks. She sits against the metal bedstead, feeling the cold bars through her hospital gown. She can see a corner of lawn through the window, a cul-de-sac of parked cars, a sapling belted to a stick as though it is injured. A nurse enters with a jug of water and a glass.

You're going home today, Ursula. Your mother's going to look after you. I want you to keep up your fluid intake, she says, smiling.

Ursula watches the nurse pour water into the glass. She is the water, and the jug, and the glass. She is the water flowing, the sound as it hits the glass. Everything is perfect.

Joyce stands on her pedals cycling into the wind along Barras Bridge towards the Royal Victoria Infirmary. She's late because she wanted to catch the midday post with a letter to the *Sunday Times* about police treatment of the Greenham women. If it arrives by Friday, a journalist friend has promised to take a look. There's a good chance they'll print it at the weekend, which will give the women much-needed media coverage before the eviction hearing. Joyce is pleased to have been of some help; now she can concentrate on her daughter. It was probably for the best Dr Tindal sent Ursula straight to hospital, it being such a busy time, but now she wants her back in Eslington Road. Joyce had felt worried when she first saw Ursula after India, all skin and bones, big staring eyes, and silent for the most part. When she did speak, she was odd somehow, distant and childlike. The doctors had first told her that Ursula had contracted glandular fever, but now it is not thought to be as serious as they first suspected, so she has persuaded them Ursula can recuperate best at home. She needs to gain weight and the hospital food isn't helping. She needs scrambled eggs, and milk, hot drinks. Most of all she needs to get back to normal. She's been saying some strange things. The first time Joyce saw her she announced she was a room without walls. Joyce pedals harder in the wind. She just hopes it isn't drugs.

At the hospital she follows the corridors to the Frederick Wing. The air is full of the smell of boiled food and bleach. Joyce tries to ignore the sounds of illness around her; coughs, hushed conversations, the squeak of trolleys as patients are wheeled to and fro. She has never been in hospital herself, except for the births of her children. Even then, Peter brought her home a few hours after each one; Joyce insisted on it. She's never liked the idea of other people looking after her; a slippery slope as far as she's concerned.

Ursula is sitting on the chair next to her bed, her rucksack beside her, packed and ready to leave. She is wearing the red jumper and jeans Joyce brought for her. She didn't want her walking home in the sari. Nothing to do with the neighbours, she's never given a hoot about them; it's just too cold in the North East for loose cotton.

Hello, Mum.

The clothes look too big on her. Joyce makes a mental note to buy more food. Ursula needs starch to put some weight on. Porridge, baked potatoes, Farley's Rusks perhaps. She used to love those; just till she's got her strength back.

There was a queue at the post office, says Joyce. The Greenham women are being evicted again. We've got new counsel, Gerald Frayn. I've been helping brief him for the hearings. I've got more time now, so I want to hear everything. We enjoyed your letters but they stopped. Jerry showed us some you sent to him.

A fly is fizzing frantically in the corner of the window. Ursula stares at it as she stands. Joyce is alarmed by how frail she is. It hits her, quite illogically, that her daughter is on the verge of death. She is gripped by a desperate desire to catch her up in her arms as she did when the crows attacked, and hold her to her body, keep her safe and warm.

We should go, she says.

I'm sad to leave, says Ursula, looking round the empty room. It's beautiful here.

Joyce is surprised to feel the truth of her daughter's words. There is something beautiful about this bare room.

Let's take the flowers, she says.

There is a vase of irises by the bed.

Kath brought them, says Ursula. Jerry's mum.

That's nice, says Joyce. How is she? They've never met. Kath rang once after Jerry and Ursula started going out, and formally invited her and Peter round. Joyce had wanted to go, but in the end they were too busy.

She's fine, says Ursula. She's doing evening classes, and getting ready for Andie's wedding. She's worried about Mike's health, but he is not as ill as he was a few months ago, so she's pleased.

Let's take them with us, says Joyce.

She picks the flowers from the vase. Ursula wraps the stems in a tissue. Their hands meet. She gazes at the blue flowers, her mother's slim hands, as though mesmerised.

Come, says Joyce. Ganny Mary is so looking forward to seeing you.

The cow-hide bag is filled with bars of Bournville and bags of toffees. It swings at Mary's side as she totters through the underpass of the motorway, into Brandling Park. She's been to Fenwick's to buy sweet things for Ursula. She didn't want to visit her in hospital. Hospitals are a mystery to her. No one she's ever known has been to one, not even to die. Her husband Wally died at home in his chair by the stove, her mother too, just lay down in bed one day and turned her face to the wall. Mary is delighted Ursula is escaping a mansion of sickness, and coming home. Joyce says she's thin. Toffees and chocolates is just what she needs. Something sweet for her little companion.

She lets herself into 35 Eslington Road. The house is quiet. They're not back. She puts on her housecoat, and heads for the kitchen. She'll put the toffees in a jam jar, tie a ribbon round it if she can find one. It feels good to bring something special home. Her mother used to bring the butter and eggs home. The door of the sitting room is wide open. Ursula is on the sofa, silent as a stone.

Ooh! You gave me a start! says Mary, hiding her alarm. Ursula is more than thin, she's gaunt and burnt by the sun.

Welcome home, chicken, she says, reaching in her bag for the toffees.

Ursula smiles. Mary sits next to her on the sofa.

For you, she says, something sweet.

She pops one in her mouth, and hands the bag to Ursula.

Where's your mother? she says.

She went to Willow Road on her bike, says Ursula. She says I need potatoes.

Always gadding off! says Mary. Oh dear, you've been away too long, love. Your mother's been worried, when she's been here, of course she's been away a lot. Everybody goes away. There's been nobody here much except me. I'm tired out with it all. One way or another I'm quite ground down!

How good it is to have Ursula back, someone to talk to, to confide in.

I blame your father. She only does it to impress him. That bloody man! If only he hadn't come along. She was quite happy at home with me before she met him, you know.

Soon she is ranging over everything she's held in all these months; how Joyce has been avoiding her, how she's been lonely, how she hates the dark house and the noisy road, how the robbers ruined her, how she misses her father, how her mother was lost to God.

It was Auntie Sissy that did it, she says. She influenced her. My mother was taken over by her bloody religion. I told her I wouldn't go to those bloody meetings.

Her voice turns hard and bitter as she imitates her mother. You're coming, she said to me. You will come. I'm lucky I've a daughter. You can't break a boy, but you can break a girl. You'll come to God in time. That's what my mother said to me! You can't break a boy, but you can break a girl. Well, she never broke me! She died before she could. I never came to God and I never bloody will!

She stares at Ursula with tears in her eyes, as her out-pouring ends. Ursula looks at her grandmother and smiles. A space seems to open up in the room.

Poor Ganny Mary, she says.

Mary frowns. She recognises something in Ursula, something from the past in the shape of her face, the smile in her eyes, but her memory clouds and she cannot place it. At least she's happy, she thinks. She puts her hand on her knee.

It's good to have you home, chicken, she says. Have another toffee.

She takes another one for herself. Yes, it feels good to bring something special home, and as she sucks her toffee, the past blows in her again, and sadness overwhelms her as she remembers how the butter came home, but home was no longer home, and suddenly Mary's back in the parlour in Padiham, taking two slices of bread, spreading the butter thick, one slice for her, and one for her father. He's mending a machine in the yard. He'll need something. She'll take it to him. She's on her way to him with it when her mother grabs her wrist like a vice.

Put that back! The Lord will work on you, Mary Tate! You greedy girl. None for you!

She snatches the bread and butter from her daughter.

Annie . . . Annie . . .

Hubert is by the door. Annie looks down at the bread and butter, a deep frown across her brow.

Don't be hard on Mary, he says.

God does not want a spoilt child, Hubert. A spoilt child is a blot.

He turns away, goes back to his machine, feeling the weight of his wife's strangeness. The winds of Pendle Hill have torn her loose from the root of herself, and now she has turned to God. There is an anger in her that frightens and crushes him.

Mary watches her mother go upstairs. She's going to pray, to read the Bible in her room. Her father works on his machine, a spanner in his oily hand. Mary goes to him, just to be close and he strokes her head with the back of his hand. She feels his strength, his reassurance that all will be well. She loves him so much one day she hopes she will marry him. He needs a good wife . . .

In Eslington Road Mary smiles bitterly at the memory. Nothing lasts. Her father fell. She clutches the arm of the sofa to stop herself falling, falling like he did, clutching his heart, clawing at his chest, his head exploding, filling with blood like a burst pipe, the meningitis flooding his brain. She watches him powerless and astonished from the hall, as he falls mouthing the final words he so desperately wanted to say to Annie, to the laundrywomen, and to Mary, his beautiful Mary, Mary, oh Mary, such a good head for numbers, my only Mary . . . but the words choke in him, I'm not ready, he cries the words without sound, as he strikes his head against the step, he's disappearing, too quick, like turning down the lamps, I can't see, I'm not ready, the laundry's doing so well, Harriet, so many good workers, the ironing machine ordered from Sheffield, and Mary so clever, you must go to grammar school. I want that for you, Mary, and so much more, to run with you into the sea at Blackpool, I had it planned, holidays, nothing but happiness for you, splashing in the waves, take Mary to the sea Annie, oh Annie . . . I hoped you'd come back to me . . . be kind to our daughter, Annie . . . and as young Mary falls weeping on to his body, holding his face, Daddy, don't go . . . Daddy, come back . . . he sees the white steps of the houses along the street, like teeth, opening wide . . . here, here I am . . .

We beat the Tory scumbags! shouts Caroline, punching the air.

She, Jerry and Tam stride happily towards the Grande Place in Brussels, the applause still ringing in their ears.

You were brilliant, Jerry! says Tam, his face shining with admiration.

Young people crowd the city. They have come from different corners of the world to represent their countries in the Student United Nations. A group of Tories in college scarves jeer as they pass.

The end is nigh! shouts Tam, jumping on to the edge of a street fountain. Caroline joins him.

Your days are numbered! she shouts into the streets.

The air smells of waffles and beer. There is a sausage seller on the corner, and a belief that socialism will soon return to Britain. Caroline snatches Neil Kinnock's book on public speaking from Jerry's denim jacket.

It worked, she says. I told you it would!

He laughs. She'd given it to him as a joke, but he'd found himself using it, trying not to judge Kinnock's jaunty advice, and written a speech full of rousing left-wing rhetoric. An emotional call to arms. In the end, he hadn't used the speech.

He knew somewhere that his fury and indignation about Tory policies would only cloud his reason, so instead he'd listened with steely concentration to the other speeches, and then spoken off the cuff, arguing each point with almost surgical logic. By the time he'd finished he knew he'd won. There is no room in politics for emotion.

Who were the suits? Caroline asks him. Come on, tell us.

Two Labour Party officials from headquarters in London had approached him after the debate. They asked about his plans for the future, exchanged numbers and addresses.

Westminster, he says.

Caroline whoops for joy.

Tam! she cries, kissing Jerry. Haven't you heard? He's going to be the next prime minister!

They pile into a bar and order tankards of blonde beer, their excited voices joining the cacophony of other drinkers. They fight their way to a gap in the crowded room, raise a toast, and drink. Tam flicks beer mats at Jerry.

After we graduate, we'll stay with my uncle in London, he says, and waltz into Westminster!

Jerry feels good to be with friends, high on victory in a foreign city. A group of Italian students from the debate invites them to join their table, and the conversation turns to the NHS. After a while, Caroline touches his shoulder.

How's it going with Ursula? she says, inviting confidence.

I'm not sure, he answers.

He hasn't spoken to her since that night after she returned from India, over a month ago. He tries not to think about her but she's always on his mind. He's tempted to find a quiet corner with Caroline somewhere and talk. But he's done this before, and it always leads to drunken intimacy.

During Ursula's long absence, he and Caroline would occasionally get drunk and fall into bed together. It happened again after Ursula left Oxford that morning. They had spent the afternoon together, demolishing a bottle of gin. Caroline had listened warmly as he told her of his confusion, kissed him as she took off her clothes.

Tell me, Jerry? says Caroline, standing close to him. He can feel the heat in her body.

He remembers them getting undressed, her bra, her waist, his drunkenness, the disappointment of it all before it had begun.

I've got to call my dad, he says, standing abruptly, we had a bet. He said the Tories would win. I've won a fiver. I won't be long.

He leaves the bar without looking back. Caroline's probings about Ursula make him uncomfortable. He needs to work things out, to find the correct argument, the exact line of cause and effect that will solve the difficulty of her, just as he masterminded his win in the student debate. He walks down streets not knowing where he is going. A ring of people are taking photos of a statue on the side of a house. It is of a little boy peeing. He watches them, struck by the stupidity of their fascination. He turns down a dark alley. A church looms up between the houses. He sits on the steps. How could Ursula leave him like that? Without saying goodbye? It was typical of her, wasn't it? He wanted to look after her, still wants to. He can't help it. He feels connected to her in a way he can't explain. There's a phone box on the corner. He fishes a phonecard from his pocket.

Hi, Mam, it's me, he says. Is Dad there?

He's just gone out for a takeaway.

Tell him he owes me a fiver. We smashed the Tories.

He knows his dad will enjoy his victory. Things haven't been easy between them since his illness. The bet had felt like a good way to engage him, to distract him from it.

I was at the hospital, says Kath. I saw Ursula. She's so lovely. You should call her, Jerry. The good ones don't hang about for ever, you know.

Mam, I've got to go.

He leaves the phone box and stares up at the sky. Above him is the pale moon, and the clouds. He sees faces in them. They're Ursula's clouds; he would never have seen them without her. He watches them twist and disappear. He will go to Newcastle and tell her everything. They'll get married, play music, and climb mountains. They'll start revolutions and make the clouds laugh with joy.

Ursula is not thinking about Jerry. She's not thinking much at all. Since she came home three weeks ago she is happy wherever she is, whatever she is doing. She demands nothing. She rests or sits quietly, spends time with Ganny Mary in the kitchen or tidying the rockery under the ash in the garden. Time is slowing at Eslington Road; even Joyce feels it. When Ursula accompanies her to shop for food, they spend time browsing in the aisles. Twice they've driven to Tynemouth to walk on Long Sands. Joyce feels at ease with her daughter. It's how she imagines a holiday might feel, and secretly she's loving their time together.

Today Ursula is venturing out alone. She is putting on a pair of trainers by the front door, still wearing the jeans and red jumper she came home in from the hospital.

Looking forward to it? asks Joyce.

Yes, says Ursula.

Are you sure that's what you want to wear? I can try to find something for you if you like . . .

I'm happy in these, Mum.

It was Joyce's idea for Ursula to see some old friends. She's begun to notice a growing fragility in her daughter, in little things, how she's turned the mirror in her bedroom to face the wall, how she evades all talk of the past and future. Joyce has tried to ask her about what happened in India but Ursula seems unwilling, or unable, to talk about it. It is lovely to spend time with her, but it's a bubble, and Ursula can't just lounge around at home for ever. She isn't academically bright like her sister so perhaps university wouldn't be right for her, but she'll have to earn a living somehow. The trip to India may have been a dreadful mistake. She's been away so long that her ties with normal life are broken. Jerry, whom she and Peter had liked very much, far more suitable than that boy in the band, seems to have disappeared off the scene completely. A shame; he and Ursula had seemed inseparable. Joyce used to wonder how they could spend so much time with each other. Now Ursula barely mentions him. Joyce's pleased she's managed to get hold of Jeanette and Ashley and delighted they are keen to see Ursula again. She's even succeeded in getting a message to Howard, whose mother used to come to CND rallies. She's not sure Ursula was ever really friends with Howard, but at least he'll be another familiar face.

Have a nice time, love, says Joyce, surprised by the softness in her voice.

She can't help but feel anxious. Ursula seems like a child setting off for her first day at school. Joyce almost offers to accompany her, but tells herself not to be ridiculous. Ursula has always been independent. It won't do any good to start mollycoddling her now.

Jeanette, Ashley and Howard are in the Carriage pub, the scene of so many of their teenage drinking sessions. It is lunchtime and the lounge is empty except for a smattering of men watching the football on a television above the bar. Jeanette shrieks when she sees Ursula.

Ursula! How long's it been? Eeeeee . . .!

A year, man! Maybes two . . .? says Ashley.

Hi, says Ursula, beaming at them all. Ashley and Jeanette are both dolled up, their blouses tight, tailored leather jackets with fur trim. The smell of their perfume is overpowering. Howard is transformed, no longer a gawky boy, but a fashionably dressed young man in bright shirt and jacket, the self-consciousness of childhood evaporated.

Hiya, says Howard.

Ah man, everything has changed! Everything, says Jeanette. We were just saying, weren't we, Ashley?

Ursula is happy to see them again. Before she left for India, she had been so absorbed by her relationship with Jerry that she'd barely seen her school friends. The truth was they hadn't been close for years.

My round, says Howard. What you drinking?

Pints! says Ashley. We're making up for lost time.

Howard goes to the bar.

And Bacardi chasers! Jeanette calls after him.

She leans in to Ursula. We're celebrating, aren't we?!

You're always celebrating, says Ashley, laughing.

Mind you've lost weight, Ursula! says Jeanette. I wish I had!

Howard returns with a tray of four pints and four shorts and they toast old friends. Ursula listens to their news and gossip as she sips her lager, feeling the bubbles tickle her throat. Jeanette is working as a typist in a law firm. She has just finished with a guy called Scott, who turned out to be a right twat, and according to Jeanette, definitely gay; Ashley is getting married to Alistair who owns a pizza-franchise outlet down on the quayside. Howard is studying computing at Gateshead Technical College, but wants to travel. His dream is to go to Florida. Jeanette makes eyes at him as they slam shots.

Howhey! she cries. Down the hatch! Again!

Ursula drains her glass. The Bacardi rushes straight to her head.

I haven't had a drink in ages, she says, laughing.

Nor me! says Jeanette. Not since breakfast!

She goes off to the bar to buy another round.

So come on then, Ursula, tell all, says Ashley. What have you been doing all these years? Did you sneak off and marry that weird lad of yours . . .? Johnny . . .?

Jerry. No. I was in India, says Ursula.

India. Whatever for? . . . God, you're brave.

I'd love to go there, Howard says. I'd like to see the Taj Mahal.

There's a Taj Mahal on Percy Street, squeals Jeanette from the bar. She comes back with another tray of shots. India! Fuck me, I'd have died, man!

I think I did, says Ursula laughing.

What do you mean? says Howard.

Ursula smiles. There are no words for what happened.

Another toast, says Jeanette. To coming home!

They knock them back, slam the glasses down.

So did you have an Indian boyfriend? asks Jeanette.

Not really. I met some Indian boys, and stayed in their village. And I met some guys with motorbikes who weren't so nice, not in the end, and I went to this place. I went to a few places actually, but in the end I was in a place in the hills, and I was with the monks . . .

Monks? says Jeanette. How many? You dirty sod!

Jeanette! says Ashley, laughing and rolling her eyes. Let her talk, man.

What was that like, being in a monastery? says Howard.

Ursula feels the alcohol warming through her. She feels just how long she's been away, and a desire to speak rises in her, to put what happened into words, to own it, to explain how it has changed her life for ever.

What was it like . . .? It was . . . I was . . . I am . . . I mean . . . Suddenly she is laughing. She can't stop. She's laughing at the ridiculousness of it all. She is filled with joy and madness, with alcohol.

I am still with them, she says. In fact I am them, you know? I am them . . .

She's gone mad, says Jeanette, turning to Howard, raising an eyebrow.

I know what you mean, says Ashley. I felt like that about Alistair when he asked us to marry him.

No, it wasn't love like that, I mean it was love but . . . She goes quiet, her words fail her, embarrass her, and she drinks to cover her confusion.

Well, you were always mad, and you're still mad and I'll drink to that! Mind, Howard, you'll have to drive me home after! Your round, Ashley.

Howard grins at Jeanette. Ashley goes to the bar and orders more drinks.

After this, I'm going on the wagon, cries Jeanette, picking up her glass. My last drink. After this evening, I am never drinking again! Never!

How many times have I heard that?! cries Ashley, laughing.

If you see me with another drink, you have my permission . . .

. . . to drink it for you! says Howard, and they laugh uproariously. Jeanette touches Howard's arm as she takes another drink. Ursula can see her anxiety. She can feel a loneliness in Jeanette, in the whole city, drinking to escape itself. The conversation is loud now and drunken as they tell stories of nights out, of lovers, fights, crazy situations. They are full of ribaldry and mockery. Ursula can't join in.

How about we make a night of it? says Jeanette. Bigg Market? Or down the quayside?

Howard suggests a new music venue on the Westgate Road. A band he knows will be playing there. They stand up and make their way outside. Jeanette notices Ursula is quiet, and turns to her, sensing judgement.

What's the matter, Ursula? You OK?

Are you? she asks innocently.

I asked you! cries Jeanette. There's nothing wrong with me!

You seem so frightened, says Ursula.

Frightened? I'm not fucking frightened.

Sorry, says Ursula. It's OK.

Too right, it's OK! It's you I'm worried about! I'm not the one who went off with a bunch of monks! You were always weird, Ursula. We all made an effort to see you today. You never even bought a round. Look at you! You didn't even brush your hair!

She links arms with Howard. Come on, gorgeous!

They lurch towards Northumberland Street. Ashley goes

after them, calling to Ursula behind her.

You not coming, Ursula? Ignore her, she's pissed! Don't forget my wedding list! It's at Fenwick's, remember? . . . There's loads of nice stuff left, plates, towels, a toaster, there's a set of candles . . . candles might be more your thing . . .

Jerry's come straight from the station, walked as fast as he could all the way. He knows exactly what he wants and why he's here. Ursula. He must win her round. Perhaps she feels the same way as him ... perhaps she's lonely without him. He'll make it up to her. As he turns into the front path of 35 Eslington Road, he feels a surge of fear and excitement. He borrowed some money from Tam in Brussels to buy her a present. He went to a jeweller's and looked through rows of gold bands with neatly clasped diamonds. None of them seemed right for her. In the end, he bought a jade necklace in a boutique in Oxford. It's in his inside pocket now, waiting for the right moment. He imagines how it will feel when he gives it to her. His heart's beating and he hesitates on the steps to calm himself. Through the bay window, he sees the lamps and books, the ornate mirrors, Ursula's grandmother, still at her place at the long table; the charming eccentricity of the house, all unchanged. Jerry is filled with hope. He and Ursula will be unchanged too.

In the kitchen, Mary too is happy. Never has Eslington Road seemed such a wonderful place to be. She has her confidante, Ursula, again. No matter how angrily or bitterly she vents her anger against her past, or present, Ursula is always happy to listen. It seems all she wants to do, her face always open and kind. There has been so little tenderness in Mary's life, she can't help but love this time with her granddaughter. She finds herself telling Ursula things she has never spoken of before to anyone; how she longed for her mother's love after the violence of her father's death, but received none, how her pretty dresses were thrown away and were replaced with clogs and overalls, how her mother hid her own grief in anger.

Stop crying, Mary, she'd say. Death is in God's hands. Grief is a sin against His Will!

Mary cries softly over the small ads as her memories consume her. She can't go to school, but must work in the laundry. She must be humble, her mother says, like the other girls. For her father's sake she throws herself into her chores with all her energy. She's up at dawn every day to open the iron gates, feed the delivery pony, unlock the sheds. There are tables to be scrubbed, floors washed, tubs scoured and lime-soaped, the copper boiler to rub with brick dust to a shine. The office needs managing too. Her mother has no patience for correspondence and bills, no head for the wages that must be calculated in a pyramid according to the women's skills and hours. Mary does it all. She spots the hot irons that have burned out, and orders new ones. Her education is forgotten.

On the laundry floor, she does the best she can. She's too young and weak to be a washer, a dollier, or an ironer, so Mary is a sorter, not like Grace Bates, so skilled and dextrous, who sorts according to colour, size, finish and fabric, or Verity Fowler who can pick out plain cotton from brushed cotton blindfold, even pinafores from counterpanes, but the lowest kind; sorting dirty whites for boil washes, and soiled underwear from stained sheets.

Hurry up with those whites, Miss Mary! shouts Harriet.

Steam's not up yet! she shouts back fiercely. The women were late this morning. Since her father died they have become lazy. It galls her. When her father was alive, they'd be fined a shilling out of five if they were so much as a minute late. The dolliers were tardy too; the coal should have been brought and the boilers stoked by 5.30.

Hurry up, little Miss Mary, shouts Eloise from one of the mangles. Four girls feed the wet linen into the machine, smoothing it flat as it rolls through, folding it the other side. Little Miss Mary, the owner's daughter. The women cannot resist their mockery.

Her father's hand-printed instructions curl on the walls, forgotten in the steam.

MUSLIN – dip twice, squeeze tightly. Do NOT twist. Iron on reverse side to avoid gloss.

His systems are slipping. Several of the women have left to work for a rival on the outskirts of town. There are only five tubs in operation now, and four wringing machines.

Mary picks up an armful of dirty whites and carries it to the tubs. The floor is an inch or two deep in water, and the room steaming hot though the day has only just begun.

Will you sing, Eloise?

Sing? Your mother will skin us alive.

Annie believes singing popular songs is blasphemous. The women will be out of a job if she catches them.

Mary puts the cottons into the copper boiler. Harriet plunges the dolly into the mass, and works it with both arms, left and right.

167

Don't let the feet scrape, Harriet, she says. Harriet scowls. Mary scolds herself. Her father would have said it in a way that made Harriet smile.

She goes into her father's office, takes a cloth from a shelf, and dusts his desk. He'll come back. He'll come back and look after her again. The women start to sing, and somehow it seems a blessing from him. She listens at the door.

Oh dishy dishy! Oh dishy dishy!

And what a dish he is! cries Eloise. The piano player at the Picture Palace! A dishy dish!

He can play anything! cries Verity. Play with his feet, he can.

And mine, if he likes! cries Eloise.

The Boy Wonder! Oh dishy dishy! Oh dishy dishy!

The women laugh and squeal.

Little Miss Mary! shouts Eloise. Take my place. I'm nipping to lav.

Mary joins the girls at the mangle, picks up a corner of a sheet and pulls it taut with Jean Grayson. The girls seem to dance with the sheets, elegant and graceful as they wind them through.

You should come, Mary, says Jean, giggling. Come and see the Boy Wonder.

Her father had promised he would take her to the Picture Palace to see a moving picture. He promised to show her wonders. Blackpool, Manchester.

I could ask Mother, says Mary.

Mrs Tate is here, girls, says Harriet, nodding at Annie, standing by the delivery shelves. The girls go quiet.

We're going to see *The Pink Rose* after work, whispers Jean. Ask her.

Mary sees her mother, and behind her, her shadow, Aunt Sissy. Mary is so dismayed at the sight of her aunt, she lets the sheet drop.

Clumsy girl! says Aunt Sissy.

Jean and the girls smirk silently.

Eloise, says Mary, holding on to her dignity, please be so kind as to take your place again. She walks with purpose across the floor, one thing on her mind.

Mother, she says as loudly as she dares. I have been invited by Jean to accompany her and her friends to the Picture Palace to see a motion picture entitled *The Pink Rose*.

Annie turns sharply and takes hold of her arm.

The Picture Palace is the devil's work, Mary, she rasps with almost passionate intensity. Mary! We've enough wickedness in us!

She looks to Sissy, seeking her approval. Mary jerks away from her. The women in the laundry carry on with their work. Annie and Sissy go into her father's office. Mary runs to the back door, hiding her tears. A new pile of linens has been delivered. She lifts out the rough and coarse calico, heavy to handle, and makes a new pile, anger and humiliation rising . . .

The doorbell brings Mary back to the present. She's looking down at her own hands, clasped over the newspaper on the kitchen table. She must have dozed off. The doorbell rings again.

Joyce! . . . Ursula! The door! She shouts, bridling at the interruption. Is nobody bloody well going to answer the door in this godforsaken house!

*

169

Jerry waits anxiously on the doorstep. It hasn't occurred to him Ursula might be out. Perhaps she's gone away. He's crestfallen for a moment, but rallies; wherever she is in the world, he will find her, no matter how far. The door opens and he sees Ursula. Her hair is longer, straight, the ends lightened by the sun. She's wearing baggy cotton trousers she picked up in India, and a long shapeless T-shirt. There is colour in her cheeks. She looks astoundingly beautiful.

Hi Jerry, she says, I'm happy to see you.

He's lost for words. She doesn't seem surprised to see him at all. He wasn't expecting this.

How was Brussels? she asks.

He thought she'd be emotional, angry at him for not being in touch with her since she got back to Newcastle, but she is smiling.

Your mum told me all about your success, she says.

I got far too drunk, and ate too many waffles, he says, and I saw a statue of a peeing boy, and yeah, we won. It was generally deemed a tremendous success.

You are always a success, Jerry.

He searches for irony in her words, finds none.

Would you like to come in?

How about a walk?

I'd like that.

She slips on a pair of flip-flops, and joins him on the doorstep.

You'll freeze, he says, wishing his words less blunt. You're not in India now.

I like to feel the ground, she says. They set off down the steps. There are goose bumps on her skin.

They cross under the motorway and walk out on to the

broad expanse of the Town Moor. The Hoppings fair has just left after its annual visit, and the earth is scarred with tyre grooves and patches of yellow grass from where the rides stood. Jerry stops by a wooden fence, a lonely border cutting across the fields.

I should apologise for how I was in Oxford, he says.

Me too. I was ill. I should have come straight home.

I brought you something.

He takes the necklace from his pocket and places it in the palm of her hand. It curls there like a tiny snake.

It's lovely, she says, smiling, delighted. She looks at it for a long time. He leans in to kiss her. She kisses him back. Her openness makes him shy. He wants to tell her how he still loves her, and about Caroline, and how he wants to make things right between them.

Ursula, what happened? he says gently. You said you didn't want to come home. You said some monks made you come home, but what about us? About me? Didn't you want to come home because of me?

He strokes her hair.

I thought we were going to be together. To live abroad. Have children.

I don't know, she says.

I thought we wanted the same thing. Don't we?

Everything is different now.

How? he says. How is it different? It doesn't feel different to me.

He tries to wish away the prickles of frustration.

Something happened to me, Jerry. I don't really understand it and I don't know how to say it, but when I was with the monks, I sat in front of a hill for so long that I became the hill. That's all there was. Just the hill. One hill. I was the hill. There was nothing else.

She looks at him, waiting for him to understand, to accept, to love her.

Nothing else? You mean nothing else is important? Nothing matters? he says. All he can feel is dull anger.

Exactly, she says, smiling. Yes, exactly!

You mean you and I don't matter?

No, we don't. I mean not like you think . . .

All the months of missing her, the pain and anxiety of not knowing, the struggle to love her as he knew he should rise up in him. Really? he says. Nothing matters? This is bullshit, Ursula! What's happened to you?

Nothing is what we think it is, she says. She shivers in the wind.

You're freezing, he says accusingly.

I'm fine, she says and walks on.

What?! So this is what it's all about, he says catching up with her, religion!

It's not religion.

Of course it is. You've seen the truth have you? The bloody truth! The only truth is that you haven't thought! You've gone to India, like a typical middle-class wanker and now that you're back you think you're bloody Gandhi. Not even that! At least he had political purpose! Tell me one good thing that comes from this kind of passive spirituality. Moved beyond consciousness, have you? You're part of some greater bloody whole?

She turns away from him into the wind. A single caravan from the fair still stands on the Moor. A child is playing outside it with a dog. Ursula feels the residue of her old self stirring inside her.

You're hurting me, she says.

How? says Jerry, his voice rising. I'm not hurting you. They're only words, Ursula. According to you, words, like everything else, don't matter. There is no good, no bad, no injustice, no fuck all. It's all the same. My words can't hurt you, but they do, and I'll tell you why. Because they're the truth and it hurts. You've come back like a passive-aggressive space cadet, holier-than-thou with your perfect world. If everything is so perfect then why do people get hurt by all the shit in the world? Why is there injustice?

He stops, takes her arm, forces her to turn to him.

Go on! Tell me! Why is there injustice?

Because we don't really see . . . she begins.

He ignites into pure anger.

You don't see injustice! he shouts, because you've never felt it, because you don't see that there is an insidious class system, inequality that drives people to despair, strike, broken communities, Thatcher, a right side, and a wrong side. Or is that not how it is on Planet Ursula? Look at yourself. You want to be different. You want to be special, and you've ended up just like everyone else, passive, unthinking, and stupid!

She tries to focus upon a sensation in her body. Anything that will let her stay on this exact moment, because it will pass. A wisp of hair falls on her face. She forces herself to feel the tickle of it.

You think this is about God? says Jerry, his voice cutting and rapid. God is nothing more than the lack of courage in the face of the existential doubt. It is plain, old-fashioned, stupid, an excuse for apathy. It's evil in the name of love. Fuck that!

173

Suddenly she can't feel the hair on her face. A line of tension down one side of her body seems to twist her spine. She walks away from him over the grooves of mud. Chip trays blow past her.

Why are you running away? He runs to catch her.

She faces him, eyes burning. A howl rips through her.

I saw something, she says, tears falling down her face, I can't help it . . .

What did you see? A vision? Jesus on the cross? A floating Buddha with a fat arse? Allah in an aubergine? The laughter in him is raw and cold.

I saw the hill . . . I . . . was the hill . . .

You're mad! he laughs. Fucking mad!

She looks into his eyes searching for words. She can't find them. There are no words, and suddenly she can't hold it any longer. Something deep inside her collapses, like a tent falling to the ground. Jerry turns and walks off across the Moor, shouting into the wind.

A hill! I was going to marry a fucking hill!

She watches him go across the churned-up ground. Her eyes fill with tears. He is right. She is stupid. She sees the mud, the caravan, the dog, the yellow patches where the rides have been. She is stupid and docile. She sees the mud on her feet. Ursula is shutting down her experience. She sees Jerry disappearing into the underpass. She sees the sky, pulled taut over her like a great grey sheet. She pushes the memories down, deep down where no one will find them. She must forget she ever felt this. She sees birds, and tyre tracks, and the pools of rainwater. She is turning her back on the hill. She is just a girl who went away to India, for reasons that now escape her, and came home ill. She looks across the Town Moor. Three men stand in a line, their metal detectors swaying together. Three figures against the sky, scanning the ground, joined by a single rhythm, searching, searching.

II

Autumn comes, covering Ursula in leaves. Winter turns her white, spring soaks her into the soil, and now summer blows through her. She's nineteen, still at home in Newcastle, the miracle of her experience in India fading fast inside her, unnourished. She no longer feels the single hair touching her cheek, or loves the buzzing of a fly, or sees beauty in the roar of the motorway. The world is separate from her again. Her friends enrol at colleges, find jobs on fruit farms, start businesses, enter government schemes, go to live in Brazil, but Ursula sits in the back garden at Eslington Road, only sensing a world she has no part in. She searches in the clouds for shape, for wonder, but glimpses it only in moments, and then wants the wind to cease, grasp the cloud and freeze it, whispering, please don't change, please don't disappoint me. Don't let my story be of the great failure to love. She aches for Jerry, the fit of their bodies. He seems to her the only thing that ever mattered, or ever will matter, but he has gone back to Oxford, possibly to London, and will disappear into the future like everyone else. Pain creeps into her body, a deep twist that stops the breath. The clouds move over her, and she cannot stop them, but even as she sits, week after week, month after month, being Ganny Mary's little companion again, even as she feels stuck, forgotten by the world, she is moving on, slowly transforming, part of the unstoppable flow at the core of things. Birds, televisions, babies, tables, toast, all slip through time as Ursula does, and so here she is, turning twenty, in the kitchen, receiving the full blast of Ganny Mary's bitter past. Her grandmother bangs her fist on the sycamore table, her face filling with the fierce and dreadful anger of God as she mimics her mother.

You are nothing, child! she cries, sucking in her cheeks. God's Will be done! God's Will! Not yours!

Ursula no longer relishes Mary's mimicry. She sees only Ganny Mary's hatred. Annie, the frightening figure who stands behind all their lives with her face of stone that never smiles, seems to hide sadness and pain. Ganny Mary sneers at her mother's memory.

Well, I told my mother, bugger God! I said, Bugger His bloody Will!

Ursula feels loneliness envelop her, beckoning almost. Joyce sends her to visit Jonathan in Brighton, who's promised his mother he'll straighten her out. She walks with him on the cliffs at Beachy Head and as he's pointing at the ships, the glimpse of France, Ursula, for a horrifying moment, sees the rocks below and their invitation. Wooden crosses mark the spots where others have answered their call, and in her mind she sees herself falling, lying broken on the rocks below, being washed away by the grey waves. As she and Jonathan walk back towards the town, she sees the chaplaincy team patrolling the cliffs, Bibles in their hands. This is not her way, and never could be. Something kicks hard inside her like a child, filling her with energy. She will not throw herself from the world, but into it.

Back in Newcastle she waitresses in a cafe, helps in a homeless shelter, runs a marathon, has a one-night stand with a man who runs a youth theatre, volunteers to help on a drama project for disabled kids, and does some acting. People say she's good and she auditions for a profit-share company doing theatre-in-education. Ursula gets the job, and plays a boy, a lady, a housewife, a doctor, a monkey, throwing herself into characters, disappearing from herself, finding a haven in pretence. She sleeps with a variety of men, some nice, some not, it doesn't matter, hardening into experience, finding brand new Ursulas, ones that can survive, be tough, ambitious for success. Joyce and Peter are entirely bemused by their daughter's choice of career. They give up trying to persuade her to go to uni, stop offering to pay fees for secretarial school, but feel relieved that at least she's *doing something*. They help her move to London where she gets an agent, Barry Noledon, who declares Ursula is *the future*, and as time moves on, she starts to shin the greasy pole with theatre jobs, and then telly jobs, until four years eight months and three days after her twentieth birthday, Ursula's a film actor, on *The Androgyne*, sci-fi, big-budget, biggest job of her career so far, with the director zooming in for a tight shot in her big scene.

Captain, give me a zero eight three ten! Copy that? Come in! . . . come in! . . . Shit! Christ! There's a malfunction in phase two. She is Ferrang from the planet Shu, sparky, possibly ill, deeply in love with Captain Bell of the *Crusader* on his mission to the Contamination Zone in Galaxy Five although no one must know. Ursula bows her head, unflinching in sacrifice. Captain Bell is human, she is Thwark, a different species, more orchid than human, and now containing a full bloom of contagious spores. She must warn Captain Bell about Skad before she dies. Sound speed. Ten seconds to impact! Aaagh! Her dishevelled heart is burning up for Captain Bell! Resist it and burn, Ferrang!! Burn, Ursula, burn!

CRASH!

It's a poor do, as Ganny Mary would say, Ursula's gone to hell in a handcart!

Poor Ferrang. Rest in Pieces. But what's this? The smoke is clearing, staggering from the pod, silver-suited, gasping in Shu speak, Hystle pys . . . skad, skad . . . she lives! How exciting! Uplifting! How entirely unexpected! She's alive! She staggers forwards, eyes of fire, face of buttery gold.

Do not enter the Contamination Zone, Captain Bell! she cries as he runs breathless towards her, wildly off-script, screaming about Skad the death angel from the galactic 9 Valley of Helix.

Navigator Lois Hardy tries to keep them apart but Ferrang can't bear it. She shoves her aside, falls at Captain Bell's feet, Ungemetllich pys! I love you, cries Ursula, tears pouring down her cheeks, the greatest actor of her generation!

Cut! Excellent everyone!

Jesus! That was intense, whispers Navigator Lois Hardy, aka Judy Monroe (*The Grafters*, *Hell Boys*, *Your Girl*), nursing her hand, don't grab me so hard, Ursula!

They are in Jefferson Studios, making shiny fool-fuel, silver-screen sparkles, three weeks into the shoot for *The Androgyne* with Hollywood up-and-comers Judy Monroe, Ethan Krevick (*The Wall of Mind*) and Ryan Tellerman (*Angel Head*, *Claudio*) directed by Keith Grayson (*Moon Girl*, *Killing Thomas*). Ursula holds her breath, as director

Keith, broom thin, bristly, calls out: Hold your positions, please. Can I see that back?

Ursula watches him turn to Camera. Silence falls. Have they served Him well? The actors pick their way reverentially through the forest of light-stands, silver-suited animals in the vast dark of the studio, towards the hooded altar of the monitor. Ursula peels off her silver mask, feeling something divine in the moment, suspended in Camera's sublime authority.

Ryan's a fucking genius, Judy whispers as they watch the playback. He'll get the big O for this. She squeezes Ursula's arm. The crew adjust and polish, busy devotees, lost in the mysteries of Camera's complexity. Ursula sits on a silver lens box and ignores the jabbing dabs of Missie, the sour-faced powder girl. She must ignore everything around her, and stay in a heightened state for Ferrang, and her fuel is limited. She is only human after all. She must give her all for Camera when it is asked of her; like the mirrors in Newcastle when she was a child, the camera is Ursula's proof of herself.

Jesus, I'm a shit actor! cries Judy Monroe, turning away from the monitor, unable to watch. I was shit! She laughs blowsily, hiding her fear, looking for love. She grossed 70 million with *The Grafters*. She has a wide trembling mouth. Ursula would like to be her. A drill hammers in the darkness.

Hold the work! barks the First Assistant.

The Focus Puller, Camera's altar boy, shakes his canister and sprays the inner workings. He peers deep inside with his torch. Ryan Tellerman, who plays Captain Bell, stands close to Ursula in a patch of yellow light. He's bare-chested, and Ursula can feel his breathing. Camera loves his cheekbones, his dark eyes. She combs her fingers through her hair, willing Ryan to give her some sign of the night before. Don't fiddle, says Missie, spraying Ursula with clouds of hairspray. Chemicals fume her mouth. The night before, after wrap, they had zoomed down the A40 into London, a fleet of Higher Beings, Ursula, Ethan, Judy, Ryan each in separate Mercs, the drivers indulging their whims, sticking close to each other in the lanes so they could make gargoyle faces at each other through the windows. Judy snorted cocaine off the back seat and passed the wrap through the car window to Ryan in his car. The thin line. The rolled fiver. Coke and speed at the same time: seventy miles an hour!

They'd gone to Ryan's private club in Soho. In the dark alcoves Ursula shone bright as a diamond as the tequilas were lined up, slammed, lined up again. They were baby birds, gagging for more of anything, everything, another shot, another line, or five, Judy whispering, giggling as they squashed into the ladies' cubicle, quietly, professionally, sucking trails, cutting more, snow on a lizard's back.

Ursula was with Ryan on a leather sofa, I just want to be the best, she said to him, leaning close, speaking too fast, you know? Not just to be best but because I would do anything, like you, to make good work. That's all. The work. That's all there is. Work and integrity. I want to make people think. I'm sick of commercial shit, you know?

Ryan's smile was full of pill-love. He'd taken Ursula's hand, and they'd left together. You know, I get muddled up with my character, Ursula had kept talking, like I really think I am her, like I don't know who I am. Do you get that?

Yeah, said Ryan, sucking on a cigarette, flagging a car on the street, the driver Ghanaian, chewing gum. In the back,

Ryan had played with her nipples through her dress. Want to dance? he said. Yeah. Let's bone dance.

They'd curled round each other, their bodies made strange by drugs. At some point, he had penetrated her.

Camera's good! shouts the Focus Puller. Great, says Keith Grayson, hugely relieved. That's lunch!

Everyone relaxes; Camera is happy, but they must remain vigilant. He is a fickle god who can turn from even the best and most devoted in an instant to bestow his love on younger, fresher believers.

They emerge through studio doors big enough for planes, blinking into the daylight, and make their way to the trailers and catering trucks that line the unkempt areas by the perimeter fence.

Look Ursula, says Judy, your new agent. What's she doing here? Must be something big!

Agent Patty waves, ginger hair like wisps of candyfloss, pale blue eyes in watery whites.

Darling, she kisses Ursula, and steps into the tiny two-way.

How the hell are you supposed to manage in these fucking little rabbit hutches? says Patty, perching on the sofa by the sliding window. You're not a fucking rabbit, are you? She sounds drunk. Ursula would never say. She is new, has only been on Patty's books three months. Ursula is a good girl.

Palkovsky's in town. Sukie Barrington's arranged a meeting. It's big. Sukie only casts big ones.

Ursula mustn't show too much desire, or she'll be sacrificed, hurled over the rockface for wanting too much, a smashed skull on the shore for boys to find. Ursula is filled with extremes, most of them hidden.

What is it? she asks as nonchalantly as she can, while her heart's beating, wanting, kicking.

Patty's eyes hold her for a moment then swim away in a dream of camellias and race days. Her first hubby divorced her, but she'll always be grateful for the garden. Bastard still invites her to Ladies Day: Come and join us, Patty, in the Corporation box. She goes collagen-pumped and gin-fizzing with anger.

Could be exciting, says Ursula, lightly, leaning back against the tiny loo door. Her silver suit chafes her armpits, she undoes the fasteners. Agent Patty has arrived before she's had a chance to change, and she now feels the awkwardness of the small trailer. She wants to take it off, but Patty would see her, her skinniness, her enhancing bra, her shyness too. Patty mustn't see what's underneath. The whiteness, the lack of knowledge. It's not a Winnebago like Ryan's, or Ethan's, Judy's, but that will come. A twenty-footer, with a bedroom and a fitted kitchen. Patty, oh Patty, you are the key. I am so lucky to have you. Patty spotted her in *Barton Towers* on ITV, said *she has legs, will go far*, poached her from Barry Noledon. Her friends said, Patty Lucas! Oh my God! Go with her! You're so lucky, so fucky fucky lucky, she's a legend. And as though to prove it, Patty had got her this, *The Androgyne*, a movie with edge and meaning, a metaphor for something. So what if the suit is uncomfortable? She's the luckiest girl in the world, just got to hold it together, let the sweat trickle and relax. She looks shapely, the costume girl said, good enough to eat, she said.

Patty?

Patty doesn't answer. Rule One of Agent Patty: always command the stop and flow of communication. Create silences, answer questions out of sequence, if at all. It's a technique she's developed over years. It helps with negotiating deals with fucking producers who take the fucking piss. Put them off-balance, get up their noses, they'll soon agree terms, just to minimise the ordeal.

What is it, Patty?

Patty may never speak ever again. She is at Cheltenham in a dream of revenge, spiking a Martini, calling him a wanker in front of his posse, winning the four o'clock by a length and a half, and throwing the money in his face. You can't buy me, fucker.

Ursula feels the pain stab in her side again. Her neck and ribs jam and she arches to loosen them. Nothing helps. She's had it since India. She blames the dhal in Tamil Nadu, the lychee ice cream in Bangalore made with well water, and more, something beyond illness, the wound of it all. She's discovered osteopaths. She'll make an appointment after wrap. They crack her. It helps . . .

Joan of Arc, says Patty at last. I mentioned you. Might happen, might not.

To play Joan?

You're hardly the Dauphin, darling. Joan, yes. Why not? Sukie Barrington likes you.

Ursula's heart skips. She wants to know everything immediately. Is there a script? Does she have to read? Is it just a meet? Reading is low status. Just a meet means you're on the list. A-listers, B-listers, heart blisters . . .

The door of the trailer opens. The runner, a young boy, dark half-moons for eyes, slides in two plates of hot food under tin foil.

Thanks darling, Ursula says. The AD's been shouting at

him all day. It's wrong. What's his name? No idea. Never mind. Ignore it all. Everyone's a darling now.

They'll want you on tape, says Patty distractedly. How's it all going here? Are they treating you well?

Ursula's space suit itches in the groin. She needs to urinate. The food is waiting under the foil. She can't eat. It's too awkward.

What is Ryan Tellerman like? Any fucking good? Patty drawls, her eyes half closed like a cat. She peels back the silver foil on a steaming pile of chilli con carne.

Fucking hell! she says. Trough food!

Ryan's amazing, says Ursula. The whole thing's amazing. Except the costumes! Ursula tries out her comic *yikes* face. But I really love science fiction so . . .

Her words are dust. Weird dust. She hates science fiction. She knows nothing. She remembers how Jerry played with words, weirdo, lusho . . . she can't remember. Her last letter to him. Never sent. The roaring silence.

And really nice too, says Ursula, trying laughter, a tremolo like Judy. I thought he'd be . . . you know? But he's not. He's actually nice and . . . think of something witty . . . Brilliant! . . . keep going . . . He'll get an O for this. Everything will . . . laugh, laugh in the voice . . . Everyone will, except these suits! It's just *so* fucking hard to go to the loo!

Patty's eyes are dead fish eyes. Nothing registers.

If they try anything, she says darkly, let me know. She takes a forkful of mush, and deposits it in her mouth. Patty's world is full of treachery.

So, Joan? Joan of Arc? says Ursula brightly. Should I cut my hair?

Patty, old fish, turns to Ursula, silverfish. Jonno will call you, she says in fish tongue.

The runner leans in.

Keith will be shooting the crash for Shelton Hardy's close-up after lunch, so if you wouldn't mind Ursula . . .

Ursula's going back in her pod, to die all over again. If she's not dead already, she soon will be from drink, drugs, emotional pile-up, head-on collisions. She needs someone to save her, to wake her up. Where is Jerry; funny, charming, intelligent Jerry? The clever lad with the way of putting things, the first-class honours in Politics and Philosophy, a PhD in record time on Deleuze and Derrida, names of detergents to his mam but his supervisor says he's an original, he'll be on the telly, in the public eye, politics, MP, QC or PM why not?

Jerry sniffs the air in Oxford where his friend Giles has begun a junior fellowship, sniffs it in Soho where Caroline's gone into advertising, wearing hairclips and deodorant, guzzling mojitos, sniffs Westminster where Tam has a research post with Tony Benn, the one true man, and finally takes a job in Millbank, Labour HQ, determined not to compromise. His intelligence and flair for persuasive reasoning get him noticed. For a year, he is filled with energy; he can see the future, and what needs to be done. He works tirelessly on a proposal for radical reform of the voting system. When he presents it to a Home Office subcommittee, he is feted as a man of vision. He imagines his proposals will be adopted, made policy, but he misjudges the volatility of the political moment. His ideas are dropped, washed away by the next wave of new ideas from people just like him. The defeat wounds him. His ideas are just as quickly lauded and dismissed a second, then a third time. He feels his own fallibility. He feels frightened. The political machine is beyond logic, and he is built on pure reason, cultivated in the Lit and Phil, hammered out in the arguments with his parents, debates with his teachers. Without reason the world makes no sense to him. He is already looking over his shoulder when his father is diagnosed with multiple sclerosis. It gives him the excuse he's been looking for. He returns to Newcastle. His dad needs him, is what he tells everyone, and himself. He will turn his back on his ambition, choosing to live under cold skies in the Byker Wall again, at home with his mam and dad, where his anger was born and his reason forged. Fuck them all; he'll start a revolution all his own.

So here he is, pinning up a poster he's photocopied at the central library: Wallsend Hub, opening 8 March. All welcome! Jerry feels nothing but hope, as he makes round pellets of Blu-tack in his fingers, thumbs it like chewing gum, and presses it on the wall. Through the window, he can see a woman and man at the bus stop. The man is smoking, his face pallid, the woman is heavily made up, all black eyes and orange cheeks, like his sister Andie. Jerry knows he has made the right decision to come back. He'll get to know people, make a difference. He will rebuild the Wallsend Community Centre and create a hub where working-class culture can be celebrated and renewed. The man at the bus stop might join the reading group, the woman the culture club, perhaps. She looks over at him, hard as a town fox. He hopes people don't get put off by the building. A bloody public toilet, his mam said. It's true it's ugly, a one-storey purpose-built unit, but the people's enthusiasm will make it stand out. He'll get some murals, commission a local artist. Must put that on the list.

Mr Cairn, the caretaker, is mopping the corridor. The tiles darken as the wet head moves to and fro.

I'll be closing early today, he says, his face pure vinegar.

Right, Mr Cairn, says Jerry.

It's all going well. He took over the place a month ago, persuaded the Council in one meeting. On you go, son, they'd said, and good luck to you. He's already lined up an interesting programme of speakers: Mannery Gates is to give a talk about ship-building; Mrs Tylle from the Council accounts department is going to talk about Wallsend in the war years. Several local businesses have chipped in; Jerry doesn't really approve of business sponsorship, but money's money as his dad says. He's spoken with the Lit and Phil about Hub members borrowing books. He even put in a call to Ursula's father, and told him his plans. Jerry! Great to hear from you! Very positive. No mention of Ursula. No need. They are all grown-ups now. Men and women of the world.

Mr Cairn, hope you're coming to the meeting. I want to hear from you too, says Jerry. Your opinions about the future of the centre are just as important as anyone else's.

I keep the keys, man, clean the toilets.

I know, so what would you like to see happen here? says Jerry.

I divven knaa. You're the one had the education!

I'm learning all the time, man, says Jerry, smiling. Education is for ever, isn't it?

Aye well.

Mr Cairn avoids Jerry's shoes with his mop head, and continues his work in long regular sweeps.

*

The pavements on the north side of the Byker Wall are icy and Jerry takes care not to fall. He passes Headland Way, Vicarage Row, the small council houses aspiring to quaintness with their coloured roofs. The church, a relic of old Byker before the Wall, stands out like a giant headstone. He turns and walks underneath the Wall, million-eyed monster with jutting balconies, home to three thousand tenants. The wind funnels in from the river in a roar. He pulls his coat round him in a hug of himself as he emerges from the North Entrance.

Hey, Jerry!

A shout from the far side of the estate. It's Mackie with a young woman walking through the children's playground.

Mackie!

They slide towards each other on the ice.

Hiya, Jerry. This is Lisa.

Hiya, Lisa.

High heels, tight jeans, low-cut top, cleavage goosebumping in the cold.

Jerry's a genius, so legend has it, says Mackie.

He is in denim, looks triangular, manly. Perhaps he's been working out. They've met since Jerry came back, but only like this, by the Wall, exchanging a few words. They are unsure of each other after so long.

Are you? A genius? asks Lisa, eyeing Jerry.

Jerry deadpans. Every millimetre.

How's the Hub? says Mackie.

How's life on the dole?

The banality of the words embarrasses them. Pigeons spray up from the white ground and disappear over the buildings.

Her Majesty's Department of Social Security is looking after me very well, says Mackie.

I might join you.

We don't accept riff-raff.

Hoi polloi.

Raspberry fucking ripple.

Jesus! What are yous on? says Lisa. She breathes out disdainfully, and looks away.

Jerry and Mackie check their grins.

I thought you were poncing about in art college, says Jerry.

I got corrupted, he says jerking his thumb towards Lisa.

Shut up, Mackie, she says, looking at the horizon. She'll go to Spain if she can, or Lanzarote, life on a lounger. She smiles, suddenly pretty, and Jerry sees her in bed with Mackie, a flash of their bodies, Mackie's lust, his jokes.

How's that lass of yours? says Mackie, reading his mind. Getting any?

Lisa whacks him.

Fucking crude. What lass? she says, sparkling.

Jerry went out with a weird lass, Ursu-la, says Mackie, grinning back.

She is no more, says Jerry.

Dead? says Mackie, sadly.

Has she died? says Lisa.

To me, says Jerry.

Eee, I thought you meant she was dead, man, says Lisa. It's not nice to joke about dead people!

Don't be thick, Lisa, says Mackie.

If I'm thick, you're a fucking meat head, moron.

She adjusts the shoulder strap on her bag.

He was born moronic, says Jerry.

'Course I was. My mother is a moron. It's her religion, says Mackie.

They all laugh. Jerry feels the relief of it. Lisa tuts, smiles at Jerry. He feels the sexual promise of her. A white Ford drives into the estate, music blaring, and screeches to a stop. A man gets out and walks to them over the icy ground. Jerry feels his stomach flip like it used to. It's Spennie, his features less symmetrical somehow, all grown up, walking fast, holding a hand out to Mackie.

Give us a tab, Mackie.

Tight tracksuit, hair cut sharply sideways.

Mackie gives him one, lights it. Lisa sighs, hair falls over one eye.

Spennie looks at Jerry. Keep calm, keep friendly.

You're at the community centre. He says it like an accusation.

The music pulses from the white car. Another man is at the wheel.

Come sometime, Spennie, says Jerry. It's called the Hub now.

What the fuck for? says Spennie.

There's loads going on, and there's advice . . .

He hears himself too late.

Do I look like I need fucking help? says Spennie. He blows smoke at Jerry, his chin jutting out. Violence is all that is on offer. Jerry looks over at the car. The man inside would be out like a dog from a trap.

Help me, says Spennie. Go on, fucking help me.

Jerry gives him two Benson and Hedges. Spennie grins.

Scrounger, says Mackie, easy, risking a taunt. Lisa sighs loudly, shifting her weight from one foot to the other. The men turn and look at her. She knows what she's doing.

Howhey, let's get chips, she says. I'm starvin', man. I only came out to get chips, man!

Her haranguing tone smacks of a domestic, cutting through the male violence.

I'm freezin', Mackie! she goes on, treading a thin line.

Spennie steps back. The tension defused. Two cigarettes is enough. For now.

I don't need any fucking help, Jerry. Get it?

He walks back across the ice to the white car.

Twat, says Lisa, under her breath. Mackie puts his arm through hers, and turns her away. Spennie passes a cigarette to the man in the car, deferential. He'd been told to confront them. Jerry sees it. No one is free. Spennie had once asked Ursula for tabs when she came to the Wall. She brazenly told him to get his own. Coming from Jesmond, she couldn't possibly know how dangerous it was. Jerry had felt humiliation in his fear. Afterwards he'd wanted to smack the smile off her face. Ignorant bitch, he'd said, infected by Spennie's violence.

Must be peculiar, coming back here, says Mackie.

Peculiar is not the word, says Jerry.

What is?

Fucking peculiar is the word.

They reach the stairwell. We'll be at the Stag tonight, says Lisa.

The lift stops at the fourteenth floor. The doors do not open; it's the same fault there's been since Jerry was eight. His mam has made endless complaints, filled out the forms.

Nothing's happened. The Council are useless, she says. The doors shut for a minute, then suddenly judder apart. Come on then, if you're coming, they seem to say.

He lets himself into the flat. His parents took advantage of the Tory policy of selling off council flats. You're helping them crush the working class, he told his father. The working class don't exist, said his mam, sharp as tweezers. You're out of touch!

No one is at home. His room has been stripped since he went to Oxford, his treasures all gone; the books, the posters, the stash of periodicals. The walls are freshly white, and festooned with fancy mouldings. Now they are homeowners, his parents have palatial aspirations. The room is a wedding cake. Cornices, covings and corbels, a chandelier with surrounding boss on the ceiling. There are plaster swirls around the radiator to look like a sculpted fireplace. His mother's collection of white china shepherdesses has expanded to fill new shelving above his bed. Blame Andie, said his mam when he first saw it. She's married now; designed Jerry's room while she was planning her big day. Her wedding is an experience Andie will never fully recover from. The beauty of it, the wonder of herself as she rustled down the aisle, the love she felt. She lives in Seaton Sluice now, twenty minutes down the coast road, in a new council house, with the twins.

A smattering of books disturb the room's virginity; Jerry's been at the Lit and Phil borrowing like the old days. Books on the Levellers, the Diggers, the early socialist movement in the North East, volumes of workers' songs, mystery plays. He lies on the bed, and opens Winstanley's *An Appeale to all Englishmen*. A humble request.

But though the devill be let loose to swell against us,
in these gentry that rule over us by Kingly power,
or law of Norman Bequest, not withstanding,
they have taken the engagement,
to cast out kingly power:
yet his time to be chained up draws nigh
and then we are assured this righteous work of earthly
    community
shall have a vast glorious resurrection out of his ashes.

This righteous work of earthly community. The words please him, the fight for equality alive now, as it was then.

He leans back on his pillow, finds a folded *Daily Mail*. His mother still leaves it for him, her little joke. He makes a note to himself, must move out. He must call that girl from the Labour Women campaign. Melanie. Mellie, she said she preferred. She was bright. And serious. There was definitely an understanding there. Working-class roots like him. She was moving to Birmingham. His thoughts gallop. How long's the train from Newcastle to the Midlands . . .?

Jerry!

His mother calls from the kitchen. She'll be putting the shopping into the freezer. She buys frozen when she can. Tastier, she claims. His dad's voice too now. Since his retirement they are always together. On Sundays they get the car out, and visit Andie and the twins.

Jerry!

He comes through. It should be comforting to be never more than twenty feet away from someone at any time. Ursula used to complain about her big Victorian house, how her bedroom was miles from the heart of things. She didn't know how lucky she was. Spoilt. There's no other word for it. He misses his student house in Oxford with Caroline and Tam, his room in the attic, where Ursula had stayed that night after India. How awkward that had been.

All that education, man, and you're throwing it away, says Jerry's father as he comes in. He thinks Jerry should be running a corporation, or making his way through law school.

A bloody day centre, man? he says. You could be making a packet!

His father puts a loaf of white sliced in the freezer, and faces him.

It's a community centre, says Jerry.

You're not even in bloody charge!

Jerry's heard it all before. He's told them how it is, had the row, but they keep on. He reaches into the shopping bag, hands his dad a packet of frozen waffles.

It's run by the community, for the community, says Jerry. There is no one with absolute power.

Bloody communist, says his dad, taking the bag off the table, unpacking a fish pie, the Sea Captain smiling through the frost.

If it wasn't for communist ideals, says Jerry, in the voice that annoys them most, you would never have had a union at the shipyards, never received redundancy money when the bosses cut the workforce, you Mam wouldn't have had this flat in the first place if it hadn't been for . . .

We own it, man!

You have been hoodwinked, says Jerry.

Don't start, Jerry! says Kath. Don't bloody well start!! The bottom line is your 'job' doesn't pay a brass farthing!

I get paid, says Jerry.

A pittance. A bloody pittance . . .! She bites her tongue, turns away. She's boasted of Jerry all these years, made people green with envy, Kerry, Fiona, other mams. They'd complain about their lads, and she'd chime in, oh Jerry's the same, he's a worry, but now he's in Westminster talking to the government, so we live in hope! She'd laugh, couldn't help feeling lucky, knowing Kerry's boy was an apprentice, still at home, and Lee and Steve on the dole. Now she doesn't know what to say. The disappointment, the waste of it all.

I think he came back because of your illness, says Kath softly. Mike puts his hand on her shoulder. Jerry sees the tenderness between them, the love in his touch.

MS is a slow worker. I've got a dicky arm, that's all. He turns to Jerry. I hope to God you didn't come back here on my account, Jerry. It's the last thing I want.

I can make a difference here, Dad.

Jerry looks down, feeling uncomfortable, runs his hands over his knees.

Don't hide from the world, he says.

Coming from you! says Jerry.

Divven base yourself on me, says his father, more gently now.

Kath puts two foil dishes in the oven, and turns the knob. The fan whirrs in a silence that holds them all. Findus pie. Peas in a saucepan. Plates. Cutlery. The mashed potato from the microwave so hot it scalds their tongues. Jerry fetches a bottle of white wine from the top cupboard. Kath takes out glasses, the good ones. It's Chardonnay, warm, and syrupy.

Your Ursula was on the telly, says Kath, sipping the yellow liquid, her distress losing its edge.

She's not mine, Mam, says Jerry.

She'll be famous and then you'll be sorry.

It's not like that, says Jerry.

What happened? You never said, says his dad. Did she dump you?

Mike, says his mam, admonishing. Do you never hear from her?

It's fine, Mam. There's nothing to say about it.

When I visited her in the hospital, says Kath. She was . . .

She wasn't herself, says Jerry. He hasn't seen her since the Town Moor. She wrote to him once. She was living in London, making her way as an actress. He couldn't help feeling she was wasting her time. She'd apologised for how strange she'd been after India, for the arguments they'd had. He'd written back, a postcard of Marx. Everything is material, he'd written, we are only our history. The ideal moment of wonder, which Marx believed in, cannot come about until everyone is equal. He'd tried to put it gently, knowing she had once felt so differently. She'd replied, promised to visit, never had.

That evening, in the white room, Jerry listens to wind. He thinks of Mackie and Lisa at the Stag. He will call Melanie tomorrow. He will be good for her, as she will be for him. Hope springs from good intentions.

He looks over north Tyneside. All the lives out there he hopes to touch. He reaches for a book. *A History of Communes*, or Shakespeare's *Hamlet*? He chooses the well-thumbed play. He loves the words, indulges in them, almost guiltily. The Royal Shakespeare Company are in Newcastle for their season at the Theatre Royal. *Hamlet* is one of the plays they will perform. He'd love to see it but who would he go with? No one from Byker, not even Mackie. He turns to a page at random and reads: 'the native hue of resolution Is sicklied over with the pale cast of thought, And enterprises of great pith and moment, With this regard, their currents turn awry, And lose the name of action. Soft you now. The fair Ophelia . . .'

5.30 a.m. Keith's black Merc crawls up Jerrup Street, E17. He watches the shop fronts – MIND, Aljebah, the grilled windows of King's the chemist, Accessorize, Carphone Warehouse, recently opened, money coming into the area. He turns into Hendik Way, a Victorian terrace, and edges towards number 65. No hurry. She'll be late. She was late every morning on the last job. No reason it would have changed.

He stops the car in the middle of the road, gets out and lights a cigarette in the curl of his palm to shield it from the wind.

Ursula emerges, sleepwalking down the front path.

Good morning, Keith says, blowing out smoke.

She climbs in the back of the Mercedes without answering and falls asleep on the back seat. Keith stubs out his cigarette, peers in at her. She's got her feet up on his seats. He knows better than to say anything. He's seen it all before. Young actors, here today, gone tomorrow, headless shits, he calls them when he's had a few.

He's at Junction 3 of the M4 when she wakes up, thirsty, head pounding. Car lights flare in the windows. She feels the twist in her body, the pain wrenching her neck. She stretches.

Late night, was it?

Keith shifts in his seat to look in the rear-view mirror. Best to keep in with the actors, you never know where it might lead. Des drove Tom Cruise for a day, now he's his chauffeur when he's over in London. Nice work if you can get it.

You don't want to know, she groans. She knows the face, rectangular above collar and tie. He's driven her before. Can't remember his name.

Where are we going?

It's an ad, love. Mobile phones.

She looks out the window at the passing cars. Perhaps she should be nervous. It's hard to know what to feel. Vodafone, Patty says, the money is good, the director's hot, and the other actor is going to be big. All the right, short adjectives.

What day is it? says Ursula. She knows it is Wednesday but she's enjoying being the airhead, the trashed high-status dipshit. The drivers seem to expect it.

Wednesday, love. They've been shooting for three days. They lost one already. There was a stink about it.

Ursula twists her back again, trying for a click.

A real shitstorm, mind my French, suits on set, the CEO flying in, effing and blinding, the whole bang shoot. Director fucked up the schedule. Cost them half a mill. How hard can it be? A four-day shoot, you lose a whole fucking day! Give me the job. I'd get it done!

At the studio Ursula is greeted enthusiastically. Make-up, costume, runners, second assistant are friendly as though their lives depend on it. She's led to a dressing room. They bring her coffee, porridge, and a bacon sandwich, find her a toothbrush, blow her hair, brush her face with cosmetics, encourage her into seamless underwear, strap a large cushion to her belly, ease a sweet daisy-print dress over it, and Ursula is a young, heavily pregnant wife ready to love her husband beyond reason, and sell Vodafones. She is led back through the darkness towards the bright new build of a perfect kitchen.

Hi, Ursula. Yes. What took you so long? says the director. He is sweating from his hair line. The crew are quiet. Behind the camera, three men in suits watch his every move.

She looks OK, he says, looking her over, glancing at the suits. Each minute costs a grand, they've told him, so no fuck-ups. Ursula, you're the pregnant wife of Kelsey here. Have you two met? Kelsey is your co-star. Kelsey, this is Ursula, your wife. Great. You look good together. This is your kitchen. Your new kitchen, full of lovely gadgets. Ursula, I want you to pretend to be on the phone but without a phone in your hand, OK? Just talk into the air, and at the same time you are getting on with your lovely kitchen activities, put some toast in the toaster, water in the kettle. Can this kettle boil? He turns to the crew. We need to boil water in this. I want steam . . .

Hi, Ursula.

Kelsey Fern rolls his eyes, sharing the moment with her. He's Scottish, a round face, boyish, eyes like warm chestnuts.

Hi, Kelsey, says Ursula.

I want this kettle practical! Let's do this! shouts a man just behind her. We need steam!

A suit comes over to the director and speaks quietly in his ear. The director nods. A grand a minute.

Forget the steam, he shouts. Forget the steam!

Ursula is positioned under the blazing arc lights. Sweat prickles her skin. Her padded costume feels hot enough to cook a chicken.

Sound. Speed. Action!

Ursula has no idea what she's doing. She would like to lie down. She puts her hands on to her back in the way she has seen pregnant women do.

I feel fat, she says, remembering her line.

You're keeping our baby warm, says Kelsey Fern from behind the camera.

She walks to the kettle and turns it on.

I can't see my toes, she says.

Cut. Jesus. Don't turn on the kettle. Remember? There's no steam. Again, shouts the director. And you're flaring your eyes.

What do you mean?

Just look more natural.

It's weird talking into a phone without a phone, she says. It doesn't feel natural.

That's the whole point, sweetheart. You don't have a phone. You two love-birds can communicate just like that, anywhere. Everywhere. You are in touch all the time. Right? The Vodafone V8 is so easy to use it's like talking without a phone. Get it?

He goes back to the monitor. Ursula hears a 'fuck's sake'. She sits by the continuity woman waiting for Camera to be ready for her. She tries to think it through. The action is ordinary, easy, relaxed. She must say two lines into a phone but without holding a phone, while she is making tea. It seems easy, but she feels hot and uncomfortable. She yawns, eyes watering, feels the twist in her body stifling her breath.

You OK? says Kelsey Fern, suddenly beside her.

I'm fine, she says. I'm just a bit . . . I don't know. I'm fine. When you're giving me the off-lines, can you say them like you're really talking into a phone?

Her tone is professional and reprimanding. She speaks loudly, wants everyone to know it's not her fault she doesn't look 'natural'.

What do you mean? Kelsey says. He seems oblivious to her motives.

I don't know . . . I don't know. I just . . . you're not help-ing, the way you're saying your lines . . . I need you to make it sound more like you are speaking to me on the phone, and less like you are in the actual room with me pretending to be on the phone. When I see you there behind the cam-era it makes my eyes do something funny, so, perhaps you should, I don't know, perhaps you could hide when you say your lines . . .

Sure, he says, smiling, totally unflustered. She feels irritated with him. Is he enjoying the fact that she feels so awkward? She's not sure. It's hard to tell. Why has he stayed on set to say his lines off camera? Must be to laugh at her. She hates herself. Why is she having these thoughts? She feels their ugli-ness, and stands up abruptly as though to escape them.

Starting positions! And Action!

I feel fat, she says.

You are keeping our baby warm, says Kelsey Fern. She can't see him; he must be hiding somewhere. His voice is weirdly distorted, pitched strangely. He's speaking with his hand over his mouth, trying to make it sound like an old-fashioned phone call.

Ursula can't help but laugh.

Cut!

Great! That's it! That's the one. Really natural. Great, Ursula. Thank God! Moving on . . .

Kelsey Fern appears from behind a flat.

Did it help? he says, smiling.

Yes, she says. Thank you.

No problem, he says. It's been good to work with you.

Yeah, you too, says Ursula. Short, but good.

He smiles. She notices how soft and pale his lips are.

Want to share a car later? Get a drink somewhere? she says.

After they wrap, Keith drives them to a pub on the Farringdon Road. Ursula orders pints, and they talk. Kelsey went to drama school. He always wanted to be an actor. It's in his blood, he says, his dad's one. He likes the life, feels the privilege of it. He's learning his trade. He's just played Romeo in a touring production. They played all around Asia.

Playing Shakespeare abroad was amazing. It's a universal language. We went to amazing places. Have you done much travelling?

I've been to India, says Ursula, stretching her neck over to one side, a long time ago, in another lifetime! She laughs though nothing's funny. I need a cigarette! Let's get cigarettes!

She goes to the bar, gets change for the machine, buys a packet, and lights one, taking a deep drag.

So what are you doing next? she says, as she sits down again, offering one to Kelsey.

Another advert.

My agent says you are the next big thing.

Mine said the same about you.

Really? Is that true?

God's honour. What are you doing next?

I don't know. I've got loads of auditions coming up. One for a film of *Joan of Arc*, but I think the funding is dodgy. It would be an amazing part.

Yeah, so many films just don't get their funding. I had this part last year. The day before we started, they lost all the money. All the sets were built for nothing.

It's crazy, laughs Ursula. There is an awkwardness between them. The conversation doesn't flow, but Ursula can't bear the thought of him leaving.

Another drink? she says.

I should get going. I need to eat something.

He stands up to go. He hates her, must hate her. A fire blazes in her head.

It's early, she says. Stay.

What are we going to do? he says, a look in his eye.

Eat, she says. Why not?

Anything, eat, smoke, drink, I don't care but please don't go. I can't be alone, now, please be a mirror to me make me real . . . He's smiling, doing up his coat, stop him . . . Don't go, Kelsey Fern, please take me in your arms, Kelsey Fern, gentle straightforward man riding your bicycle through life. Don't leave me here with nothing no love no words, no sense of me. No you, no touch, no arms, strong like rope yours are, perhaps they can hold off the fear, the terrible uncertainty . . . Can they? Can you? . . . He's saying goodbye, moving to the door. Ursula, do something, say something, quick, stop him, anything . . .

Kelsey . . . ? she says. I have a fantastic cunt.

Jerry leans against the brass banisters in the foyer of the Theatre Royal Newcastle, eating pink ice cream and fending off negative thoughts. The Hub is not flourishing as he'd hoped it would. The reading group has three members: Ted and Maureen Jackson, and himself. Ted and Maureen regard history in the same way trainspotters regard train timetables, totting up facts in small spiral-bound notebooks. Whitley Bay was used by the Home Guard in 1943. *Tick*. Gladstone visited Tynemouth in 1844. *Tick*. So far no one has turned up to the debating club, or taken advantage of the deal he's done with the Literary and Philosophical Society to borrow books. He had hoped local groups would spring up of their own accord, make a hub in the community where ideas could be proposed and shared. He tries to cultivate positive thoughts; there are some encouraging signs. More people have started coming through the doors: a group of teenage girls is rehearsing a dance show; the mothers' group is every Wednesday morning; and Mr Cairn the caretaker and his friends watch the football on the new TV. After his initial reluctance, Mr Cairn has become a strong vocal force regarding the Hub. When Jerry wanted to use some of his modest Council funding to commission a local artist to create a mural above the front entrance, Mr Cairn told him the idea was crap and demanded Jerry use the money to buy a big TV with surround sound. When Jerry said no, Mr Cairn discovered a latent gift for political manoeuvring and put it to the vote. At the April policy meeting, he flooded the room with his friends and the motion was carried. A huge Sony was bought, and placed in the common room. 'Now all we need is Sky!' said Mr Cairn. 'Let's put it to the vote . . .'

Please take your seats. The performance will begin in two minutes.

Jerry makes his way to his seat. The Theatre Royal is a haven to him. He's pleased no one signed up for the Hub Theatre Club, though he can barely admit it to himself. He needs a night off. The Royal Shakespeare Company's production of *Hamlet* has received controversial reviews, and Jerry is excited to see for himself whether 'Mark Rylance wearing shit-stained pyjamas, mooning, jeering, spitting in Ophelia's face, is too wild', or if he's 'hawk-eyed, sardonic. Intelligent and anarchic in equal measure.' He bought a good seat on return at the box office. Royal circle, front row.

Perhaps Melanie likes the theatre. He phoned her in Birmingham a couple of weeks before. She is training to be a social worker. He told her he admired her, and promised to visit the following week. She was clearly happy to hear from him. They are both trying to work out whether they are suitable life partners. This feels entirely comfortable to them. Shared beliefs are important, political allegiances, a kiss and a cuddle of course, a joke or two. Jerry's looking for a partnership he can depend on. Ursula never gave him that.

He takes his seat in the crimson auditorium among the

well-dressed theatregoers, and stares at the deep folds in the curtains at the front of the stage. He can't help feeling a prickle of bitterness towards Mr Cairn and his friends about the TV. He'd invited them to the theatre, but they all declined. *Hamlet*? What's that? A cigar? said Mr Cairn. Jerry almost enjoys their mockery. He imagines them all sitting with him now along the row in their suits, gazing at the vaulting ceiling with its cherubs and golden swirls, full of derision, but unable to resist the exquisite hush of anticipation as the curtain lifts.

He leans back in his seat as the house lights dim. The actors are already on stage, modern soldiers on a lonely turret. Ursula is an actor, just like them. It still perplexes him. He wonders whether she can 'drown the stage with tears, cleave the general ear with horrid speech, make mad the guilty and appal the free, confound the ignorant, and amaze indeed the very faculties of eyes and ears', as Hamlet says about the band of actors he invites to perform for the king. His mam saw her in an advert for Vodafone. She has chosen a path, perplexing and utterly beyond him, as she always has. He reaches for her but she disappears.

His mind is only half on the play, and it passes in front of him, pictures in his eyes. During the interval he stays in his seat, while people squeeze past him, his thoughts circling back to the Hub. He gave up a career in the Labour Party because it was full of career politicians, shit-head Tories in red ties. Jerry didn't want to compromise. He's no better. He compromises every day . . . Shut up Jerry, you think too much, his mother would say, like bloody Hamlet on the stage. The second half starts. When Mark Rylance puts his head in his hands agonising with his future, Jerry feels the reflection of himself; and the play grabs him. Hamlet's tortured soul, his fear and prevarication, expressed in such rich language, lifts him out of himself, and his own thoughts vanish.

When the final curtain comes down, he leaves the theatre as empty as a blown egg. His anxiety gone, he moves with the crowd down the steps into the cool night. A group of drunken girls, arms linked like sailors, floats past. A woman is unchaining a bicycle from a lamp post.

Jerry? Jerry . . .!

It's Joyce, one foot on the kerb, one on a pedal. Were you at the play? she says. I've been so busy I didn't think I'd make it but here I am.

Me too. I'm in a daze . . . sorry! It's good to see you, he says, stopping, loosely putting his hands in his pockets. He's pleased to see her. How are you? How's the campaign going?

Very well. Against all predictions, it looks like Reagan did something good! He was determined to build bridges with Russia. A Bible-basher of course, so it's all about bloody God, but . . .

Christ help us if that's our best hope! laughs Jerry.

She smiles. She looks older, more worn but it seems to Jerry that passion for her cause lifts her. Her hair is short and choppy. He's sure she cuts it herself. She is effortlessly elegant, like her daughter.

I thought Rylance was excellent with the verse, didn't you?

Yes, I love how he threw it away . . . he hesitates. You can't really think Reagan's overtures to Russia have been honourable? He just wants influence in the Eastern Bloc.

Of course, but Gorbachev knows that.

Gorbachev's no better than the rest, says Jerry, yearning for debate.

Cynicism will only get you so far, laughs Joyce. Politics may be a blunt tool but it is the only way to effect real change in people's lives.

He had almost forgotten. They walk up Northumberland Street, and he can't stop talking. He tells her about his struggle to run the Hub, about how hard it is to be back in Byker.

Compromise is always hard, says Joyce. Too hard for me, it's why I'm CND. We never compromise. Political compromise is the fire ideas are forged in. Look at the National Health Service, compromised since the day Bevan founded it, yet it is still the one truly socialist ideal in the country, making a real difference to people's lives, every day, year in, year out. There is something beautiful in that.

They reach Eslington Road. Joyce chains her bicycle.

Come in for a drink, she says.

He looks through the window, as he did so long ago, at the dark hallway, the mirrors and books, the paintings and posters on the walls. He forces the memories of Ursula to be still. If Peter is home he can ask him about funding for the Hub. He follows her inside. Everything is as it used to be, but there is a quietness now. The children have gone and there is something almost stale about the house, as though the life is ebbing from it.

Is Peter here? he asks, catching himself in one of the mirrors.

He's been in London today, but the trains are awful so . . .

That's privatisation for you, calls Peter from the sitting room. Bandits! That's what these new train companies are.

213

He emerges into the hallway, reading glasses perched on his nose.

Jerry, good to see you! I've been at the TUC all day. A fascinating talk on Socialism in the Digital Age.

Jerry follows him into the book-lined room, glowing with lamps, and they discuss new technologies and their potential to revolutionise everyday experience. To Jerry it's like an enchantment; debating issues with broad-minded people unafraid of the world, passionate about making a difference. Joyce balances side-saddle on an armrest as Peter sits at his desk. Jerry finds himself confiding in them about the difficulties he faces with the Hub, hungry for their approval and advice.

You give people what they need and they don't bloody well want it! says Peter. Grassroots work is always tough!

I admire you, Jerry, says Joyce. You mustn't give up.

He imagines for a moment that he is part of this house and family, Ursula's husband, talking to Peter his father-in-law as Ursula, a mirror of her mother, sits side-saddle beside him. Time slips by as they settle into a flow of conversation that ranges effortlessly from the Middle East to the Winchester by-election. Eventually Joyce stands and stretches, her arms straightening, her hands splaying outwards. There is something girlish and unguarded in the gesture. Jerry watches, smiling, seeing Ursula in it.

You'll join us for supper, I hope? she says.

In the kitchen he's surprised to see Ursula's grandmother is still sitting at the table in her lampshade hat, her face obscured by the brim, as though she hasn't moved since he last saw her. Joyce and Peter behave as though she is not there. Joyce goes to the fridge and takes out a cooked ham. Peter carves.

You know, Jerry, what you're doing in Byker is the purest kind of politics, he says. Idealism is nothing to be ashamed of.

The phone rings and he goes to answer it. Joyce! John Grange, he calls.

Open the wine, would you, Jerry? says Joyce as she hurries upstairs. Help yourself to some ham.

Jerry looks around for a wine bottle. Mary sits motionless beneath her brim, stolid with hostility. He crosses the kitchen, peers at a bottle of olive oil beside the bread bin.

Do you remember me? he says, directing his voice to the hat, loudly, unsure whether she may be hard of hearing. I'm Jerry, I used to be a friend of Ursula's.

The hat remains unnervingly still.

Would you like a glass of wine?

The hat grunts in a downward inflection of despair.

He can hear Joyce's voice on the phone upstairs, We can't, John. If we do, we'll be pushovers, and pushovers is one thing we are not!

Her tone has something of the contrived hauteur of Margaret Thatcher. Perhaps the two women are from similar backgrounds. He remembers Ursula telling him that Ganny Mary had been a shopkeeper. Shopkeepers were always trying to improve themselves.

He spots a wine rack on the windowsill behind the kettle, and carefully removes a bottle. He looks in the cutlery drawer for a corkscrew, but can't find one, opens a drawer in the table full of newspaper cuttings. The table rocks as he closes it, and Mary looks up, her face, owl-like, with big, hyperthyroid eyes. He smiles and stretches towards the plate of ham with a fork. Before he can reach it, quick as a lizard, she darts forward and spears his slice of meat with her knife. The aggression of her movement shocks him, and he suppresses the instinct to laugh. Had she had the knife ready, waiting to make her move? He watches her fold the ham in her tortoise mouth, and chew slowly.

Mary sighs, a tender sound. Jerry thinks he can see a tear on her cheek. She is lowering her face, concealing herself again in shadow. He remembers how she fell when he and Ursula were teenagers, how Ursula ran to her, cradled her in her arms. He'd not known what to do, feels the same now, torn between moving forward and moving away. He feels an almost intimate urge to reach out, to hold her, as he thinks how Ursula is conditioned, flavoured by this, this suffering. He feels how the connection across the generations drives, blinds, never rests, but its inner workings frustrate him, they are hidden from him.

Mary, he says gently, are you sure you wouldn't like some wine?

She looks up. I went to a pub once, she says, the lines and corners of her face softening.

Wine is kind, she says with a hint of Lancashire hauteur, or so I believe.

Depends on the year, or so I believe, he replies.

She looks as though she might almost smile.

Sorry, Jerry! Sorry. Joyce bursts into the room. That was John Grange from CND North West. Finally he has agreed to do something together. He wants me to help organise a demonstration.

Excellent! says Peter, following her in, picking up the wine bottle, taking the corkscrew from a hook by the oven.

Let's raise a glass. Joyce?

Bloody hell! exclaims Mary. Oh bloody hell! When will you be done with that politics?!

There is a pause in the room. For a moment, everyone seems to hold their breath. Peter looks at Joyce.

Tell me about *Hamlet*, he says brightly, I haven't seen it for years . . .!

You've no bloody right! says Mary. Who the hell do you think you are!

Joyce does not seem to have heard her mother speak at all as she offers Jerry the breadboard.

Do have some, Jerry, she says. Butter's in the dish.

Oh God! cries Mary in anguish. When is it going to end?

Joyce vigorously cuts thick slices of bread. Peter looks to the ceiling like a man fighting for air.

It's all wrong. All wrong!

Mum, stop this now! says Joyce sharply, hardness in her voice. We have a guest! So pipe down, will you?

I think I'll just finish off upstairs, says Peter, and slips from the room.

Go on! Go, you runt! Mary shouts to him as he goes. Oh, Joyce you're not nice! You're not nice. And you're not an independent woman! You shouldn't have married him. You used to be nice.

Don't be ridiculous, Mum! says Joyce.

You could have been a teacher. We could have been happy!

Happy! You? says Joyce. You've been bitter and angry your whole life!

Jerry takes a large glug of wine, and moves to the door.

I better go . . . he says.

Stay, Jerry, says Joyce. There's steel in her voice. Do you see much of Ursula?

Not for years actually, says Jerry, struggling to be casual.

Of course. One gets so busy, says Joyce.

I don't even have a number for her.

She got away! shouts Mary, Ursy got away from all of you! She bangs her fist down on the table, spilling the wine.

Shut up! Joyce snaps. Her inhibitions gone, she leans on the table and points at her mother furiously. Nothing is how you say it is! Nothing!!

You don't know! All you buggers! You don't know what I know.

Jerry moves to the door. I'll let myself out.

No one stays! cries Mary. There's no love! No love! No love!

I'll get Ursula's number for you, Jerry, says Joyce, quickly moving past him up the stairs. You should see her. Really. It is hard when one is so busy.

He turns back to Mary.

Goodbye, he says, and she looks at him, eyes shining, lucid, imprisoned, a pulse within her that cannot escape, a bird beating desperately in her trying to get out.

He says a quick goodbye to Joyce and Peter, and leaves. He is happy to feel cool night air on his skin, the fury of the basement burning in him, Mary's look, the women's words penetrating him like a curse. As he turns the corner at the end of Eslington Road, he knows a sudden clarity. He must be free. Ursula and her whole family drag him down, confuse him. There are too many knots and he cannot untie them. He will forget her. All of them. He's on a different track. His strides lengthen, his arms swing as he strides away from Jesmond once more. Mellie is the woman for him. When they met in Birmingham, they talked with ease and affection. Mellie wants to go slowly, not to rush into anything, but he knows now she's the one. He will take the cross-country train to see her again. He drops the paper Joyce has given him with Ursula's number on it in the road and the wind blows her away.

In the kitchen, Mary sits stabbing at the ham, waiting for Joyce. It seems to her she's spent her whole life waiting for Joyce, for things to be better, waited all her life for something to be glorious.

The house is silent. Everyone must have gone to bed. She thought she heard footsteps an hour ago, but it's hard to tell. Sounds melt away, lose the hardness of fact. One thing is for sure, Mary will not go to bed, not to that pokey room that smells of polish, and that narrow coffin of a bed. In Padiham her bed was wide and yielding. She'd lie in it thirteen, sometimes fourteen hours on the trot. Conventional bedtime has never been for Mary. She'll stay up all night if she wants, an owl, haunting the kitchen, hunched over the small ads. She'll drink a gallon of dark tea, a bottle of brandy, eat a bag of sweets; just try and stop me. She butters some bread, spreads it thick like cheese, and masticates slowly.

Where is Ursula? *Like a daughter to me*, she croons, nursing the sentiment. She's gotten away from this terrible place. Good for her. Mary's seen her photograph in a magazine: Ursula in a bright red dress on a rooftop, looking out over the London skyline. Up and coming, it said. Saw her on the television, the magic box, must be making a nice bit of money for herself. Joyce says she's bought a place in

London. Not married. Quite right. Ursula is just like she used to be. She has her wilfulness, her daring. Mary unpins her hair, slowly unplaits the long strands, and as she does she's walking through Padiham with her mother and Aunt Sissy. Her mother's Bible is burning in her pocket. She feels it knocking against her leg as they march past Old Mill on Factory Lane, past Bridge End with its great engine room churning. It is the route Mary knows well: the laundry to the Brethren Meeting Hall.

Mary doesn't know what she will do with the Bible, only that she had to take it. She'd been in the laundry office dusting her father's desk when she saw it in the drawer on top of the stationery – her father's stamps, the writing paper, his ledgers scored with figures. She'd felt a wave of anger. It had no place in her father's world of progress. Heart beating, she'd stolen it, put it in her pocket.

Annie and Sissy keep their focus dead ahead as they pass the beer houses, the Black Bull, the Swan, the Weavers, the Starkie Arms. A group of men sit on the pavement smoking, holding cups of beer, stripped to their vests.

Orders are falling, says Annie as they turn on to the cobbles leading up from the Calder.

The laundry was Hubert's, not yours, Annie. Love not the world, neither the things *that are* in the world. Machines are the work of men, not God. God dealt Hubert the ultimate punishment for his pride!

Annie stops suddenly.

I have sinned, Sissy, she whispers. I must confess it now. My Bible. I couldn't find it.

This is not a good sign, says Sissy, brushing down her black crape. You are wayward Annie. We must be vigilant.

Sissy is always saying things like this to her mother. She presses her own Bible into Annie's hand.

God will see to you, Annie. Come. We must not be late.

Forgive me Sissy, says Annie.

As they approach the doorway the smell of aniseed, ginger and raspberry fills the air. The Brethren share a door to the street with Patty Henshley's sweetshop. Mary peeks in and sees pans of bubbling caramel, sacks of sugar, women in white aprons wiping their faces as they stand at rows of twisted sugar and trays of boiled sweets.

At the prayer meeting, she tries to sit still on the bench. A handful of Brethren sit facing each other, men at the front, women at the back, their bodies as stiff and straight as upholstered chairs. No one speaks. The silence frightens Mary. She never knows what will emerge from it, a hymn, a mumbled prayer, or one of the men bearing witness in a loud, haranguing voice. Her mother sits on one side of Mary, her Aunt Sissy on the other. The smells from Patty Henshley's sweetshop below permeate the bare room. She longs for the meeting to end. The smell of caramel rises through the floorboards and feeds her imagination. She feels the hard sweet ball of gobstopper and rolls it between her tongue and the roof of her mouth. She sees herself run downstairs and stuff her mouth with toffees and barley sugar.

It is safest to keep her eyes downwards. She stares down at the floor. Aunt Sissy's black shoes poke out from a long black skirt. Nobody is dead but the women still wear black blouses pinched at the waist with wide belts. Mary wishes she could wear pink and blue. Her mother says it would be an impertinence to God.

A man on the front row opposite is staring straight at

her. She can feel his eyes on her. Mary is afraid he is going to speak to her, and closes her eyes tightly to blot him out. Aunty Sissy prods her. The man stands up, takes in a deep breath, sucks through his teeth, and begins to sing.

> *Saviour and Lord, we love to sing*
> *Of all thy wondrous suffering.*

Annie and Sissy join in, shrill and tuneless.

> *When sin had done foul wrong to God*
> *And thou in Grace did bear the rod . . .*

Mary spots a patch of sunlight on the floorboards from one of the skylights. It is a golden ellipse, like a perfect honey drop, smooth as a piece of sea-washed glass. She wants to pick it up, to own it, taste it. All she wants is this, something precious and golden, to hold and keep. Something beautiful, something delicious. She moans aloud.

SLAP!

Annie hits her across the face. All the Brethren look round at her, their faces pale, severe. Mary runs, pushes away her mother's grabbing hands, kicks past her aunt, and clatters down the stairs, her mother's Bible bouncing in her pocket. She runs past the Padiham Picture Palace, her mother's voice banging in her head as she tears through the streets, you'll have no supper tonight, no bread no butter no gravy no currant bun no jam, no love, nothing, no salt, no pancake, no milk, no tea, no pie no bacon no person, no one to care about you.

At Old Mill, by the Starkie Arms, she climbs on to the

Calder Bridge. She takes out her mother's Bible, holds it at arm's length above the railway below, the train line her father spoke of with wonder, how it united the country, fanning out to all the great cities, Burnley, Blackpool, the metropolis of Manchester, London, the great capital. She hurls it on to the track.

Her heart leaps into her mouth, half expecting it to burst into flames as it hits the ground with a crash of thunder from the sky, and the earth to open and swallow her up.

Forgive me, she whispers. Please God forgive me.

She peeks over. The Bible lies on the track, its pages lifting in the wind.

God does not answer. So be it. She will not walk with Him. She will walk in the world of her father, and relish its pleasures. The sun glints on the track below, and in her mind she can still see the lozenge of gold on the floor of the Brethren's meeting hall. As the frustration of her mother still burns in her cheek, she commits her life to her own god, and makes her vow: mine will be a life of beautiful things.

Be a normal girl you say, like the others, but I have seen and heard things you cannot even imagine; mountains that stand up and walk away, the sun fly down and land in my hand. I have known love as vast as the vanishing sky, and it has shattered me. How can I be normal? My love is nothing like your idea of love. My God is nothing like your God. You ask me to gather potatoes in the fields, sweep the floor, paint my face, plait my hair. There are other women for this work! Do not ask me to put up my sword or give up my soldiers! How can I unswear what I know? I see it, touch it. Now! For ever!

Ursula falls to her knees as she looks to heaven. She is bursting, yielding multitudes of colours through the prism of herself, unadulterated, a thrashing punk, a blaze. She makes concrete shatter, and the earth collapse in a single breath.

Burn me! Build up the fire! Incinerate my body! Your hatred is nothing! My spirit is with God. Only God, only I am I. Listen to them! Burn me, they cry! Burn her! Burn her! The people shout, but it is they that burn! They burn with the hatred of the bishops!

What bishops?! Who is this?

She finishes her speech, wipes the tears from her face. Her

head tipped back, she feels the air on her neck. She's cut her hair short with scissors the night before to become Joan.

Hevel Palkovsky watches her. He's a small man with shiny shoes, a Polish film-maker, made it big in America with the sleeper hit *Child*. Wealth hangs off him like badly fitted clothes. Ursula, he thinks, hmmm. Intense. Not as sweet as the Irish girl he saw earlier, so rosy and pretty, but she's got something. The way she fell to her knees and looked to heaven, yes perhaps . . .

Ursula gets to her feet, her body somehow smaller now, curving, no longer filled with the passion of Joan.

I think I could do it better, she says, I'd love another go, if you have time . . .

Hevel admires Ursula's breasts in silence. There was a time when he'd have taken advantage of the unguarded desperation to be liked. In the old days he would have invited her to rehearse the scene in his hotel room.

Thank you, he says, I have seen all I need. He's thinking of his wife, Teresa. She's flying in that evening. He will lie down with her in the hotel room instead. Her comfortable body. There's been so much trouble with this project. The green light was nine months ago but since then funding has collapsed, they lost the lead actress, found a new backer, and now the whole thing has to be recast in a week, before the end of the financial year. Hevel wishes he had been an academic like his brother Karl. A life of ideas, in cosy rooms, surrounded by beautiful, adoring students. He has started taking Valium again. He focuses an imaginary frame around Ursula's face, sees chainmail, the Bishop of Beauvais in the back of shot. Yes, perhaps . . .

Ursula gathers pages into her bag, buttons her jacket.

Thank you for seeing me, she says.

She does not notice Hevel's weariness. She is consumed only with how badly she did her speech. She felt she strained, and let her desire for the role infect Joan's purity. If only she could have another go.

She leaves quietly. Sukie Barrington's house is done out like a showroom in a furniture store. Everything is tasteful, expensive and cold. It feels like a house no one lives in. She peers into a kitchen decorated with hand-painted Italian tiles. Voices come from the conservatory.

Sorry I was late, Sukie! I've been stuck on set all day filming *Troy*. It's exhausting, but it's worth it.

Helen is a marvellous part, says Sukie Barrington, emerging from behind a daisied curtain in a short skirt. She smiles at Ursula with bright red lips. Judy Monroe is behind her.

Ursula! cries Judy, rushing to hug her, I didn't know you were up for this! Hevel's sweet, isn't he? What have you done to your hair? I really like it!

Her make-up is subtle, her hair pinned. To Ursula she seems effortlessly beautiful.

He's nice, says Ursula. Really nice.

Thanks for coming, Ursula, breezes Sukie Barrington, not making eye contact, polite, but too polite, cool, thinks Ursula, not giving her 'special' look. Ursula panics; she will be overlooked. Judy will be Joan. She will never be Joan. I am no good she is good I am no good she is good I am no good she is good.

This way, Judy, says Sukie Barrington, climbing the stairs as fast as her skirt will allow.

Urs, let's catch up! says Judy, turning. I'm going to Soho this evening. Want to come?

I'm meeting someone.

Oooo, let me guess. Ryan?

No! Ursula laughs, too brightly.

Who?

No one special, she says.

Sounds interesting, says Judy, floating a smile, as Hevel opens the door, and she's kissing him, left and right.

Hevel! You must be exhausted. So sorry I'm late . . .

Jerry sits on the grass, leaning against a tree. He has arranged to meet Ursula by the southernmost pond in Regent's Park. He is wondering why he has done this. It's Mellie's fault. Why not? she said. He's often mentioning Ursula. He should see her again. It'll be a good way of being sure you want to commit to me, she said. He had laughed. There was no point, he insisted, he hadn't seen Ursula for years, there were no skeletons there. Mellie, always one step ahead, told him his reluctance was a sign of entanglement. She kissed him and told him she trusted him completely. He'd left his number with Ursula's agent, half hoping she wouldn't respond. She'd called the next day.

He leans back against the tree and waits. There is vibrancy in the leaves, the greens seem brighter than usual. The flowerbeds are a kaleidoscope of intense blooms. He knows it's because he's excited. He looks across the park, and sees her, bounding over the grass towards him. He breaks into a smile. What a dreadful haircut, like a helmet. His heart fills with delight for her.

Sorry I'm late, says Ursula, kneeling down next to him and kissing his cheeks, both sides. My audition ran over. How are you?

How are you? he says, beaming, despite himself.

Great. Really busy.

A busy body.

Busy bee.

In a body.

Thank you. That's kindly.

She looks quite wild, he thinks. She's cut her hair herself. He remembers the perm the first time he met her. She's always messing around with her hair, trying to look like someone else.

What you reading . . .?

He holds up his book. *The Philosophy of the Welfare State.*

Bet that's a page-turner, she smiles.

It is actually, a slow one, he says. Auditions must be . . .

They're weird. Sometimes you do something brilliant, and it's not weird, at least you think it's brilliant, and you get sweet fuck all, so it is weirdly weird.

She laughs, looks at him. His body, the simple fact of him. She'd like to bury her head in his shoulder. She's learned to hide her doubt but it gathers in her like wind-blown pollen. She stretches her neck to one side to release the tension in her shoulders.

Do you think you'll get the part?

I doubt it, says Ursula. If I don't, who cares? There's loads of interesting stuff around. How long have you got? I've an appointment with my osteopath.

Not long. I've got to buy a suit, he says, seeing her body on the osteopath's table. Why does she have an osteopath?

Is it an extravagance? Is she hurt? He is filled with curiosity about her, and how she lives.

This is my favourite park in London, she says, way better than Hyde or Primrose Hill. It's got boats! A park without boats isn't a park at all! Sorry, I'm feeling wired. I've been up all night preparing to be bloody Joan of Arc. Tell me everything. What about you? How's the community centre? she says.

Dead.

As a dodo?

Deader.

He sees her hand on the grass, the green blades between her fingers.

That's great news, Jerry. Now you have failed, you can get on with *ruling the world*!

She puts on a funny voice, mock Russian, or German. Nothing stays the same for long with her. Was it always like this?

Yes, I must get round to that, he says. It's so weird seeing you.

Weirder than weird, she says. You know we never split up properly.

I know, he says. Let's. Officially. Right now.

Jerry, I don't want to go out with you.

Me neither. Ursula, I don't want anything to do with you.

Great, she grins.

A heron swoops into the willows, its huge nest like knotted hair in the branches.

It feels good to break up after we've broken up, he says, clasping his book under his arm. Less painful.

We can be friends straight away, she says, her hand

moving to the back of her neck.

People who say they'll be friends usually can't stand the fucking sight of each other.

She checks to see if he's smiling, suddenly aware of how fragile the connection is between them.

Getting married, are you? she says.

What? He's taken aback.

The suit.

No, I've got an interview tomorrow, he laughs, relieved, putting the book in his briefcase, shielding his eyes from the sun.

Let me be your guide, she says, standing. I know a suitable place for suits.

There is allure in her offer, a sweet sense of promise. What's the harm? He hasn't been looking forward to buying a suit, just planned to grab something off the shelf. With Ursula it will be fun. He's touched by her willingness to spend time with him. Perhaps friendship is a possibility for them. He feels grateful to Mellie for suggesting it.

Lead on, he says cheerfully. Where are we going?

The evening sun slants into Upper Regent Street. Jerry's shadow steals in and out of Ursula's as they walk. In Selfridges they move through shoppers with bright yellow bags and the dazzling array of goods.

Suits suits suits . . . Ursula says, laughing. This way . . .! This way . . .!

In the men's department, she borrows a tape measure and moves round him, like a wardrobe designer.

Relax! Don't fidget, she says, putting on a posh teacher's voice, measuring the length of his arm.

He stands, awkwardly, legs slightly apart.

Can't we just try some on . . .? he protests feebly, delighted to be fussed over. Tape measure in hand, she circles him, fingers lightly touching his neck, his waist, inside leg.

Ursula . . .! he cries out, laughing, as her fingers reach to his groin. Come on . . .!

No need to be shy, young man, she says, I am a professional, you know!

I'm not shy, he says, as she turns away flicking through some suits on a rail, I'm very shy!

Try this! A Paul Smith. Three-piece, with wide lapels.

Pinstripe? he cries, appalled.

You'll be like the dad in *Mary Poppins*.

Lush, he says, as he disappears behind the curtains of the changing room.

What's the interview for? she says.

A job in the NHS.

Not a doctor, I hope.

A manager.

Really? she says incredulously. That's so . . . surprising.

He can't tell if she's being serious or not.

I should have done it years ago. The National Health Service is an ideal made manifest . . .

He emerges from the booth, his head on one side. The suit is huge; for a man twice his size.

This is for a fucking elephant, he says.

She puts her hands over her mouth and laughs.

Jesus! he says. You don't know what you're doing, do you?!

I'm sorry! she says. I'll get you another one . . .

They look together through the aisles. Jerry doesn't want to stand out, he says. It's important that he's ordinary and unthreatening to his colleagues. They finally decide on a grey suit. Ursula resists mocking him. As they make their way down Bond Street, the day is turning into a sultry evening. They skate happily along the surface of themselves, avoiding their pasts, or more profound feelings. The suit is in a rectangular bag with hard plastic handles, swishing back and forwards between them, following the rhythm of their banter.

I thought it would never end, says Jerry, happily, not knowing where they are heading, not caring.

Next time, we'll go to a charity shop . . .

Next time?! I'm never going to another shop in my life, he says.

We should become tailors. Make our own stuff. Weird stuff.

Dress the same. Save trouble.

That's school uniform.

Big babygros for everyone . . .

There is a queue of cars on Shaftesbury Avenue. They pass the Coach and Horses. Jerry remembers drinking there with Tam and Giles when he was living in London. Tam had pledged to support Jerry to become a Labour MP, and help him rise through the ranks. They'd made a toast to a better future. When Jerry turned his back on politics, and returned to Newcastle, Tam became an MP, as though his disappointment in Jerry had forced his hand. Jerry feels the stark fact of his retreat for the first time, and reflects on it. With Ursula beside him, perhaps he would have chosen differently. He feels brave beside her. He always has. She makes a dash through the cars into Chinatown, quick and impulsive.

He follows, catches up with her in the light of a window

of hung ducks and chickens, roasting brown and sticky. She seems radiant to him.

Let's get some dinner, he says, not wanting their time together to end.

God yes! We must celebrate the suit! And we can make a night of it. I could take you to my club, she says.

Your club! Who are you?

I'm the queen of Soho! You can kip at my place, she says breezily.

She doesn't want to see Jerry's hesitation.

We can drink cocktails, and walk home along the canals . . .

She's high on his company, the osteopath long forgotten.

I need to call Mellie, he says.

Who's Mellie? she says.

My girlfriend, he says.

A sound escapes her. He hears it. He should have told her. He knew it would change things.

Sure, she says. Go ahead.

She waits while he goes into a phone box. Tourists with backpacks, weary with the heat, move past, following their guide. Through the window of the restaurant, a Chinese woman is making dumplings, her fingers twisting the little parcels into rows. Jerry's voice is in her ear.

I have to go, he says quietly.

Sure. OK, she says.

Mellie is stuck in Leeds. The trains are on strike. I have to pick her up. I'm sorry.

What does she do? she says.

She's a social worker.

Fantastic.

233

It is the wrong word.

I mean, fantastic that you and Mellie are both in the same line of work.

She looks back into the window. The Chinese woman has vanished.

I'm pregnant, she says lightly.

She has barely acknowledged it until that moment, let alone known that she would keep it. Everything is so tenuous; Kelsey, her work, herself, somehow. She had bought a pregnancy test last week; a blue line had appeared in the window, so faint she could almost believe it wasn't there. She'd been so busy with Joan, she'd avoided thinking about it.

What . . .? Jerry gasps, stunned. You're . . .? What? What are you going to do?

I'm going to have a baby, says Ursula. Suddenly she knows it for sure. She will have the baby. Jerry has Mellie. So what? She doesn't need him. She doesn't care. She can do anything she wants. She feels wonderfully reckless.

Kelsey will be a great dad, she says.

Who's Kelsey? says Jerry, unable to hide his confusion.

I met him a year ago on a job, she says, we've been seeing each other, on and off. Having a baby will be a chance for me to grow up, Jerry, to take on some responsibility. Who wants arrested development? So last year . . .

Behind the banter she is desperate to believe what she's saying. A child will restore her to wholeness, heal what happened in India. She needs this: a baby will calm her in both mind and body.

Jerry can't speak. One arm clasping his briefcase, he steps off the kerb.

This was fun, she says. We should do it again sometime.

Sure, he stammers. Listen ... yes ... I'd better get going ...

Me too, says Ursula.

Thanks for shopping. The suit is suitably horrible. Bye.

She hugs him on the edge of the pavement. He pulls away, waves briefly as he crosses the road, and disappears into the crowd.

On the motorway, driving north, Jerry erupts with speed, his thoughts crystal clear. Everything is fine. He did what Mellie asked, and saw Ursula. His heart is no longer clouded. He and Ursula are over. They always were. He idolised her. Why? She could never have made *him* happy. He was always on the outside of her; outside Eslington Road, his nose pressed up against the glass. All he wanted was love and she left him. Went to India. Left him. He feels the swell of injury. And when she came home, he wanted to love her, but he couldn't work out how. He got it wrong. With Ursula everything was always wrong. It will be different with Mellie. He mustn't lose her. Mellie is the answer. She is his equal. They will make a home together. They'll buy a house in Newcastle, a big Victorian house, their own Eslington Road, sweat and pain in every brick, sand gathered by his own ancestors, but a house for the future, filled with ideas, and talk, and people. An open house, a house of culture. Classless. Idealistic, and Northern. They will put in huge windows so they can see the sky. Trees will fringe it with green. They will have a beautiful kitchen of marble and wood, and he'll bake. There will be a piano next to a window, and he'll sit in his book-lined rooms in his grey suit, and he'll work in hospitals and he will matter. He will make a difference.

Ursula is walking away too, her life unfolding in every step, as she leaves Soho, through the housing estates behind Euston, past two women in saris with their three thin boys on bicycles. She walks through the heavy evening, the heat rising from the concrete, feeling the heat's drag, through the storm that breaks over Islington as the cells divide inside her. Kelsey is trustworthy. A baby will join them. She keeps walking, into her future, her body changing and growing. Judy Monroe is offered Joan of Arc but turns it down. Hevel asks Ursula to play the role, and the baby grows. She shoots in Prague and the cells divide and the costumier lets out her waistband and Joan is touched by God and falls to her knees and cries in ecstasy as the brushwood is lit under her feet, as the flames engulf her, the cells in Ursula divide and multiply. She bleeds and burns for Camera, and back in London, filming over, flat hunting, heady with hormones, flushed with success, cells become eyes, ears, fingers, and eight months, two weeks, and twenty-one hours later they cut her open and he's here, a blood-soaked lamb, held aloft like a prize, keep still say the doctors but she's reaching out for him, taking this prince from the void, into her arms and whispering, Gabe, Gabe! Like the dawn.

III

I promised you love. You long for its warmth and its certainty but when you reach for it there is nothing. Perhaps this is how it has always been, people searching for it, knowing it must be, has to be there, but glimpsing it only in teasing pinpricks, firefly moments that fade as quickly as they appear. How can I catch them for you so they can be held? Here is one now, a particular moment, in the morning light of a small flat in Hackney. Ursula is gazing at her son. His eyes are so empty of desire, they brim only with pure, bright existence. Until now he has been known mainly by weight and size, seven, eight, nine pounds, and a number of centimetres, recorded on percentile charts by a rota of maternity nurses who proudly announce him to be average. But now Time is starting to notice Gabe; it is six months since the eagle of his birth threatened to carry him off, six months since Ursula wrenched free of the talons, and dropped back to the slab, bloodied but alive, holding Gabe close, shocked into love. He is six months old and growing less amphibian and more human every day. Ursula sits with him in the brown velvet chair gazing at his chubby legs, little fat ankles, and the blue eyes as he looks through the window at the sycamore tree. It grows close to the building and its leaves flatten against the panes; a city tree on a corner of grass outside the low-rise block, lacklustre and pale, struggling with poor soil and scarce sunlight. Gabe loves it; to him, it is a tree of wonder. Its lines are his stories, branching out from his past to his future, the dot-to-dot of him.

> *I'll give my love a cherry that has no stone*
> *I'll give my love a chicken that has no bone*
> *I'll give my love a story that has no end . . .*

Ursula sings as he moves towards the breast. She lets him suckle till he's drunk with milk.

> *A cherry when it's blossom, it has no stone.*
> *A chicken when it's pippin, it has no bone.*
> *The story of our love . . .*

He'll sleep soon and she can rest. They'll lie in bed curled up under the duvet.

> *The story of our love, it has no end!*
> *A baby when it's sleeping, it's no crying!*

The front door opens and Kelsey's home, joining in the last line. Ursula hears him peeing in the bathroom, flushing the chain, turning on the taps, making the pipes hiss through the flat.

Too true! A Gabey when he's sleeping is no crying! he laughs.

He emerges, drying his face on a towel.

How are we this morning, my loves? he cries, swooping

for a kiss, flicking on the kettle. Coffee. I need coffee. And eggs! Have you taken your fish pills, Urs? Good for the breast milk. Here . . . and he is putting two golden capsules in her hand, filling a glass of water.

How did it go? she asks.

Couldn't have gone better. Andrew Skelter loves the whole idea of *Big Dog*! He's going to set up some meetings. Molly is going to design. He thinks we could get the Bush or the Upstairs Duck.

Kelsey's been working on *Big Dog* for a year now. It's a theatre show written with a friend from drama school. He dreams of them having their own company, making their own work, empowering themselves, but swings constantly between intense hope and utter despair. Ursula tries to block it out. Kelsey's anxiety stirs her own about being stuck with the baby. She worries she'll be forgotten. She won an *Evening Standard* award for Best Newcomer for Joan but since then . . .

Andrew sends his love, by the way. I think he fancies you. He's a good soul.

To Kelsey everyone is a good soul, a good sort, or a great fellow. She used to find it boyish and attractive. It had seemed generous, but now she hears only fear behind it, that life is somehow unbearable to him.

Kelsey moves into the middle of the room, reaches his arms to the ceiling then plunges down, his body flat to the floor, face into the carpet, then rears up into a back bend.

Got to get the old bones moving! he cries. Two shows today!

He's in a new play at the Kracken, a fifty-seater in Balham, profit-share. The reviews are good, and there's talk of a West End transfer, Broadway perhaps. When they'd first met, Kelsey taught Ursula his Grotowski stretches. He'd teased her for never having been to drama school. She'd loved the dynamism of the poses, the way they made her breathe so deeply.

Andrew thinks *Big Dog* could be a film, he says, jumping back to his feet. He's got a contact at the BFI. Early days, but you never know!

Sshh Kels, she says, rocking Gabe gently. I'm trying to get him down.

Coming from you! he says, moving on to all fours like a cat, making his back arch and curve, I couldn't shut you up yesterday! White dwarfs, red dwarfs, supernovas. Gabe was wired!

She had drifted into the Science Museum and slipped into a lecture room to breastfeed. She found herself in the middle of a talk about stars. She sat in the dark, Gabe at her breast, watching spawn-like blooms, exploding supernovas, distant shadows containing billions of galaxies, each one far vaster than our own. A lecturer spoke from the low light of a lectern, his voice hushed as though astonished at his own audacity for attempting to communicate the mystery of the universe. He spoke of how the universe began, of how it has no end, and Ursula thrilled to the vastness of it all, without horizon, voice, or boundary. She was electrified by the bubble that billions of years ago suddenly appeared, and filled up with energy until one day it exploded, throwing out a fiery cloud that cooled into gas that gathered into burning stars. She cried at the supernova, the dying star, and how its destruction sent its dying breath floating away in cooling mists that turned to dust and planets and moons.

Everything comes from stardust: rock, metal, air, cloud, chairs, animals, herself, Gabe . . .

And when she'd got home, she was bursting with it.

I have the feeling that I understand everything and I always have done, of course everyone knows we are made of stardust but I experience it, we all do, we all can, but does it matter? Does this experience mean anything? Does it . . .? Kelsey, does it?

But Kelsey couldn't listen. He wanted to be with Gabe; he cooed and rocked him in his arms, blocking out Ursula's voice until her questions subsided, unanswered.

Gabe has fallen asleep. Ursula puts him in the baby-carrier.

I think I'll take him out, get some air, she says, tying the straps round her waist. Kelsey suddenly looks up from the floor with hurt in his eyes.

Why the fuck can't you be happy for me about *Big Dog*?

She is shocked by the injury in his voice. A resentful silence hangs between them, one they will only know more and more as, young, careless, intolerant of each other's weaknesses, they misfire, dying stars imploding into dust clouds, tiptoeing along the edges of each other, never easy in themselves, until the thread of them is stretched to breaking point. Ursula doesn't answer. Nor does she question. She falls silent. Questions will only jeopardise the delicate equilibrium they manage between them. Like the bubble in the void she keeps them inside her.

Will Ursula explode? Shatter into a billion planets? This is not the time. Her connection with Kelsey simply breaks like a plucked string, and they fall away from each other, tumbling into space. She is reaching but there is nothing to hold on to, no one to break her fall, not Jerry certainly, they've never been further apart, he's with Caitlin now, in Newcastle. Mellie didn't last. Caitlin's a human rights lawyer, red-haired, bright as a button. They're married, honeymooned in the Hebrides, bought a big fuck-off house in Jesmondia as Mackie would say, and Ursula falls for a lifetime it would seem, holding Gabe tightly against her. Jerry's finding his perfect home in the NHS, wielding his sword of radicalism and reason. He fights market-led policies, arguing that only humanity can be a workable policy, refocuses on patient care, cutting waiting times, doubling cancer-detection rates; he rises through the ranks, and is whispered, not for the first time, to be one to watch. He's at home one night when he sees Ursula's on his television playing a patient in a hospital soap and he decides to call her out of the blue. When he's next down in London they meet up, for old times' sake, and so now they're on the South Bank with Gabe, three years old, flying a balsawood plane in a perfect arc, a present from Jerry, the first time he's met the boy. Gabe gallops underneath the plane, his coat undone, craning up to see it, shouting, Up!

Great, cries Ursula skipping along next to him, picking it up when it lands. Fly it down there. Let's see where it lands.

It's sunny but the wind is blowing hard. A free-runner in the distance, a kid, somersaults off stone steps on to the scrap of shore by the mud-brown river. Gabe launches the plane into the air and it nosedives to the ground.

Ursula takes the plane and throws it upwards. Gabe laughs as it loops the loop then soars. He runs after it towards a line of bollards by a car park. Jerry watches him, enthralled, dreaming him his son.

How was your meeting with the big guns at Westminster?

asks Ursula. Her tone is playful but he feels the praise in her mockery. She is wearing a blue summer dress. Her arms are bare and she's put a scarf round her shoulders like a shawl to keep herself warm. She never seems to wear the right clothes. Her attire seems always out of place, either too flimsy altogether or too layered with mysterious types of knitwear, but always beautifully so.

Was it fun? she asks.

It's a riot, he says. A riot of clowns.

A cauldron of crows.

A knuckle of gangsters.

A thunder of hippopotami.

A gap in the buildings opens up and the sky is broad over the city. A mountain of cumulus towers over them. They watch it in awkward silence, neither daring to name it nor to mention the past that exists between them.

How's Kelsey?

He's fine. We're working things out.

Gabe is looking back at her, holding the plane. He stretches out his arms like wings and runs off again.

And you? How's Caitlin? she says.

She's wonderful.

A real plane is above them, pinned impossibly to the sky. Ursula is watching it when she hears Gabe crying. He is running towards her, the propellers of his toy splintered, a wing sheared off.

It's OK, Gabey, it's OK, she says, holding him tight as he sobs.

How about some hot chocolate? Jerry says gently. He takes the broken plane, turns it in his hands. You know this happened to the Wright Brothers all the time. They invented aeroplanes but it took a long time to get them to fly. Their experiments often involved crashes and setbacks like this.

Gabe stares up at him. Jerry's words are too long for him to understand but he's caught by the certainty of them, the way they have value. Ursula lifts him up. She carries him on her back, and they find a cafe.

Gabe eats shortbread and drinks hot chocolate. Jerry quizzes him on his favourite subject, jungle animals. Eventually he falls asleep in Ursula's arms and she places him on a chair next to them. Jerry and Ursula share a beer, and talk. About anything and everything; about George W. Bush, drinker turned preacher, tectonic plates, the shared genes of Arabs and Jews, warring siblings. They find meaning in the smallest details, the infinite in the mundane, in random words. As evening falls they are still there talking, their lives forgotten, feeling the charge of each other flow through them until Jerry runs for his train, their planets separate once more, and they fall back into their lives. The meeting is soon remembered for what it was, an afternoon with a good friend and Ursula and Jerry continue to move apart while orbiting each other. Love slips from the grasp, never held, never enough, only cherished in the mind, which is how Mary remembers it now, sitting in the kitchen at Eslington Road, still plaiting her hair, more slowly as time stiffens her fingers, as the past pulls her back to the dark horsedrawn days when she, aged fourteen years, six months and eight days precisely, as yet unsalted by resentment, stood on the cusp of love. She is at the booth of the Padiham Picture Palace, and takes a penny from her pocket, her heart thumping with her own wickedness.

Just you? says the man in the booth. There is mockery in his voice.

Just myself, says Mary, the perfect measure of haughtiness and sweetness.

Feature's started. You've missed the short.

Nevertheless, she says tartly, not knowing what he means, but placing her penny firmly on the counter. It is the act of a girl who cannot and will not be crushed, as though the death of her father were a mere interruption, and her mother's religious zeal a mild inconvenience; here is the real Mary, at the matinee of *Zorro*, alive, defiant, and free.

She opens the inner door and is instantly hit by the smell of straw, tobacco and alcohol. At first, she can't make anything out in the darkness, and then the whole Picture Palace opens up to her. Couples sit kissing in the long rows. Groups of mill workers, men and women, are drinking beer. A man rolls an empty bottle down the aisle. It clinks as it joins hundreds of others glinting in the light from the screen, piled up against the pianist's rail. The auditorium is like a stable. Straw and sacks have been laid on the floor to soak up the water. Mary's feet crunch on the shells of a thousand monkey nuts. There is an undercurrent of conversation and banter. Somewhere a baby is crying. A vendor in the aisles is selling chocolate and candies. The projector whirrs at the back of the room. To Mary it is a wonderful pandemonium. She tiptoes through it all, recognising faces from the laundry, and sits on the end of a row. The Chief of Police, Captain Gonzales, is telling his bloodthirsty men how he will kill Zorro.

ZORRO – THAT Z MAKER! says the card angrily.

Captain Gonzales makes an elaborate mime of how he will defeat his enemy, cutting the air with his sword, and plunging it into Zorro's body. His men look down at the imagined corpse of their enemy. Mary is thrilled to see their lust for violence, their glee as they rub their hands and laugh, dreaming of bloody revenge.

Suddenly there is a loud banging. Everyone in the cinema screams. Someone is at the door! Gonzales and his men freeze. The piano player slams the lid of his piano down hard, over and over again as Zorro tries to break down the door. The pianist is so close to the screen, he's almost part of it. He seems to Mary to be possessed by a kind of glee as he works, his face turned to the silvery light. There's a painted sign above him, DIRECT FROM NEW YORK! THE BOY WONDER! PIANIST WALTHER MORELY. MASTER OF THE IVORIES!

On screen Captain Gonzales puffs up his chest and storms across the room to the door. The piano player crashes out mock-heroic chords. The door bursts open and Zorro appears, his face masked, sword at the ready. Gonzales' men creep backwards, terrified. Zorro laughs; a sword fight ensues. At the top of a flight of stairs, he pins Gonzales to the wall, scornfully flicks his hat from his head, and kicks him down the stairs. The piano player glissandos on a glockenspiel as he falls, and bangs a drum as he collapses in a heap. Mary stands up in her seat along with the rest of the audience and cheers loudly, in heaven.

Over the next few months she goes back as often as she can. Her mother has closed the laundry and bequeathed it to the Brethren as their new meeting hall. The elders felt the room above Henshley's sweetshop was no longer appropriate for worship. Annie and Aunt Sissy are so busy overseeing the laundry's conversion they barely notice Mary's absence.

The cinema becomes her refuge. She loves Lillian Gish, Norma Talmadge, Pauline Frederick, Charlie Chaplin, Harold Lloyd, Buster Keaton and Harry Langdon. She sees things she could never dream of happening in Padiham, Pearl White hanging from a bridge, riding a boat down the rapids, falling off a cliff, being tied to the railway track. She doesn't just watch the screen, she watches Walther Morely, the Boy Wonder. She is fascinated by the way he anticipates the action, how he moves from one sound to another, one instrument to the next, timpani for the appearance of a villain, a bell for a telephone, jarring piano chords for inner dread, his face mimicking the expressions and fortunes of the characters as he plays. When he fires a gun with real gunpowder, Mary screams. A lady in front of her faints and has to be escorted out. She watches with delight as Walther removes the lower panel of the piano and scrapes his feet down the open strings to accompany a stampede of Red Indians. He slams the lid for the returning cannonfire of the soldiers. She thrills at the great *crack* he makes with his slapstick when Charlie Chaplin trips and falls, but he plays tunes sad enough to break her heart too, and Mary cries in the dark. Her mother says it's a sin against God to be unhappy. She lets the tears come freely, relishing her misery, her secret rebellion.

Walther the Boy Wonder seems as transported by the scenes on the screen as his audience is. When Lillian Gish is left by her fiancé, he stands up and shouts, Look how she loves him! She'd kill herself for love!

One day after watching *Song Bird* for the fourth time in a week, Mary stays behind in her seat. The Boy Wonder plays a sad waltz as the hall clears into dusty light. President Starkie, manager of the Picture Palace, comes over to him. He has a long stick which he uses to rap the knuckles of boys who misbehave in the rows. Rumour has it that he was once a strongman in music-hall. Mary has seen him lift a boy clean out of his seat and carry him out under one arm.

Beautiful, Walther! he says as the music swells.

Rachmaninov, says the Boy Wonder, I thought we could use it for *The River*.

Got owt for the lion? asks President Starkie.

Certainly I do. He picks up a home-made contraption from behind the piano. It's a metal tub with a string protruding from a hole in the middle. He holds it between his legs, pulls the string taut and runs a shammy leather sharply down it. A lion roars. Mary almost cries out in fright.

Wonderful! says President Starkie. That'll get the ladies going, Wally! You're an attraction as much as the films. I've got someone going round the pubs talking about you.

Mary tucks her head down as President Starkie walks past her up the aisle. Wally stays playing the Rachmaninov over and over, modifying it, making it lighter, darker. She is a robin hopping towards a crumb, coming closer to him by degrees, until she's standing at the rail. He carries on playing, the same phrase over and over. Suddenly, he swivels on his stool.

Boo! he says.

She jumps in fright, and cries out.

Wally laughs. I've heard that scream! You're in a lot, aren't you? What's your name?

Mary, if it's anything to you, she says, recovering her composure.

It is, Mary. What can I do for you?

Thank you Mr Morely, I'm interested in taking lessons on the pianoforte.

Come up here and sit beside me then, he says with a wink, there's no time like the present.

She climbs the steps and sits on the stool as far away from him as a young lady should. He places her fingers on the keys and shows her how to play five notes of a scale. She glances at him as he talks. He's older than he looks when he's playing, but his eyes are pale and kind. His hand touches hers briefly and she pulls it away. He flicks over a page from the album of sheet music on the stand. It's all just dots and lines to Mary.

Joseph Carl Breil's *Dramatic Music for Motion Picture Plays*! says Wally. A fella in Leeds gave it me after he was called up. It's a beauty. From America.

Leeds. America. Beauty. Mary is mesmerised. Wally leafs through the music. He plays a few bars of each piece, enthusing about them, 'Hearts and Flowers', for romantic scenes; 'On the Quarter Deck', rousing, for soldiers. 'I Love the Moon', for gardens or general background, 'Wedgwood Blue', for longing, oh and 'Glow-worm', my favourite, two alternative endings, so clever, listen, one for hopelessness, listen, with a plagal cadence, one for hope rising, like this, with an unresolved cadence. Beautiful, isn't it? And here's *Peer Gynt*, a classic for suspense.

Mary is entranced. She picks out a sheet.

That's *La bohème* by Puccini.

What's that for?

Love.

Play it, says Mary.

He plays it twice and she asks for more.

Don't you have a home to go to? he asks.

Of course, she giggles. But I'm staying for the next show.

You can sit up here with me then, he says.

I'm a respectable girl, says Mary, smiling.

And I'm a respectable reprobate, Mary, he smiles, happy in your company.

She stays for the next two showings, and comes back again and again, sometimes staying all day in the Picture Palace. She absorbs every story and makes it her own. She sees charming heroes who make her warm and yearn, girls in gardens mooning for lovers, sad-eyed daughters preyed on by villains, valiant fathers who sacrifice all for the love of their families. Here redemption and rescue are possible. And best of all, the Boy Wonder gives her hope. During *The Spy* there is a chase sequence ending in a train crash. He asks her to help with the sound effect. He has a huge metal tub, full of biscuit tins and broken bottles. Mary sits next to it for the whole film, still as a stone, waiting for her cue. When the train crashes on the screen Wally nods to her, and she pushes the tub off the stage. Her timing is perfect. It crashes to the ground just as the train does. The audience bursts into applause. Mary curtsies in the silvery light. This is what she wants. This is what she will have. A beautiful man, and a life of beauty. She deserves nothing less.

Plants grow and wither, buildings crumble, new ones appear, people get taller, shorter, lie down, die, get born, two, three, four, calendar years pass, and Gabe is seven, running in the playground. There's no stopping him, he's dodging friends playing 'it', mousy hair, the blond wisps gone, no one can catch him, his legs are so strong now. The bell goes. He runs into the classroom, sits at his table. Running and stopping are all the same to Gabe. He's fresh as a daisy in a gale, unlike his mother. Ursula's stuck in the middle, somehow never running nor still, never touching the edges, older now, on an endless track to school, tube, studio, home, gym, osteopath, car, playground, reaching out for phone, charger, socket, keys, zip, fridge, bed, dreams, her shoes, and today for the outstretched palm of Tim Hoddell from Benham and Hodge Insurance.

Hi, great to meet you, Tim. Hi. Hi. Hi . . . Hello! . . . Yes I think we have. Your face is familiar! . . . Thanks. Thanks. Thanks for thinking of me . . .

This is Ursula the voice-over artist. She's at the Sound Studio in Soho greeting a team of strangers like old friends. Tim, recently divorced, on antidepressants, the nights are the worst; Saskia and Sarah, blond execs from the Rubber Tree Agency who hide their laughter lines in the ladies' mirrors; the unnamed Creative in the black T-shirt slumped in the corner of the sofa with a handshake as weak as his conviction; and Tuke, the bearded bear of a sound engineer.

Okey-dokey, Ursula, says Tuke. Shall we?

Ursula follows him into the recording booth. He slides the door closed behind them, cutting out the outside noise. She can't breathe for a moment, as though the lack of sound cuts out the air.

This shouldn't take long, he says. As long as they behave!

He nods at the team on the other side of the glass, and smiles conspiratorially at Ursula. It's always like this with the sound engineers. They give secret signs of complicity, *we know we're better than these monkeys, but let's do as we're told, take the money, and run!*

She sits at a table in front of a mic with a red foam head. Tuke adjusts the height and goes back through to the mixing desk. Ursula watches Saskia and Sarah talking to the Creative, who slumps ever lower on the sofa. Tuke presses the button for the interconnecting mic.

Hear me, Ursula?!

Perfect, she says, brightly.

Green light coming . . .

She looks down at the script as the light in front of her goes green.

Big Insurance without the small print? Unbelievable! she reads. Benham and Hodge. No-claims bonus guaranteed for five years. Terms and conditions apply.

The light goes red.

Ursula, says Saskia, leaning in to the mic on the other side of the glass. That was great, but a little too soft.

Tell her to make it bouncier, says the Creative.

Stronger, says Sarah.

Not too strong, says Saskia.

I want bounce, says the Creative.

Did you get that, Ursula? says Tuke with a wink.

No problem! says Ursula.

Going for another take. OK! says Tuke, giving her a thumbs up. Here comes the light. It goes green. Ursula reads it again, giving it bounce.

Big Insurance without the small print? Unbelievable! Benham and Hodge. No-claims bonus guaranteed for five years. Terms and conditions apply.

Great, Saskia leans over to the mic. We'll play back. Hold just a minute.

Ursula waits. Too many people, as usual. Two is enough, someone from the ad agency and a sound engineer. She feels the tension on her left side. The twist's been getting worse. Her new osteopath has told her that she has a scoliosis, a rotation in her sacroiliac, a shortening. Her hand reaches to her neck.

All right, let's go again.

Less bounce, says the Creative.

The green light comes on. Ursula finds the right distance between mouth and mic to stop her voice 'popping', keeps a smile in the voice and tries the line with slight rising into-nation.

Big Insurance, without the small print. Unbelievable! Benham and Hodge. No-claims bonus guaranteed for five . . .

She's grateful for the money. When she and Kelsey split up, he'd been an actor earning just about enough. Now he's retraining to be a carpenter and he can't contribute. Her own career has dwindled to the odd part and a few voice-overs. The past mocks her present. She massages the muscles of her shoulder.

Going again! says Tuke. The green light. Ursula switches to her voice of quiet authority.

Big Insurance without the small print. Unbelievable! Benham and Hodge. No-claims bonus guaranteed for five years. Terms and conditions apply.

Jesus, says the Creative.

They go off mic. Ursula is left in the dead of her headphones. She watches them all gesticulating behind the glass. She sips her water and flicks through *Hello!* left on a chair. There's a picture of Judy Monroe in a blue dress at a premiere. Jealousy strikes her like a whip, and she closes it quickly. Kelsey was right to get out of show business. They should have worked harder to save the relationship. She should have. For Gabe's sake. They'd been so happy at the beginning. Ursula had felt she would finally be the magnificent creature she knew herself to be, a wonderful mother, a successful actress, and a loving wife. There was no need to compromise a career because of the baby. Work was money, status, meaning; every working woman in the country knew that. She'd leave Gabe with a nanny, hear him cry as she closed the door. It had felt like part of herself was unravelling. The umbilical cord seemed to trail along behind her as she walked away. For what? Tight budgets, tight schedules, tight, brittle people.

Ursula . . .?

The mic crackles to life again.

We think it should be funnier, says Saskia.

Tuke jerks up both thumbs again.

Okey-dokey! Going again.

Big Insurance without the small print. Benham and Hodge. It's unbelievable! No-claims bonus guaranteed for five years. Terms and conditions apply.

Did you put in an extra word? says Saskia.

Did she? says Tim, nervously. It's forty-five, it should be forty-three . . .

I said 'it's unbelievable' instead of just 'unbelievable!' Sorry, I thought it might be funnier . . . says Ursula. They've gone again. Lines from the Madeline books she reads to Gabe come to her.

In the middle of the night.
Miss Clavel turned on her light
and said, 'Something is not right!'

She looks at her watch. She mustn't let this run over. Kelsey is doing a course on the other side of London, so she is picking up Gabe from school every day.

Ursula . . .?

She grabs the headphones.

Yes, hi . . .

Okey-chokey, says Tuke. We're going back to bouncier! Ready?

Sure, she says, taking a deep breath.

Big Insurance without the small print. Unbelievable! Benham and Hodge. No-claims bonus guaranteed for five years. Terms and conditions apply.

Wait for the light . . .

Jesus! says Tim, aren't we recording? That was the best one!

Sarah and Saskia stare accusingly at Ursula through the glass. The green light comes on.

Big Insurance without the small print. It's unbelievable! Benham and Hodge. No-claims bonus guaranteed for five years. Terms and conditions apply. Wait. Shit! I said 'It's' again. Fuck. Sorry, she says, laughing. The team are not laughing. Tim, Saskia, Sarah, and the Creative look at her, disapproving grown-ups watching a child. She is their zoo child, caged in her airless box.

Green light! says Tuke.

Big Insurance without the small print. Unbelievable! Benham and Hodge. No-claims bonus guaranteed for five years. Terms and conditions apply.

Stop!

Too fast, too quiet, too soft, too funny, too crazy, too manic, too loud . . . It is 2.30. Gabe. She has to go. She takes off her headphones and knocks on the pane.

It's 2.30. I've got to go. I have to pick up my son.

You can't, says Saskia, we haven't got it!

I think we got it on the first take, says Ursula smiling, and as their jaws drop she grabs her coat, pulls open the heavy door and takes the stairs two at a time, grabs a handful of complimentary sweets from a glass jar at reception, and runs for the number 19.

He is in his green coat at the school gates. His piano teacher, Miss Penny, is beside him looking anxiously down the street. It's Friday, the other children have gone, she's planned an Indian meal with her boyfriend, wants to get home, but there's no one she can leave the boy with. Ursula runs up, more breathless than she needs to be, making a show of the struggle she's endured to get there.

Sorry, Miss Penny! So sorry! Traffic.

Miss Penny lets out a perplexed sigh.

You weren't worried, were you, Gabe? says Ursula, taking his hand. He pulls it free.

Thank you, Miss Penny, he says, his politeness upbraiding Ursula.

You're very welcome, says Miss Penny, doing the same. I hope you have a lovely evening, Gabriel.

We are going to watch a DVD about dinosaurs, says Gabe. Aren't we, Mum?

She'd promised to buy it while she was in town. She's forgotten. Her phone rings in her pocket. She takes it out. A bright fish, buzzing. It's Agent Patty.

Come, Gabe, she says. I've just got to take this. Thanks again, Miss Penny.

They walk along the high school fence, Gabe tugging at her arm as Ursula holds the phone to her ear.

Ursula? Patty's voice is thick with boredom. A movie. *Jagged Love*. I know, God help us, but Will Chaser is directing. Shoots in Australia. He's agreed to see you this afternoon.

Ursula's heart leaps up. Camera is calling. Camera wants her again. Gabe tugs at her arm.

I don't know if I can, says Ursula, I've no childcare.

Darling, I've bent over backwards for you on this one, drawls Patty. Do you want to be a voice-over artist all your life? Jonno will give you the details. I want you to do this, Ursula. Stop worrying so much and smile. That's what I do when I worry at night. I just lie in the dark and smile! And she's gone, and suddenly Jonno is on the line telling Ursula she should go to the Central Casting Suite immediately. She'd be mad not to. It's a proper film. She hears herself saying yes. Gabe kicks the school fence behind her.

You didn't get it, did you? he says, narrowing his eyes.

The dinosaur DVD. Computer-generated dinosaurs roaming a desert landscape. The terrified ankylosaurus hiding with her young as pterosaurs close in. They'd watched the first episode at a friend's. Gabe has mentioned it to her every night for a week before bed.

Gabe, I have to call Daddy, she says.

But Mummy you promised . . .!

Kelsey? I've got an audition. I'm really sorry but it's just

259

come up. Can you take Gabe?

I can't, says Kelsey, I'm leading a team today. It counts towards my final assessment.

Please, Kelsey. I wouldn't ask but it's a film . . .

Urs, no, I'm sorry I . . .

He is talking to someone in the background. She can hear banging and drilling.

I've got to go. I'll pick up Gabe next week. Kiss him for me.

He hangs up. Her mouth feels dry. She turns to Gabe, exasperation rising in her.

I knew you'd forget, he says. You always forget!

A taxi appears, a beacon of hope floating towards them. Ursula puts out her hand. It'll be £20 from here to the West End, she'll cut back on something. Coffee. Wine. Anything. She feels the tug of ambition.

Come, Gabe, she says, pushing him in the taxi. I promise we'll get the DVD after Mummy's meeting. Everything is going to be fine.

On Wardour Street, he lags behind her, his attention caught by a lorry driver shouting at a cyclist, a patisserie shop full of glazed tartlets, a poster of Spiderman. Come on, Gabe! Come on! says Ursula, pulling him along, running up the steps to the Central Casting Suite. They burst through double doors into a reception area crowded with people. Four different productions are casting, two TV shows, a commercial, and *Jagged Love*. The plastic chairs are filled with grey-haired men, Goth teenagers, and a gaggle of models plucking their eyebrows, changing tights, applying make-up.

I'm hungry, says Gabe.

They squeeze on to a corner seat. Gabe gawps at the models, the hardness in them; their bodies and faces, polished and tweaked.

Ursula? A young woman with a clipboard comes over to them. Mel will see you now. This way . . .

She turns to Gabe. I've got to go in now, she says, I won't be long. Just wait here.

Tears well in his eyes.

This lady will keep an eye on you, says Ursula, smiling over at the woman with the clipboard. It's only for five minutes, and then we'll get the DVD.

I don't want to . . . he says.

The door opens and three men enter, laughing. Gabe looks round fearfully.

Mummy, don't leave me here.

She gives him a squeeze. Don't be silly, Gabe, you're a big boy now. She smiles towards the clipboard woman. Coming . . .

I want to come with you, Mum.

You can't, Gabe.

Please . . . he says, starting to panic. He grabs her skirt.

Stop it, Gabe, says Ursula, too loudly. Wait here.

She turns away but he's crying, a great burst of tears and sobs, I'm not staying here! The models look over, frowning, children a mystery to them.

The clipboard glances at her watch anxiously. If it's a problem . . .

He's fine, says Ursula quickly, he's not normally like this, he's just tired.

I'm not tired! shouts Gabe, lashing out at her.

That's enough! She bends down to him, holds his wrists tightly, and whispers fiercely, That's enough! There'll be no DVD. Stop it.

But you said! Mummy . . .! He's choking, desperate, grabbing her. Everyone is looking at them. She prises him off and pushes him down on to the chair. She remembers the sweets in her pocket, grabbed as she left the voice-over studio. She thrusts them in his hand, and follows the woman with the clipboard inside.

All through the audition she can hear him crying. She tries to concentrate but her emotions are blown. Will Chaser talks to her about the film, about love, about resonance, but she doesn't hear a word.

When she comes out, Gabe is sitting happily on the chair, eating the sweets, his outburst forgotten. He smiles, happy to see her. She takes his hand without a word and leads him out. She drags him down Oxford Street, and buys the DVD in anger.

Back at the flat, he falls asleep in front of the television. She strokes his head, willing the day to pass with every stroke. She kisses his cheek, puts his clothes in the washing basket, gets fresh ones for the next day, lays them out next to his bed, feeling the weight of their solitude, their tiny team against the world. She is frightened she can't hold him, keep him safe. It's been like this since Kelsey moved out. Their flat is a life raft and they are drifting further and further from shore with no anchor. Gabe needs unfailing love. She can't find the ease in herself to give it. She loves him in bursts, switching between rushes of wild abandoned affection, and the feeling of being trapped, even bored. She hates herself for it. She hears other women speak of feeling split between home and work, but their complaints don't even begin to articulate the rift and separation she feels inside.

Her jacket and handbag hang over the back of a kitchen chair, ready for the morning, a puppet of herself. She and Kelsey had couples therapy when they were struggling to stay together. In one session, Kelsey had asked her, what's wrong with you? Who are you? The therapist had turned to her and said, Ursula, do you know?

She stops by the fridge and stares at Gabe's felt-tip picture of a house and a fire-breathing dragon. It was she who had ended the relationship. Kelsey had been washing up, piling pans on the draining board, talking about the future. He was tired of the rat race in London he said, they should go away, take a road trip, anywhere, Europe, America. Gabe would love it. She imagined the three of them on the open road, and felt a sense of panic. That night she told him it was over, she needed some space. It was not him, she said, it was her. When he moved into a flat round the corner she felt nothing but relief.

She opens the fridge door and stands in the light of it, staring down at her own torso. Her T-shirt moves up and down with each breath, lighter and darker as it rises and falls. She hasn't seen Jerry for a long time. They used to meet up regularly. They'd become friends, and during the time she was splitting up with Kelsey she'd come to rely on him for support. She'd never met Jerry's wife, Caitlin, but there was no tension or awkwardness about their friendship. Sometimes, when Ursula phoned the house, Caitlin would answer and they'd always share a joke before Jerry came on the line.

One day, about two years ago, Jerry was on one of his work trips to London. Ursula met him at King's Cross as she often would. His train was late and there wasn't as much time as they'd expected before his first meeting, so they walked to his hotel for a coffee. As they were dropping his bags in his room, he got a call cancelling his meeting. They ordered room service, and sat on the bed until a table covered in white linen was wheeled in by a waiter. When they were alone, Jerry touched her hair.

What are you doing? she asked.

I think I don't know, he replied.

They spent all afternoon in bed together, blind to their lives, and they slept that night like they used to, curled in each other's arms. In the morning, they'd walked to the station. It didn't need to mean anything, he said. She agreed. No one need know. It didn't change a thing. They felt the lie of it as they spoke.

He wrote to her three weeks later, full of shame and sorrow. He'd told Caitlin everything. She'd been deeply hurt by his betrayal. He realised how selfish and wrong he'd been, and how much he loved his wife. His infidelity had forced them to examine the nature of their marriage, and they'd spoken the truth about their feelings for each other. It had been deeply cathartic, he said. They had worked through the baggage of their pasts, and found a new love for each other. As she read his letter, Ursula could see the moment of their reconciliation. She imagined Caitlin, whom she'd never met, womanly, soft-faced, after days of crying, in the small hours. She saw his earnestness, her forgiveness, their grateful collapse on the bed, and she felt the stab of it. Jerry concluded his letter saying he had to cut Ursula from his life. He couldn't see her again. Ursula knew he was right. She had meant to throw the letter away.

Ursula's heart nearly jumps out of her body when Patty tells her that Will Chaser has offered her the part of Hedwig in *Jagged Love*, opposite Jack Jones, Golden Globe winner and star of *The Beauty of the Night* and *R.I.P. Helen*. He said she had exactly the right anxious quality he was looking for. Ursula accepted the part straight away and quickly arranged things for Gabe. She is to fly to Sydney in two days' time for a six-week shoot. Gabe will stay with Kelsey while she is away, but not for the first two weeks. He has a new girl-friend, younger than Ursula, a special-needs teacher and a singer, and they have booked a holiday, so Ursula is leaving Gabe at Eslington Road with Grandma Joyce and Granddad Peter until Kelsey can pick him up. Ursula is taking him up to Newcastle to leave him there. Gabe is nervous about going. Ursula hasn't exactly fostered a bond between Gabe and his grandparents over the years. She has seldom returned to Newcastle, always finding excuses not to come. It occurs to her that she is withholding Gabe from them to protect him from their lack of interest. They are still so focused on the world outside the family, on CND and politics, as they were in her own childhood. She does not linger on feelings about her upbringing or the stirring of memories.

She and Gabe are on the train to Newcastle. They are superheroes. They must protect the train from the evil Claw and his men. Gabe has made a den under the table with Ursula's coat, and they take it in turns to shoot at their enemies through the windows as they attack across the rushing fields.

At Newcastle station they walk in a crowd of people towards the entrance. Taxis form long queues under the stone arches. People greet relatives and load cases into car boots. Gabe is quiet at Ursula's side as she looks for Joyce. She hasn't come to collect them. Ursula tries not to feel annoyed. She'd begged her mother to make Gabe feel special so that he would feel comfortable about staying. They make their way back inside to the metro, and take the train to Jesmond.

Ursula holds Gabe's hand tightly as they walk up Eslington Road, the dull roar of the motorway beyond the concrete bank.

Will there be baddies? asks Gabe as they reach the house. The bay windows reflect the trees like dark mirrors. The CND sticker is still there, faded now.

Of course not, she says, laughing a little too hard. Just Grandma, Granddad, and Ganny Mary.

He grips her hand as they walk up the front steps.

I remember Ganny Mary, he says. When will she die?

I don't know. No one knows.

When will you die? asks Gabe.

Not today hopefully, says Ursula, ringing the doorbell.

Will I die? asks Gabe. Is it like being ill? Who will die today?

It's always like this. When he starts asking questions, he can't stop.

Why don't we know? What happens when you die, Mum? Why don't doctors know?

She smiles resolutely, wishing he would stop. The door opens.

Is Nelson dead? Is he under Nelson's Column?

Joyce looks at Gabe, smiling, immediately engaged.

Nelson is buried in St Paul's Cathedral, I believe, Gabe, she says. Come in. What a long journey! I'm sorry I couldn't meet you. We're running a little over . . .

It's over a year since Ursula's seen her mother but already she tenses at her bristling energy. She feels the familiar sense of dissatisfaction, of wanting it all to be different, for her mother to be quieter, more intimate, like she'd been after India. A tenderness had developed between them then, and Ursula longs for it again. Gabe is following his grandmother as she chats away and leads him into the sitting room. The Jesmond peace campaigners are holding their weekly meeting. All the old faces smile out from among the books and lamps. There is a tray on the folding card table with a teapot and the remains of a wholemeal cake. The CND faithful are still meeting, fighting, campaigning against American Foreign Policy, and the catastrophe of Blair.

Ursula, you remember Sarah and Chris, and Ernst, don't you?

She remembers them all. To her as a child, they'd seemed such tremendously important people.

We saw you on the television, Ursula! says Chris, his hair thinning now but still long, exactly like his wife's. Ursula recalls how she always thought they were twin brother and sister.

Last year, I think it was, says Sarah.

You were being pushed off a cliff, says Ernst, peering at her over his glasses.

I'm going to Australia to make a film. She's grateful she can say it.

How exciting! What is it? says Sarah.

And this is Gabriel, she says, anxious that he should not be left out. He hides behind her legs, twists her coat around his fingers.

Hello Gabriel, says Chris. How old are you?

You are seven, aren't you, Gabriel? says Peter, appearing in the doorway.

Gabriel edges further behind Ursula, and doesn't answer.

Hi Dad, says Ursula. He's tired from the journey. We'll go and get ourselves sorted.

She takes Gabe's hand.

I'm seven and a half, Gabe pipes up indignantly as they go.

Peter smiles. Then you're old enough to conquer the giant!

What giant? says Gabe, turning back.

There's one on the quayside, says Peter. He's come all the way from Sweden!

A new art installation, says Joyce. The Council commissioned Kira Lonngen.

We'll go and see him, shall we, Gabe? says Peter. See what he's got to say to us!

He won't talk, silly! says Gabe. He's not real, Granddad.

Ursula is relieved to see his shyness dissolve. Everything will be fine. Her unease about her parents' indifference is unfounded. She takes Gabe down to the kitchen for something to eat. The back door is open and he runs out into the garden. It is cold in the shadow of the house, the sunlight only filtering through the ash tree in patches. The grass is overgrown. Several crisp packets have blown in from the street. Gabe clambers on to the rockery, and picks up a pebble.

Ganny Mary and I made this together. We brought all the stones back from our trips, Gabe. Tynemouth mainly. This one is from Pendle Hill. Ursula picks up the orange stone. A skim of dark moss has grown on one side.

Who's that? Who is it?

Mary is sitting on a deckchair in her brown housecoat amongst the fallen leaves. Above her the great ash tree is now lop-sided and ragged: two big branches have been pollarded after complaints from a neighbour. She peers out anxiously from beneath her mushroom hat.

Hello, Ganny Mary, says Ursula.

Ursula, is that you? says Mary, looking at Gabe.

I'm not Ursula, silly! I'm a boy, says Gabe. He jumps down from the rockery, picks up a stick and swishes it through the long grass.

I'm here, Ganny Mary, says Ursula softly, shocked at her grandmother's frailty. Her eyes are milky with cataracts.

This is Gabe, my son.

My feet are bad, says Mary, irritated, oh dear . . .

What's wrong with her eyes? Gabe says.

He scrambles on to the first branch of the tree, and hangs over it, gazing down at Ganny Mary.

We've just arrived, Ursula says. I'll make some tea. Come inside. She takes Mary's arm to help her up.

Mary stares through the clouds in her eyes at Ursula, the tree, the boy in the branches. She used to try to wipe them away, but she doesn't bother now. Everything is cloudy now, people, places, time. Especially time. Ursula now, Ursula then, Joyce, Annie, Mrs Noonan. The young woman holding her arm might be Ursula. Or possibly Marigold Deacon from the Whalley Road, or her husband, Graham. Everything is possible. She strokes the face with curiosity. Yes, this is Ursula . . .

We went up Pendle Hill, she says. You came home.

Yes, says Ursula quietly.

Mary shakes her head. It's not Ursula, it's her mother, Annie. Annie who went out that night on to Pendle Hill, and came back changed for ever, Annie who was blown apart until the Brethren got hold of her and blackened her heart. Poor mother, poor Annie. She pats Ursula's hand.

Mummy, poor Mummy . . .

Ursula is too shaken to say anything. Her parents have not told her Ganny Mary is like this, so altered, so lost. Gabe swings down from the ash tree.

Gabe, I want you to play something on the piano for Ganny Mary.

Mummy, no! he groans.

Come on, she cajoles him. For everyone. I'm sure they'd love to hear you.

The house is full of bitches, says Mary, matter-of-factly. Bitches, all of them . . .

Mary stares at the peace campaigners through the window, seeing the Brethren in their circle, knuckle-white in their fervour. The peace campaigners are standing up, leaving, saying their goodbyes.

Bitches! shouts Ganny Mary.

Gabe starts hopping on one leg.

You're getting so good at hopping! says Ursula brightly, trying to make it all normal for him. See if you can hop all the way to the piano! Come on! I'll race you!

The piano has been relocated to the back hall. It stands now covered in books and newspapers, and obviously hasn't been played for years. Ursula remembers Jonathan and his friends working out solos by The Doors on it, painstakingly picking out note after note: she and Jerry had sex on it once and recorded it on Peter's dictaphone. Radical Sex Sonata, they called it. She clears a stack of leaflets from the lid and opens it.

It might not be in tune, says Gabe as he sits at the keys and plays a scale.

It sounds drunk.

Play something, she says, hoping it might ease the strangeness of being there, hoping her own discomfort doesn't show.

What about the Mozart?

He sits up straight at the piano, as Miss Penny has told him to. Ursula smiles at him reassuringly, and he starts to play.

Joyce and the peace campaigners are at the front door taking leave of each other. They stop as they hear the piano, and some turn back. Gabe plays with a grace beyond his years. There is gravity in his phrasing that surprises Ursula though she has heard the piece many times. Music is something he can just do. It comes effortlessly to him, unexplained.

The boy wonder, says her father, looking over the banister.

Mary shuffles in and sits on the chair by the telephone, her head on one side. The Boy Wonder, is it? Her boy wonder. This tune, so long ago. Yes, it's from Carl Breil's *Dramatic Music for Motion Picture Plays*! She hears Wally's voice, soft as he explains it – this is for idyllic scenes, Mary, for sunrises, sunsets, and rural beauty, for parent and child, brother and sister, children at play. It is a piece for everything that is good. She hears his words like a song. It's the music of love, Mary. His music transformed her. It gave her breath and life and beauty, and on the day he told her she was more beautiful to him than music, she felt her feet would never touch the ground again. She was sixteen. Annie came to the Picture Palace, and dragged her out by her ear. She told Mary she was to beg God to forgive her. That's when Mary had told her, turned on her, shouting she could keep her God, she hated God, she was marrying Walther Morely, Boy Wonder from New York on two pounds a week and rising, and nothing could stop her. Together, and for ever, they were going to live in the light.

Her mother never spoke to her again until the day she died. Mary didn't care. She was going to be free. She'd do as she pleased. She and Wally married the next week and moved into a room next to the station. One of his friends was a film-maker in Scarborough making a film with sound. He needed a woman to play a part in it and Wally suggested Mary. She was beside herself with excitement. Wally borrowed a friend's motorbike and they drove all the way to Scarborough, Mary's arms clinging tight round her new husband. The film was called *Dangerous Edge*. As the camera rolled, Mary had to walk along to the clifftop, look over the edge, and scream in terror at the top of her lungs.

Cut! said the director. Excellent!

I told you she were a good screamer! cried Wally.

The next day he had put down a deposit on a shop on the Blackburn Road. It was Mary's dream. She would sell beautiful things: china dogs, vases, pictures, tapestries, mirrors. She dreamt of an emporium.

Everything went wrong. *Dangerous Edge* was one of the first films with sound. Within five years the talkies arrived and Wally was no longer needed at the Picture Palace. Mary became pregnant. Nothing sold in the shop; the people of Padiham hadn't the money for beautiful things. Wally didn't seem to care. He took a job repairing wet batteries and took them round the factories. He needed a workroom so they split the shop in half, one side for Mary's ornaments and laces, the other side for the wet batteries. Neither side thrived. Wally remained cheerful, but he'd no head for business. He was always doing favours for people, not getting paid. Anger grew inside Mary. She miscarried three times before Joyce was born.

She wrote to her mother about her first grandchild but heard nothing. Mary felt the rejection like another death. At home with a little baby, she began to feel trapped. Wally had promised her beauty and given her poverty. He had failed her as all men fail. Even her father, clutching his heart like that, and falling like a pillar. If he'd lived, the laundry would have thrived. Mary would have gone to school, married above her, and never have become bitter. She couldn't help the violence, the hurling of pans, plates, the iron poker at Wally. Damn him! Damn him! The Boy Wonder with his sweet enticing piano music . . .

You runt! You tricked me! she shouts, reaching for Gabe

at the piano. Stop it! Stop your bloody noise!

Blind with rage, she tries to clutch him, thrashing out at thin air, flailing, spitting with frustration. Gabe bursts into tears and runs to Ursula as Joyce pushes Mary back into her chair.

Stop, Mother! Stop! Enough!

Mary feels the hands pushing her down, trying to imprison her. It is her mother again, always trying to stop her being happy. She goes mute, obedient, sits back in her chair, like a good girl. Yes, she'll have a cup of tea as her mother suggests. She drinks it meekly, but deep down she is despairing. She feels her mother's hatred of her. She can't stand it any more. She won't stay craven any longer, forever waiting, a dupe for all the bitches and the runts. She will leave Eslington Road and Newcastle, and everything will be different. Her life will be glorious, as it was meant to be.

The giant! cries Gabe.

They're standing by the old television studios, high above the quayside, looking down at a gigantic sculpture of a man. He rears up in the Tyne as tall and imposing as the bridge's iron girders. Water pours from his metal limbs as though he is surfacing from the depths.

Shall we go down and take a closer look, Gabe? says Joyce.

Yes, Grandma!

He takes her hand and they set off down the steep steps. They are all buoyed up by his wonder. Ursula is glad they have come.

What's his name, Grandma?

Odin. He's the Norse God. The guide of souls.

Ursula walks next to her father. She watches Gabe listening to his grandmother, enthralled by her. Ursula can't help wondering if she ever experienced Joyce like this as a child, both comfortable and charismatic. Perhaps she did in snatches. Her father touches her arm.

I'm glad he's staying with us. Joyce will have a chance to know him. We both will, he says.

They follow Gabe and Joyce down the banks to the quayside. Her father has always been such a mysterious presence to Ursula; deeply laconic, or simply absent. Perhaps she never made enough effort to know him, her relationship with him influenced by Ganny Mary's bitterness too. There's something in his look now she's never noticed in him before. He smiles, delighted, at the sight of Joyce chatting away with her grandson, and Ursula realises what it is. After all these years, he is still entranced by his wife.

A crowd has gathered at the foot of the giant and there is a carnival atmosphere. Everyone has come to see the Geordie Giant as Odin's been dubbed. There are mums pushing prams, grannies and granddads, teenagers sprawling on the harbour wall, a school party making sketches on clipboards. Ursula can smell her childhood, sea in the air, and chips and vinegar.

Gabe, can you see? He's made of wire, says Peter.

The giant looms above them, his face crisscrossed with strips of metal like a cage.

Is he God?

He's an artist's idea of a god, says Joyce firmly.

Mummy says God is not who you think it is, says Gabe. Is that true, Grandma?

The God questions have been coming for months now. Long interrogations into the night. What is God, Mum? Is he a person? Is he coming? Is he religion? Gabe's classmates in London are from every faith, Muslim, Sikh, Hindu, Jewish, Christian. When Ursula asks Gabe what he thinks about God, he just shrugs and says he feels him.

Peter takes Gabe to the water's edge. Ursula turns to her mother.

Thanks for agreeing to have him, Mum, she says. He seems so comfortable with you both.

Of course he is, says Joyce, and we're delighted to have him. He's a lovely boy. He'll be fine.

A great jet of water shoots up from the giant, spraying the edges of the crowd.

Mummy! I'm soaking . . .!

Gabe is running to her, hair dripping. She's about to dry him when she sees Jerry arm in arm with a woman, bobbed red hair, knee-length boots, a cream coat. It's Caitlin. They are walking towards her.

Jerry sees Ursula at the same time; Ursula with her son, Gabe, pulling him in to her, laughing, playful. He can see her in the boy's face and in the way he moves.

Jerry!

Joyce has seen him. She's calling, waving. Panic courses through him. This can't happen. They mustn't meet, Caitlin and Ursula. Not like this. He tries to steer his wife away.

What is it? she asks.

It's too late. Joyce and Peter are coming towards them through the crowd.

Jerry, what a lovely surprise!

Joyce, he says, smiling helplessly. This is Caitlin, my wife.

Good to meet you, Caitlin. This is Peter. Ursula is here somewhere . . . She looks round. Ursula is pretending not to have seen Jerry, drying Gabe's hair.

Ursula! Gabe! It's Jerry, Joyce says, beckoning them over. Gabe breaks free and runs to her.

This is Gabe, my grandson, she says, stroking his head. Jerry can feel Caitlin stiffen at his side. What do you think of our giant, Jerry?

Ursula hangs back, trying not to catch Jerry's eyes. He

can almost feel her heart beating as fast as his own. Caitlin looks down at her feet.

What does it say about art? says Joyce loudly, sensing uneasiness.

What does it say about public funding! rejoins Peter.

Granddad! cries Gabe, rolling his eyes. The giant can't say *anything*. It's made of metal, and it's got no mouth! Look!

They all look up at the wire head of the giant, grateful for the distraction. There's an indentation where his mouth should be. Jerry feels Caitlin pull on his arm.

We must be going, he says, good to see you all.

Gabe turns to Ursula. Mummy, you said I could have ice cream.

Stay for ice cream, says Joyce, looking at Jerry and Caitlin. Odd couple, she thinks, Jerry never used to be shy like this, and his wife is blushing, almost on the edge of tears.

I'm sorry, we're meeting friends, says Jerry and steers Caitlin away through the crowds, shutting Ursula out of his mind, leaving all the questions of her discarded on the quayside, and she watches him disappear into nothing over the thin sickle of the Swing Bridge.

In search of clues to herself, Ursula puts the earth in her hand and turns it like a pebble. She's done it before: one small turn to a beach in Lancashire, another and the sea sparkles in Tamil Nadu, and now she turns it a full 180 degrees to Chinaman's Beach in New South Wales, Australia. The breakers roll in from the horizon on to the sand. She's lying on the shore pretending to pretend something about a pretend woman in a made-up story. Jack Jones bends over her and strokes her face. She slaps his hand. He throws her on to her back. She cries out in agony or joy, it's hard to know. He tries to kiss her. She reaches for the piece of driftwood to strike him. Enough! she cries playfully or furiously, Jesus! Sebastian!

She is rehearsing with Jack to prepare for one of their scenes together. Jack plays an artist called Sebastian who has tortured relationships with women, and Ursula is Hedwig, a married woman having an affair with him. Hedwig has no definable characteristics and rarely speaks. The little she does say is inconsistent. In this scene Sebastian has brought Hedwig to the beach to make love to her as the tide comes in. Her only scripted line is one about a gallery owner that is without any discernible motive but is apparently crucial to the plot. The director, Will Chaser, kneels down close to Jack Jones. Jack is the money. Will sees only Jack. Jack is a rare creature. Jack doesn't like loud voices when he's in character.

I like the way this is going, Jack, whispers Will. Joy, anger, fear, I'm getting them all.

Will stands up, rubs his hands together, and looks round.

Righto, he says. Into position for a take.

He nods towards Ursula on the sand, the waves lapping at her feet, naked apart from a flesh-coloured thong.

Get Ursula further into the water, he says.

Jack Jones stands in a towel in front of the camera and closes his eyes. His descent into character is almost holy. He never looks at or speaks to Ursula unless he is in character.

Will! Will, says Ursula, getting to her knees, pulling a towel round herself. I'm just not sure what Hedwig is feeling during this scene.

You're doing great, he says, walking away.

Patty said Will Chaser knew Ursula *was* Hedwig the moment she walked in for the audition. It's a real break for you, Patty had drawled. There might be some nudity, she added, but Will Chaser has integrity, and Jack was nominated for a Globe for the horse tamer in *The Wild*. So, he must have integrity, too.

Let's shoot, cries Will. The crew swarms around Camera.

Ursula, we're gonna need you in the water this time, says the third assistant.

No problem, she says, shuffling down on the sand until her legs are in the waves.

A little more, says the third AD looking for confirmation from the camera operator. Ursula takes off her towel, and moves in until the water reaches the tops of her legs.

It's cold, she says. Are we rolling?

Two caterers in aprons stagger across the sand with trays of sandwiches and fruit.

Food! says Jack Jones, dropping suddenly out of character. I'm starving! There's nothing like adultery to make a man hungry!

The crew laughs as though he's said something hilarious. He runs over to the tray and takes a slice of pineapple and a bagel.

Stay where you are, Ursula. Jack won't be long, says the first AD.

They must all wait until Jack is ready to shoot the scene. The sun shines through the clouds making tiger streaks across the ocean. Laughter rises as the caterers respond dutifully to Jack Jones's jokes. Great guy. Approachable. Hilarious.

It's dark when they wrap. The crew invites Ursula to watch English football in a pub, but she declines. At her boxy apartment in Sydney's financial district she takes a hot bath and makes sardines on toast. She wonders whether to call Gabe. Their parting still haunts her; he'd begged her not to go. When she'd finally torn herself away he hadn't said goodbye. It's hard on the telephone. Last time she'd called, he refused to speak to her. Joyce told her he was busy, but she could hear him saying no.

She reaches for the telephone. It rings for a long time, and Ursula is about to hang up when Joyce answers. She and Gabe have been out for the day, she says, as if Ursula should have known. And now Gabe is having a story with Granddad. Ursula insists on speaking to him. Eventually he comes to the phone.

How are you, Gabe? I miss you, she says.

He's instantly tearful. I want to come home, he says.

I know, I know, me too, she says helplessly. I'll be back soon.

When? He starts to cry. Joyce comes back on the line.

It's hearing your voice, she says. He's been perfectly happy.

She tells her their news; how Peter has been taking Gabe to museums, how they've visited Holy Island, how there is a little boy the same age on Eslington Road who's played with Gabe, how they've made a camp in the garden under the ash tree.

That's great, Mum, says Ursula numbly.

These calls must be expensive, says Joyce.

Mum, you're not leaving him with Ganny Mary, are you? He's scared of her.

Of course not. Why ever would you think that? She keeps herself to herself . . .

You used to leave me with her! says Ursula, emotion surging in her.

Only when I was busy, says Joyce, perplexed, defensive. Kelsey is coming for Gabe tomorrow. I don't know what you're worried about. You can't control everything, Ursula. Especially from the other side of the world!

Ursula spoke to Kelsey a few days ago to make sure of the arrangements. He accused her of doing the same thing when she'd asked him not to introduce Gabe to his new girlfriend, Judy. In case it wobbled him, she said. Stop trying to control everything, Ursula, he'd said . . .

A sheet of paper is slipped under her door. It's her pick-up time for the next day. She knows now this will be her last job. She doesn't enjoy it any more. Camera has finally lost his allure. She will retrain as something, move out of London, find a new relationship. When I get home, she thinks, I will be a better mother, daughter, granddaughter. She lays out the lives in her family and tries to find her place in their constellation. The more she thinks about it, the less she knows. The pain in her back twists and nags her. She thinks of Ganny Mary; the last time she saw her. Her terrible sadness and anger. She realises she barely knows her despite the time they spent together; her mother, Joyce, too, absent even in her presence. Has she ever really known anyone in her family? Perhaps she has never known anyone at all. It's her own fault, always roaming off, escaping, reaching for something – acting, Kelsey, motherhood, Australia, India . . .

India; it rings through her still. It changed everything, in an instant, a single blow that shattered her into a million pieces. She had tried to make sense of it. After she'd got home, she'd gone into a church in Newcastle, not knowing where else to go, searching for answers. An elderly priest was putting out prayer books.

I need to talk, she'd said.

Would you like me to hear your confession? he said.

I'm not religious, I'm not Catholic.

You need to be confirmed for me to hear your confession, he said, but we can talk here. He'd gestured to a wooden bench at the back of the church. Ursula was so relieved to find someone who might understand, to whom she might begin to express what had happened in India, she felt she was going to burst into tears.

Something happened, she started. To me. I disappeared. I mean everything did. I still feel it. Like I don't exist.

The priest nodded, but said nothing.

It sounds crazy, I know, she said, suddenly embarrassed. I'm not very clever, you see. I mean I thought it must be about God . . . and that maybe you would know . . . you see I don't know what I'm talking about, but it feels like I touched something . . . like I am God, you know, and so are you. Am I making any sense? I mean not God like that of course, but . . . I . . .

The priest had reached into his pocket and pulled out a small Bible.

Everything you are searching for is in here, he had said, this is the word of God.

She'd read it hungrily, searching for answers. The words filled her in turn with fear, wonder, and bewilderment, but she couldn't find what she was looking for. She didn't know what to look for. The world of the Bible, so punishing and alien, meant nothing.

Police sirens wail across Sydney Harbour. She stretches her body, arching back to ease the twist in her spine. She'll find an osteopath, get an appointment. A lifetime of treatments trails behind her. Nothing brings lasting relief. When she gets back to London, things will change, things will be better. She'll be better. Everything will be.

Maestro! Wait!

Bill Flanaghan corners Jerry by the water dispenser as he fills a cone. He's just outlined his proposal to the North East Health Authority to allow GPs' surgeries to diversify to alleviate the pressure on A & E departments.

That was inspiring, says Bill, left-field, but inspiring!

Jerry pushes through the double doors and heads for the stairwell. Flanaghan follows him out on to Percy Street. It is already dark. People are making their way home or to the pub after work. The lights of Eldon Square blaze brightly. Jerry loosens his tie.

Drink? says Flanaghan. I'd love to ask some questions about your proposal.

No thanks, says Jerry. Caitlin's waiting at home.

He can feel Flanaghan's ambition behind the warmth, his attempt to manoeuvre himself into a better position in the organisation, ride on Jerry's coat tails. Jerry isn't perturbed. He's seen it all before, doesn't get involved in internal politics. Only his ideas truly matter. They are deeply wrought and intimate to him. He has no impulse to share them. The bedrock idealism of the NHS brought him this far, and it keeps him here still. Goodnight Bill, he says crossing the road towards Leazes Park. It's a chance to gather his thoughts. The committee's response to his proposals was excellent and as he walks he sifts through them to make sure he hasn't missed something. The towering floodlights of St James's Park blaze in the stadium as he heads up Blackfriars and a great roar from the Gallowgate end lifts into the night. He is moved by the swell of it, the tribal connection. He'd like a drink, but not with Flanaghan. He'll call Mackie. Of all his friends, Mackie is still the one Jerry wants to see most. He owns a bric-a-brac shop on the Shields Road called Stuff. Earlier in the year Jerry had helped to get him out of trouble. Mackie had been dealing home-grown skunk from the shop. The police had warned him several times, then finally arrested him. Jerry's friend Tam from university was now a criminal lawyer, and Jerry asked him to represent Mackie. He'd got off with a caution.

Jerry arrives back at his house in Jesmond, the wind gusting against him, and turns into the garden. There are piles of cut privet in the front path. Baz has been. Jerry pays him to do four days a month, but the garden never looks tidy. He always leaves the job half finished. He has learning difficulties. Jerry won't let him go, but he needs to find someone else to come in and finish the job when Baz has gone.

The house is a large detached Victorian in sandstone. It was a shell when he and Caitlin bought it, and they have relished its restoration. Their happiest times were after they got married. They lived on the top floor, while the builders gutted the rooms below, and rebuilt it from the bottom up, according to their designs.

He can see her through the window in the sitting room

at the large oak desk. He knows how the evening will go. He'll open some wine and tell her about his meeting. She'll tell him about family visits, assessment meetings, care orders, her struggles with the Council. She's campaigning for greater communication between Social Services and relevant charities, to ensure greater support for children, but it's an uphill battle.

Hi love, he calls as he lets himself in.

Hi.

The huge kitchen is all marble and wood. There is an Aga with copper pans hanging from racks. A box of fresh meat and veg from the organic supplier has arrived, two legs of lamb for Saturday night; they've got twelve coming, mostly Caitlin's friends. They love to give dinner parties. Jerry's family is coming on Sunday, his mam, dad, Andie and four kids. He likes to fill the house with people. Caitlin doesn't want children. The last time they'd spoken about it she said there were enough in the world. She couldn't justify adding another when so many were neglected and needed help. He pours himself a glass of wine and walks through to the sitting room.

How did it go?

They've agreed to a pilot.

Congratulations, says Caitlin.

He kisses her. It means a pay rise. They'll make more improvements to the house, possibly buy a little place by the sea.

I'll just check my emails, he says.

He goes to his study in the annexe, where books stretch from floor to ceiling. They knocked two rooms through, put in skylights. It is his haven. He has speakers in the ceiling for Bach, Willie Nelson, Schubert, Brian Wilson. Checking his emails is a euphemism for spending time alone. Caitlin calls it his shed.

He turns on his desktop and moves his cursor over a file titled *POP*. It's his book: *The Philosophy of Power*. He's been writing it for months, sometimes into the small hours, feverishly chasing down his thoughts. Caitlin never complains, just goes to bed without him. He moves the cursor and opens *Mentor*, a nationwide project he's leading to match troubled kids with adults who can offer guidance and support. To Jerry it's a perfectly rational idea, but he's also passionate about connection, the thought of expanding a child's experience, educating them. A kid from Byker perhaps, like himself, hungry for the world.

The phone rings downstairs. He lets it, hoping it will stop. Caitlin is probably doing the same. Perhaps she's in the bath. He picks it up.

Jerry, it's me.

Ursula. Her voice is tight as a wire.

Where are you?

Australia. It's Ganny Mary. Mum just called me. Ganny Mary's gone missing. She left the house and hasn't come back. She must be wandering around the streets somewhere.

She's probably having the time of her life, he says.

He hears her laugh. It pleases him.

She's not well, Jerry. In her mind.

What do you want me to do? he says, perplexed.

I don't know, I'm sorry. I thought maybe she was in a hospital somewhere.

Have you called the police?

Mum has.

They'll contact the hospitals. It will be fine, Ursula. Don't worry. They'll find her.

I'm sorry, it's just so weird being so far away. I can't do anything . . .

I'll call your mum. See if I can help.

Thanks, she says. I know. I shouldn't have called.

I'm glad you did, he says.

When Jerry puts down the phone, Caitlin is in the doorway.

Ursula's grandmother has gone missing, he says, trying to sound matter-of-fact. She's in Australia. She wanted to know if I could help.

Caitlin looks at him in silence. A sigh falls through her, like a leaf.

What are you going to do, Jerry?

I thought we could start with the hospitals . . .

About Ursula.

Caitlin, she's in Australia. She needs some help . . .

She turns away. He hears her walk upstairs. He should go after her, talk with her, but he feels the grip of a desperate loneliness. It's unbearable, like a howl within him. He grabs his coat, and leaves.

If he's gone looking for Mary, he'll not find her. She's long gone. She's not staying around for Jerry, or anyone. She's leaving godforsaken Newcastle on the greatest adventure of her life, had a clear-headed moment of realisation in the basement of Eslington Road, a spot of sun falling on her cheek, a piece of dark choccy in her mouth, suddenly knew with absolute certainty that she should have been happy: there has been too little of it in her life and she will have it.

She's been in the biscuit tin and taken the roll of five-pound notes tightly bound by an elastic band, she's got two bars of Bournville from the bedside drawer and a rain hood, and she's left the house, heading down Eslington Road, along Osborne Road, and into town. Well, she's had enough. Her mother kept her away from happiness for too long, and Mary won't stand for it a moment longer. She is going to Tythe Farm on Pendle Hill to get butter, and when her father wakes in the morning it'll be on the table in the brown pot. Butter with the sun in it. She will bring him downstairs and show it him and they will laugh and eat breakfast and be happy.

She missed several turnings, caught the wrong bus, tottered down Pilgrim Street, but at last she's arriving at

Newcastle Central Station, undaunted. A football match has just ended and men in striped scarves flood the concourse. Mary moves slowly amongst them with clouds in her eyes towards the ticket office, in a dream of VE Day. The war is over and everyone is celebrating, drinking beer, but she can't stop, one hasn't time. Isn't that Mrs Petheridge and her sons? And May Kenton too, thieved money from her brother-in-law they say, wouldn't stop for her any road, brought a disgrace to her family, and the town. Time slides together and apart. A man, a nice man, in a uniform, a guard, or perhaps a soldier, how they've suffered, helps her buy a single ticket to Padiham and walks her to the train. Thank you, Jonathan, she says, patting his cheek, a good boy really. At Burnley she takes the bus, as she's done before so many times, from Padiham to Burnley and back again, to buy lace for the shop. She can see the public library through the clouds as the bus passes, people sitting at the Formica tables reading the *Gazette*, shortbread in the serving hatch. It was a good place for her, the library; she'd find books on antiques, travel guides to Switzerland, books of beautiful worlds. The bus weaves through out into the lanes towards Pendle Hill. She rings the request bell, looks up towards Tythe Farm. Butter. She deserves nothing less.

The earth is hers. The curve of the grass track opens up to her as she climbs, a gesture introducing the hill. The air is cold in her lungs. She breathes deeply, barely feeling the rain on her skin. Something is changing in her body. She takes off her shoes. She feels young again. Her strides become longer, surer, her mind clearer. She feels the freedom of the place. The copse is a beating heart. St Agnes seems a shining castle in the distance, and in front of it Tythe Farm. There will be cake.

She stops to catch her breath by the blasted tree with its angled and spiked branches. Beyond it is the scree where her mother lay down. Clouds thicken in Mary's eyes but suddenly sunshine strikes through them and she sees a figure on the path, a woman in a long skirt climbing upwards. It's her mother, Annie. She turns back to Mary, and she sees her face, lit with joy. Mary pushes through the bracken towards her. Suddenly the steepness is nothing, she's running, a child again, happiness flooding through her, running to the mother who blighted her but who loves her still. She's seen her smile before, just the same, on the night she came back from the hill like a stranger, torn and ragged, but she's seen it on Ursula's face too, after India, the exact same smile. Wondrous! Her mother loves her! The Brethren tried to shut her love and smile away with their cant and their dogma, but it survives! Annie holds out her arms as Mary stumbles forwards, her feet slipping on the rocks and she falls into her mother's embrace, the past opening up to the future as her body falls, striking her head against a rock. Mary doesn't mind. She can't even feel it. She feels only her mother's love, and all the hurt washing away, the hand on her hair, and a soft voice, as her heart slows, Mary, my precious Mary . . .

Ursula gets out of the taxi outside Kelsey's flat in Dalston. The £30 fare galls her and she takes a deep breath as she pays it; it's important she is strong for Gabe after being away for so long. It's been a fraught time; she begged the film company to let her fly back for Ganny Mary's funeral, but they refused. They said she'd to stay in Sydney until the end of the shoot. When it was clear they were never going to use her, she booked a flight home as soon as she could, and footed the bill herself. It was delayed in Hong Kong for forty-eight hours and she hasn't slept. The journey is still far from over; she and Gabe go to Lancashire this afternoon to scatter Ganny Mary's ashes on Pendle Hill.

Kelsey answers the door.

Hi, Urs! Come see the little man, he says and offers to carry her case. He leads her upstairs, asking how her flight was. She can hear Gabe as they approach the half-landing. The door to the roof terrace is open. Something is different: there are pots of flowers, trays of herbs, a vegetable patch made out of railway sleepers, a child's brightly coloured gardening tools in the soil. Gabe is on the decking playing with Lego, utterly absorbed as he presses the coloured bricks together. After such a long absence, the very fact of him astonishes her. He looks older, more substantial. She kneels gently at his side.

Hi, Gabe, what are you playing?

He glances up, then turns back to his toy. She longs to hold him, for an embrace to fold into, but she knows how this works. He is punishing her for being away. She must be patient, and gentle; he'll come round.

What are you making?

He shrugs and moves away.

I've missed you . . .

She picks up a piece of Lego and holds it out for him.

Kelsey calls from the kitchen.

Gabe! We're making lemonade! Want some?

She can hear him laughing with his new girlfriend, Judy. Gabe runs past her, a Lego jet roaring in his hand. She feels a wave of exhaustion. He needs time, and there isn't any. Joyce has arranged for them to spend the night with her at the Starkie Arms in Padiham. Before she'd left, Ursula had promised Gabe the first thing they'd do when she got back from Australia was see the re-run of *Star Wars* at the cinema but now Bethany must fly back to New York. Joyce wants everyone together so they can walk out early on to Pendle Hill and scatter the ashes. It's the last chance the family has to do it together.

Kelsey is making coffee in the kitchen. Judy is twisting halves of lemons on a squeezer.

Like some? she says, smiling at Ursula. She's young, maybe twenty-two, with strawberry-blond hair and pale blue eyes. There is a lightness in her voice and movements.

I can't stay, says Ursula. How's it been, Kelsey?

Gabe's a pleasure, says Judy, stirring sugar into a glass

jug, the spoon clinking against the sides. He's such a gorgeous kid.

Gabe picks up a guitar and makes a chord.

You're getting good! Judy says, taking him some lemonade. Kelsey doesn't play a musical instrument. It must be Judy's. There are signs of her everywhere: a cardigan, an Indian headscarf, some posters on the wall. It dawns on Ursula that she has moved in. It shocks her that Gabe has been living with another woman.

How is your mum, Ursula? says Kelsey, pouring hot water on to a thick layer of coffee in a cafetière. He looks different. Getting out of show business suits him. He was never truly happy with her. At the beginning perhaps, before Gabe . . .

You know how she is, says Ursula, fine. She's always *fine*.

Her mouth still feels dry from the flight. Her clothes are crumpled. She should have gone home first, taken a shower, got some sleep.

Gabe, we should go. We've a train to catch. Bring your Lego if you want, she says, moving to the door, taking the handle of her case.

I'm not going, he mumbles.

He goes into a bedroom and shuts the door. Ursula stands there, suitcase in hand.

Go easy, says Kelsey quietly. It's been hard for him.

It's always like this, says Ursula. He just needs time to adjust.

Kelsey gives Judy a look and she disappears into the bedroom after Gabe. Ursula hears her as the door closes. Come on, Gabey, let's find those pictures to show your mum . . .

He's having to adjust too much, Ursula, says Kelsey,

coming over to her. You expect him to fit in with your life. It's not good for him.

He's fine, she says. We'll be fine.

You sound like your mum, says Kelsey.

Ursula pours herself a glass of lemonade. Like Joyce? Her attempt to be strong has none of her mother's conviction. She is so sure of herself, her trajectory through life has always seemed untroubled, certain, full of forward momentum. Ursula feels quite different. Now more than ever, she is unsure that anything is ever really 'fine'.

I've talked to Gabe a lot since you left, says Kelsey, smiling. He wants to stay here for a while. I think he should. He needs to feel settled.

Here? says Ursula, her emotions rising. No. Absolutely not. I'm home now. There's no need. Gabe! Gabe, come on, let's go . . .

He emerges from the bedroom holding a picture of dragons. Judy is behind him.

Get your coat, love.

I'm not coming, he says.

Gabe, come on. Grandma is expecting us.

She holds out her hand for him.

Daddy? Daddy! He runs to Kelsey and holds him tightly.

Ursula feels alone, an outsider. Gabe is not hers any more. She opens her mouth to speak but suddenly she's crying.

Sorry . . . she splutters, fighting to stop the tears, but they force themselves out in great ugly sobs she can't control. She sees Gabe looking at her in horror and turns away, rubs her face, tries to smile, to speak . . . Gabe . . . but the tears come faster.

Lush, says Mackie, picking up an old pewter tankard. I've just got this in. It'll sell you knaa. Some daft fucking wanker from Jesmond like you will buy it and put it on his fucking Aga.

He and Jerry are sitting at the back of the shop on the Shields Road, surrounded by junk. Broken desks, office chairs, piles of magazines, a wardrobe with its door hanging off showing a stack of vinyl records inside, objects on every surface, toby mugs, broken tennis rackets, a basket full of thimbles.

I wouldn't touch it, says Jerry, smiling. Pewter, man. Too grey.

It's not grey, man, it's yellow. You're fucking pissed.

Jerry pours another whisky. He loves to hear Mackie vent his spleen. He balances the bottle back on the child's desk painted with an Alpine scene, and leans back in an office chair.

I'm not pissed, he slurs.

Pissed is not the word, man, says Mackie.

I'm not pissed, I'm fucked.

You are a fucker, says Mackie. His bloodshot eyes look into Jerry's for a moment. And do you want to know why you are a fucker? Because you've got a lovely wife, uptight mind but lovely, you've got a fucking mansion in Jesmondia, and you're fucking miserable, you twat. You've got the world eating out of your sweaty hand, you're rich as fucking Croesus and you're sitting here with me among all this shite, you fucking twat.

Around Jerry the objects shift and change; before graduating to the whisky, they've been smoking Mackie's home-grown, a demonic skunk. A line of figurines, like his mam's, looks down at him disapprovingly from the top of a wardrobe. A shepherdess, a lady with a pitcher, a tiny Buddha, and a dolphin standing on its tail. He looks along the line of them, silently eyeballing them one by one. They eyeball him back.

What are you looking at? says the lady with the pitcher.

Fuck, Mackie, says Jerry, your stuff is talking to me.

Mackie nods understandingly.

What's it saying?

Jerry bursts out laughing. It's good to get away from it all, from the pressure of work, the strain of his marriage. Since Ursula's call from Australia he and Caitlin have been spending more and more time apart, at work or with friends. The will to make things better between them has deserted him. Their intimacy has all but gone. He wakes in the night in panic about his life. Time is flying and he cannot stop it.

Oh my God! . . . I *am*, he splutters. I'm a twat. I'm a fucking wasted twat . . .!

The laughter consumes him. He cramps up in the chair. Mackie laughs too, at Jerry, sitting in his junk shop, falling to pieces.

Look at all this shite and tat, he says. They giggle uncontrollably.

Look at it all. Fuck! says Mackie. We're in a boat!

A boat made of stuff, says Jerry.

On a sea of shite.

A stuff boat, on a shite sea . . .

Their sides ache, they're beside themselves, but too stoned to stop. The stuff around them seems dead, alive, alarming, absurd. Everything is untethered. The Alpine mountains on the desk slip into ghoulish faces; a news reader, a politician, a bald man crying. Their laughter peaks and falls away in waves, and as dawn breaks they are silent, the haze of a hangover emerging, the furniture stubbornly itself again, dusty cupboards, chairs, ceramics, stuff. They smoke cigarettes, the curls of smoke rising meditatively in the airless room.

I wanted kids, says Jerry.

I've got some. Have mine, says Mackie.

He leans forward, and starts to delicately crumble hashish soft as brown sugar into a Rizla paper.

It's nowt to do with kids, says Mackie. He licks the paper and rolls it gently.

I should never have got married, says Jerry.

You took the wrong one off the fucking shelf, man, says Mackie. He lights the spliff, and draws deeply into his lungs. It should have been the weird one . . .

Ursula?

Aye. Because you are weird and two weirds make a wong, a wight, a parrot . . .

He offers Jerry the joint.

No way, says Jerry staggering to his feet. Fuck . . . I'm fucked!

300

You think about her. I know you do.

I've got to go. He almost falls as he staggers forwards.

You are more stoned than my stony arse, says Mackie.

You are more of an arse than my hairy fucking arse, says Jerry crashing towards the door.

Go on then, go the fuck back to Jesmondia and think about your perfect life, like my arse thinks about having a perfect shit one day.

His eyes glaze over, the words slurring into sound. He'll pass out soon. Jerry's found him often enough after a binge, at the back of the shop, asleep at the helm.

I deny all charges, he says, making his way out past a cracked mirror and a gnome on a toadstool. On behalf of the committee, I'll have you know, he says, turning back, I never think about her.

It is freezing outside. He staggers down Shields Road, through Heaton and Sandyford, and into the west streets of Jesmond where the cars on the motorway are awake and making their ceaseless roar. Something of Mackie's words is still in him as he turns from his route home into Eslington Road. The sun is low and dull in the winter sky. He steps into the front garden, and stands at the window, a boy again, peering into the gloom of the interior, seeing Ursula as he did the first time. He'd felt excited. She was so intriguing, so strange. He remembers his walk all the way back to Byker, how the world was transformed. He looks into the window again and sees Ursula through time, with all her crazy hairstyles, her different disguises, in all her searching through the years. Her eyes are full of humour, always trying to catch him out, or full of passion as she argues some point of politics or ethics she barely grasps, burning with intensity as she becomes hopelessly, defiantly lost. She is tilting back her head now and he can see her throat, the skin of her neck and chest. He longs to touch her. She smiles at him with such warmth he is no longer outside but inside, with her, inside her, part of her.

The front door opens and Ursula's father emerges carrying a briefcase.

Hi, Peter, says Jerry, quickly coming from behind the hedge.

Jerry?

I wasn't sure if anyone was in . . . he says, coughing a little, his mouth parched from smoking. He smoothes down his hair and steps on to the path.

I'm just off to London, says Peter. I'm the only one here, I'm afraid. They are all in Lancashire to scatter Joyce's mother's ashes.

I'm sorry. I didn't know. When did she . . .?

A few weeks ago. She went missing, walked out of the house one night, just like that. The police think she was trying to get back to her home in Padiham. Found her at the top of Pendle Hill, of all places.

What happened? asks Jerry.

She'd climbed up there. God knows why! She was losing her mind, I'm afraid. Anyway, now they're all climbing back up to scatter her ashes . . .!

He shakes his head, mystified.

They're staying in the Starkie Arms. Unsavoury establishment, but the only place in Padiham with rooms.

Is Ursula there? Is she back from Australia? asks Jerry.

Yes. Another wild goose chase, as I understand. She does seem to make a habit of those . . .

Peter laughs at the incomprehensibility of his daughter.

Anyway, I must run. Good to see you, Jerry . . .!

Jerry watches him go off down the street towards the station. Beyond him the Town Moor stretches away; miles of rough unkempt land without people or animals. Jerry remembers how he left Ursula there after they argued. He sees her crying in the middle of the desolate expanse. He'd felt so angry he couldn't reach her, he'd just left her, laughed at her, called her mad. The memory makes him ashamed. He stands there in the middle of Eslington Road, arms loose at his sides, not knowing which way to turn, an unfamiliar sense of bewilderment spreading through him.

Two post-office workers sit behind a wooden desk. Four nooses hang from a clothes rail in front of them. Ursula is in a post office in Bangalore waiting to renew her visa. Bruce Forsyth, David Bowie and Ganny Mary sit cross-legged on the floor beneath the nooses. Ursula watches as they put them around their necks to hang themselves. She puts a noose around her neck too but inside she is panicking. She doesn't want to hang herself.

I won't, she cries, I won't do it.

It's OK, says David Bowie, it doesn't matter.

He's right, says Ganny Mary, nothing matters.

What do you mean?! cries Ursula. I matter!

The post-office workers tell her not to worry; hanging only takes a few seconds. She sits under the rail, places the rope around her throat and lets go . . .

Ursula wakes terrified, deep in the dream, still protesting, her head jostled by the movement of the train. She lifts her head. She's on the early train from London to Burnley. Out of the window a power station billows smoke on the horizon. On the table in front of her lies the letter she'd been writing.

Dear Gabe . . .

She hadn't been able to find the right words, rested her head for a moment, and dropped into a sleep, like falling into deep water. She'd left Gabe at Kelsey's, walked away alone, trying to control her tears, wheeling her suitcase down the street. Kelsey had told her to go home and rest. She needed to talk to someone, he said. He told her he wanted Gabe to live with him for a while.

A baby is crying somewhere further down the carriage, the sound piercing the quiet like a siren. When Gabe cried as a baby, she would take him into her bed, and sing to him. Now when he cries she doesn't know how to comfort him. When she and Kelsey split up, one of the mums at school told her that Gabe was a lucky boy. At least it's amicable, she'd said. Yes, amicable . . .

She picks up her pen again. Dear Gabe . . .

She'd missed his concert at school while in Australia. He'd played a piece of jazz.

Miss Penny said you need to practise with a metronome . . . She can hear Gabe's response, I'll do it later, Mum, and her reply, You'll do it now, Gabe! Her strict tone upbraids her. She can hear Ganny Mary mimicking her mother Annie: You'll do as I say, child. Life is not for your enjoyment!

She takes a fresh sheet of paper and starts to write:

Dear Gabe, I saw three big kittens on a station platform today. They were old-fashioned collecting boxes for Help the Blind with slots in them for coins. They were made of painted metal, and their colour was faded on the heads where hands had patted them over the years. I used to love them as a child. Once I put all my pocket money into one, and made three wishes. I wished I could have superpowers and jump as high as the moon. I wished I could have a pretty face. And I wished that you would come. I wished for a boy to love and cherish, and my wish came true.

She reads it through. She imagines Gabe reading it, and doubts the words, crumples up the paper. She can't trust herself to write anything at all. She feels a sudden fear he's lost to her for ever. The twist in her body aches, and she shifts in the seat. The train slows on the outskirts of a town, passing rows of back gardens. There is a blanket in the window of one house, a vase on a sill of another, two beer tins by a back door, kids' bikes, a watering can . . . How do people live? How do they cope with their dreams, losses? How do they love? Her mind collapsing, doubt tumbling through her, questions jostling, questions that mustn't be asked, that have no answers, questions that break, annihilate. What am I? Where am I going? I don't know. I don't know anything, I don't know . . . suddenly she's crying.

The train stops in a jolt, and she looks out. A tree is moving in the wind. A few leaves are still on the branches, lemon-coloured, trembling on thin stalks, waiting for winter, and the clarity of cold. This is it, at last, Ursula, it is beginning . . .

It's a miracle they've made it. Joyce can't remember the last time it was like this: all three of her children in the same place at the same time. They've all come from such different parts of the world: Jonathan from Brighton, Bethany from New York, and Ursula direct from Sydney, without a raincoat so she's glad she's had the foresight to bring the spare one from Newcastle. She's pleased they've made such an effort. It's important they give her mother an appropriate farewell and she's planned everything to the smallest detail. Ursula had been supposed to come up the night before with Gabe to stay in the Starkie Arms but she arrived this morning without him. She seems subdued. Joyce stifles her concern. She's just jet-lagged. The film in Australia was clearly a mistake. She's left Gabe too long, and missed the funeral too, which must have been hard. She and Ganny Mary were thrown together a great deal when she was little. At least she's here now. They all are, except for Peter, and that's for the best. He and her mother never saw eye to eye and there is no point pretending otherwise. He braved the funeral and that was enough.

Are you sure you don't want me to drive, Mum? asks Jonathan from the back. Three times now. He drove up early from Brighton in his new car, keen to see how it would perform on the motorway. He offered to drive them all to Padiham in it, test the built-in satnav, he said. Joyce insisted on taking them all in her old Ford. It is important to remain in control. When they were children, she'd bundle them all into the car and drive out into Northumberland for long walks; they'd return home quiet, as they are now, three small faces peeping from sodden anoraks.

I'm fine. Thank you, Jonathan, she says, smiling into the rear-view mirror. Absolutely fine.

The funeral at Dunne's Crematorium had gone well. Mr Philips from the funeral parlour had been extremely accommodating with the arrangements and helped her choose the coffin, the urn, set the date and time, and order the hearse. Joyce had requested a non-religious service. She'd invited only her cousin Kathleen, and her second cousin Tom, who still lived in Padiham. Over the years, her mother had fallen out with most of the family. Still, what's past is past. The important thing now is to scatter the ashes.

She drives through Padiham; the wet streets seem bleak through the steamed-up windows, as though the rain has washed away the will of the town. When she was a child it had seemed alive with lights and noise: the mills turning, the huge chimney stacks belching smoke, the streets buzzing with people. Most of the shops are boarded up now. Another husk of Britain's great industrial heartland, left to wither and die. It makes her blood boil.

Did you tell the woman we've changed our plans? asks Bethany, breaking into her thoughts.

Tessa? Yes, we're meeting her near the river at one thirty, Joyce says.

She checks the time. It's just before one o'clock. Plenty of time. Tessa is one of the women who found her mother on the hill. She'd talked to her on the telephone. She was staying at the retreat centre at St Agnes behind Tythe Farm and found her when she was out walking. She was lying on her back. She had no shoes on and her eyes had been pecked out by crows. Joyce had been shocked when she came to the morgue. They'd done their best to make her look decent, but she could barely look. She'd decided not to tell the children. Tessa told her she'd made a pile of stones on the hillside to mark the spot. Joyce could tell it had been hard for her and had asked her to join them for the scattering. Tessa had accepted. Joyce hoped it would give her some peace of mind.

Rain splatters on the windscreen, obscuring the road ahead. She's glad of the change of plan. It would have been impossible on the hill in this weather. They will scatter the ashes on the site of the old laundry instead.

She slows the car. All the roads have changed. A housing development sprawls along the river. She pulls over next to a wooded path that leads to a footbridge.

Let's see if we can get to it from here, she says.

The wind hits them as they get out, blowing them back as they cross into the wood, their heads down, pulling their coats around them, the rain hard against their faces.

Joyce stays at the back as they follow the path in single file. Her children walk ahead of her. Jonathan strides out in front in his good walking gear. Joyce recognises something of herself in him, his propensity for action, the desire to get on. Bethany climbs the steps of the bridge in her light-green coat and woolly hat, behind him, her pace never varying.

Ursula walks behind her sister carrying the urn, her hand over the lid to keep out the rain. Of all her children, Ursula worries Joyce the most. There has always been a restlessness in her, a rashness that Joyce finds perplexing. The way she went to India like that. When she got back she was not just ill; she had changed. There had been something fragile and wonderful about her then, as though she had moved beyond the bonds of family, but ever since she has seemed to falter. Joyce watches her; the rain is plastering her hair to her face, as she holds the urn tight in her grip. She looks exhausted, on the edge of herself. It strikes Joyce that she hasn't said a single word since she arrived.

The wind blows hard along the river, bringing more rain. They reach the site of Hubert's laundry. It is part of the housing development now. Pendle Hill looms above them. Joyce shivers to think of her mother up there.

Hello!

Tessa waves to them from the iron gates of new flats, her body bending into the wind. Joyce is surprised to see she is black, West African perhaps; she heard no trace of it on the phone.

I'm Tessa. You must be Joyce . . .

Yes. Thank you for coming out in this weather, Tessa!

Don't worry, I've become used to the rain here! she says, laughing.

Her head is bare, her hair held back in a bun. She turns to the family.

Thank you for letting me share this with you today, she says simply.

We're glad you could join us, says Joyce. This is where my grandfather's laundry stood. My mother spent her happiest days here, as a child. They pumped water in from the river. It's different now, of course.

They look through the iron gates at the matchbox homes.

Right, let's do it, says Jonathan, moving off towards the river. They follow him to the bank and stand in silence, the rain falling hard, making the rushing water spit and boil.

Are you going to say something, Mum? asks Bethany.

I don't think so, says Joyce. You go first, Bethany.

Ursula holds out the urn to her sister. Bethany reaches inside and takes a handful of the ashes. She opens her palm and the wind whips them away. Jonathan is next. He removes a glove, puts it under one arm, takes a fist of ash and releases it with a flourish. Joyce watches as Ursula looks into the urn, as if unsure of what she should do. She takes a handful of ash and opens her fingers slowly. Some of the ashes blow across the water, but her hand is wet and some sticks to her palm. Joyce takes the urn from her, and empties it into the river. The last of the ashes lifts in a sweeping arc across the water to the hill beyond.

Goodbye, Mum, she says.

Her words are so ordinary, their tenderness takes her by surprise. Her mother is dead. She has not let herself feel anything until this moment.

Let's get back, says Jonathan quietly. He puts on his gloves and sets off towards the car. They follow him slowly.

The formality of the moment has passed, and they are released into speech. Joyce asks Tessa where she is staying.

St Agnes. It's a retreat centre now. It used to be a priory.

My mother and I used to walk up there when I was a girl, to Tythe Farm. There was a wonderful garden. A special place. I remember Mrs Littlewood used to provide food for the sisters. I don't suppose she is still there?

The garden is. I don't know about Mrs Littlewood, says Tessa.

The sisters?

They've all gone.

Mrs Littlewood, the priory, her family, her past, all gone. Joyce feels a sudden deep loneliness. Tears well in her eyes. She scolds herself. This is not the time.

Jerry is a man of action, in the fast lane, driving at speed down the M1. Sleeplessness makes him reckless. Mackie's right. Two weirds make a wong. He is filled with certainty. He must be with Ursula. He will find her, and tell her. They should always have been together, never have let each other go.

He leaves the motorway, taking the road to Ripon, weaving through Skipton, Harrogate, towards the industrial valleys of Lancashire. Nothing can break his resolve. When he finds her, everything will make sense. They will join together and it will be perfect. The strength of his conviction baffles him, nor can he put it into words, but he no longer resists it. With a kind of faith, he negotiates the ring roads of Burnley, and finds his way to Padiham. The rain is falling so heavily he can barely see the signposts.

He pulls up outside the Starkie Arms on the main street between two boarded shopfronts. He runs inside, jacket over his head, half expecting to see her right there behind the door, waiting for him. He is met by silence and the smell of stale beer. All the doors off the narrow hallway are closed. There is a coat stand without coats. Worn red carpet on the stairs.

Hello . . .? he calls out.

A tall boy emerges from one of the rooms.

Hi. I'm looking for someone, says Jerry. One of your guests. A family. They are staying here. Joyce, Ursula . . .

No one here now, says the boy, in a strong East European accent.

They were going to climb Pendle Hill . . .

The boy shrugs and disappears into one of the rooms. Jerry's eye is caught by a faded photograph of the Padiham cricket team on the wall. They are men of stature with moustaches, wearing whites. He looks the men in the eye. He'll climb the hill. Climb it until he finds her.

He steps out into the rain and sets off down the street. He's not sure which way to go for the path on to Pendle. Within a minute he is soaked to the skin, his clothes clinging to him. He barely feels it. This rain is nothing, almost refreshing. He heads towards what looks like a garage in the distance. He'll ask directions. A group of people in anoraks walk towards him. He recognises Ursula's brother, Jonathan. It's her family. It's her. There's Joyce talking with a black woman. Ursula's sister, too. He calls out, waving, bounding towards them.

Hi there! Hello . . .!

They look at him, perplexed.

What the hell are you doing here? says Jonathan.

Where's Ursula? Where is she?

*

She's going, going, nearly gone. There'll be no way back this time. At the river, her family and Tessa make their way back towards the town but she trails behind, walking slowly as though unsure of her own footsteps. She looks up at Pendle Hill stretching away from her in grey veils of rain, remembers the trip she made with Ganny Mary when she was a little girl: the lavender cake, the man with the peas, the sisters in black skirts walking among the ruins and is suddenly wild with longing to climb up, wind-battered, stride the fell. She hesitates, in turmoil. She can feel something on her hand – Ganny Mary's ashes stuck to her wet palm. Should she save this grit of her grandmother? Hold on to it? Wipe it away? She clambers down the bank, falls to her knees and plunges her hand in the rushing river. The cold makes her bones ache but she keeps it there, her fingers lambent white, alien – tiny bubbles rising.

Her mother is in the distance with Tessa and her brother and sister. They are crossing over the footbridge. She sees them frozen in time, exposing their struggles, their hopes, Bethany's regrets, Jonathan's longing, Joyce's good intentions and fierceness, Tessa's searching, lives like strands of air, insubstantial as clouds, little lives, light as balsa. Her body starts shaking, uncontrollably, tears are falling down her cheeks, making salt in her mouth. She touches her face, wet, fishlike, tries to stop her tears, stop it happening, to control herself. There are pebbles under the water on the riverbed, small, hard, definite. She wills them to anchor her, starts to count them. One, two, three, four . . . They are endless. Each one is different, with its own shape, colour, place. Ganny Mary is dead. Fear streaks through her, she sees her dying on the hill, the shocking pain, helpless-

314

ness, the falling body. What kind of pebble was Ganny Mary? Was she a good pebble, or a bad one? What is good? What is bad? Answer me! Water rushes over the pebbles, the strong current carrying sticks and debris. Nothing can be grasped, or known, like the branches of the ash tree. Her feet slip on the mossy stones, suddenly the sun flashes a diamond on the side of a house across the water, Pendle Hill gleams green, and the pebbles lift as one from the riverbed into the air like birds. Ursula runs up the bank – as fast as she can. Rocks, houses, cattle in the fields breaking through the earth's crust, breathing and cresting all around, coming alive – nothing matters, nothing but this running, opening, letting go, fear vanishing – this is it, Ursula! Run! – across the bridge, past the bus stand, over the stile, bursting through the trees, pushing back branches as the oil slick of memories, luminous, slippery, the millions of connections, the stuff, sum of, snagging her, hats, toffees, Bethany with dolls, Jonathan high, Howard in the playground, Peter on a train, Joyce at a window, Wally, Mary, Hubert, Annie in whalebone, deepening back through time, people, histories, the cruel power of men, hardness of women, as the twist in her spine snarls – let go! – like prayers – let them all go – Ursula! – on to the wide grass of the hill across the tussocks to the path that curves the rain, washes the wind – I'm with you – wet grass delighting, slopes falling upwards, and look across the hill – thousands come – the laundrywomen in their long skirts, Jeanette and Ashley, their tight minis ripping, falling away from them, Caitlin, Bethany, Mellie, Joycilli, Andie, their stories shedding like papers behind them, Joyce, leaflets dropping from her pockets, Annie flying, Bible in her hand, pages coming loose, fluttering behind her like gulls, and Ganny Mary, Mary, a girl again, running beside her, breaking with you, your laughter on the wind, men too, shedding their gender, forms sprinting, set free by this hill, women with broken bodies, Joan and Patty, voices from inside pouring out in streams of sound, all running, past the turn to Tythe Farm, the lightning tree up the path of wonder – run! – feel the infinity of moments, in childbirth, in the majesty of pain, in a headstone, in shattering loss, in singing at the tubs, bubbles rising, and in Ursula in the Himalayas, smashed against the sky, this is it, push above the storm, break for the summit, this heather, this scree

birds
hill
sky . . .

And out of nothing a voice, unheard, silenced years ago, grows stronger, the voice of a woman who climbed up Pendle, and was changed for ever, stripped bare, blasted to nothing, speaks out for the first time, louder and louder – my name is Annie Tate, wife of Hubert Tate of Tate's Laundry, Padiham, Lancashire. On the 15th February 1911, I climbed Pendle Hill. I had walked on the hill many times since I was a girl, first with my mother and my grandmother, then with my own daughter, Mary. On this day I went alone, and walked towards the summit. All of a sudden, I was lifted by a force that came from inside me and outside me and, in a single moment, I knew everything that I thought to be true was not. I saw the beauty of life in a single shattering blow. I lay down on the ground and let it fill me and it was beyond anything I have ever known in my small life. I saw that nothing exists. The clear sky and the rock are me. I am not Annie. I never have been, and never will be.

I felt wild with ecstasy. I could see the very insides of the grasses. I rolled on the grass. I jumped from tussock to tussock and ran in the heather. Every cloud blew through me and sang in me. I danced and was the blustering wind. At Tythe Farm, I met Sister Grace, one of the sisters from St Agnes, and we sat amongst the ruins of the Abbey. She rejoiced with me. There was no need to talk, but every word we spoke was full of joy. As darkness came, I came back down the valley, to Hubert and Mary. They did not understand. Hubert was repelled by my joy. He feared first for my honour and then for my sanity. He sent for his sister Sissy and in time the hill was taken from me. I came to believe that my experience had been an aberration, and the breath of Satan. I had not touched the hem of God but my own madness. I could neither sustain nor understand my experience, and in my confusion let religion take its place. Power and joy was taken from me and I was made small. I let the Brethren have my heart, but they took God from me. I became filled with hate, and turned from all joy, from my husband and daughter, from what I knew to be true, from love. This is my deepest regret. This is my testament. It is my gift to you, Ursula.

It is twilight when Ursula walks out of the woods and steps over the stile. The rain has stopped and drops of water splatter from the trees as she follows the hedgerow along the road towards the lights of Padiham.

Her feet barely seem to touch the ground. She feels she is floating as she steps on to the pavement by St George's Church, which Hubert, man of substance, attended so regularly, with his Annie, pretty at his side. Ursula sees the church spire, feels the life in its bricks, the stories of the men who laid them, the people who passed though its doors. As she walks by the low wall, where moss grows deep green, she holds all the world effortlessly, and knows the wondrous lightness of existence in an instant.

She finds herself entering a corner shop on the edge of Padiham. The shelves are barely stocked – rows of tinned vegetables, a few breakfast cereals, milk in a small fridge, two pork pies. The shopkeeper sits behind a counter of sweets and chocolate bars, and a low pile of *Padiham Gazettes*. An old man, drawing deeply on a cigarette. Death is in his eyes. Ursula looks right into the heart of him, like a mirror to herself, and sees his whole life, the difficulties, the failures, the longings, and sees they are her own. She gazes at the shelves, the goods sitting there, and they are all dancing. She looks at the floor tiles, and sees they are nothing but her own skirt. Everything is part of her, and she part of them. A happiness fills her, one she hasn't felt for many years. She picks up a drink, wildly orange in colour, its bubbles dancing inside, and she smiles at the shopkeeper. He smiles back, sudden as a baby, smoke rising from his fingers, agreeing with her, nothing matters. Only this, only momentum.

She leaves the shop, sips the drink, and heads towards the Starkie Arms.

Ursula . . .

Jerry is on the other side of the road. He sees the bottle of Lucozade in her hand. The wildness of the hill in her, an impossible openness. She is everything to him. It has only ever been her.

I've been looking everywhere for you . . .

She smiles at him. He takes her hand.

Come . . .

Where are we going?

Not far.

His touch delights her and she squeezes his fingers.

He'll take her to the sea, to the village they went to when they were young, to Fairleigh; where everything had made sense, before everything changed, before India, Oxford, before they became themselves.

They follow the road towards the coast, and Ursula sleeps, curled up on the passenger seat. Jerry drapes his coat over her. They'll walk on the beach again. Last time they'd argued, jumped in and out the sand dunes, whirled like dervishes. He winds through lanes, headlights picking out the hedgerows. The village is a thin ribbon along the sea. He stops outside the Ship Inn and leaves her sleeping. The air is full of peat and salt. A notice in the corner of the window says BED AND BREAKFAST. In the lounge bar, men nurse pints among the brass hangings. As Jerry enters, the barman stops his story and the room falls quiet. He'd like a room, he says. Ursula walks in behind him.

Make that a double, says one of the drinkers.

The landlord hands them a key and they climb a flight of creaky stairs. The room is at the end of a narrow corridor overlooking the road. A ribbed bedspread covers a lumpy bed. Yellow curtains hang short at the windows. The room is hot and dry, the windows double-glazed, the air sucked shut. Jerry opens one and the wind blows through the room.

Something happened . . . she says.

Tell me.

You won't understand. I shut something away.

I don't want you to . . .

I need time, to listen, to understand . . . It's part of me . . .

I know.

I felt it in India. You said I was mad.

I was afraid, Ursula.

Gabe comes into her mind. His rejection is like a blow, and again she feels the grief of it, and its history trailing back through generations, the failure to love a child enough.

Jerry strokes her hair.

Let me be with you, he says. I have to be. I always have.

She hears the need in him, and feels a certain hope. Hope that the chain of failure might be broken, not wholly, or quickly, but somehow made better. She feels it like kindness. Outside the sea glimmers under the moon. It hangs there as it has always done, as though waiting for them, endlessly changing, endlessly still. A cloud passes over it.

A chariot, whispers Jerry.

I love you, she says, looking into his eyes. Her heart opens to him.

They kiss, slowly, without fear, and suddenly they're laughing, in a rush of emotion, falling on to the bed, crashing on to the shore of each other – and, as they do, they touch the moon and stars, and all that exists in the heavens above them. The yellow curtains, the polyester sheets, the two white cups and tiny kettle fly away . . .

This is just the beginning. There will be many. The future is coming. Ursula and Jerry will leave Fairleigh, and drive south. The road will open in front of them like the promise they feel, and, as they drive, they will talk, of everyone and everything, of Jerry's sister's youngest boy refusing to take off his new football shirt even in bed; of his dad's illness and how he's agreed to use his wheelchair along the front at Tynemouth; of how Gabe wants to stay with his father and not come home to Ursula. Everything will seem to them connected: Joyce and Peter, and their plan to sell Eslington Road and move to Northumberland; Mackie in his world of junk; Caitlin and the pain of separation. Their love for each other will make everything seem part of them, and they in turn will be part of it all.

In time, Ursula will return to Pendle. Jerry will go with her, and Gabe too. She will have found a way to reach her son. He will be starting to trust her, and Jerry. They will all walk to the lightning tree together, and the summit beyond. She will tell them how she helped Mrs Littlewood take lavender cake to the sisters in the priory, and how Ganny Mary came for butter as golden as the sun. They'll walk in the kitchen garden where Annie sat with Sister Grace. She will stay for two nights at the retreat centre, alone, in a simple room, and feel struggle and beauty in the silence. And on the day she leaves, she will walk in the grounds, through the ring of oaks, where people say witches danced, to the nuns' graveyard. She will sit by the plain headstones that stand untended in the long grass, and feel humility in the simple numbers and unadorned names engraved on them: Katherine b.1906 d.1978. Uchenna b.1945 d.1992. Grace b.1854 d.1921. She will look out over the ruins of the medieval Abbey spread out like a puzzle in the grass, towards the Celtic standing stone in the distance, and know it has always been like this: people stopping, listening, for the roar of God.

Acknowledgements

Thanks first and foremost to Hamish for his never-ending love and support. Thanks to my sons, Samuel and Louis, for their patience throughout the writing of this book, and for just being themselves. I am grateful to everyone at Faber, especially my wonderful editor, Hannah Griffiths. Huge thanks to Rebecca Carter, oldest friend and literary agent, for her enthusiasm, and invaluable suggestions. Thanks to John Gaynor for his Zen teaching, and insightful comments. Thanks to dear friends Wes Williams and Michele Camarda for their fulsome responses to early drafts. Many thanks to Usman Khan and Francesca Simon for their great advice. Thanks to Spencer for letting me borrow his empty space. Thank you to Jamie James – best reader ever, and greatest encourager. Finally thank you to my mum, Pamela Woof, source of inspiration and love.

Also by Emily Woof

ff

The Whole Wide Beauty

Katherine Freeman has drifted far from the life she had imagined for herself. Now married with a small child and working part-time as a teacher, she has left behind her career as a dancer. Then she meets Stephen, a poet and colleague of her father, and they begin an intense affair, reawakening Katherine's feelings of passion. Yet their love puts everything at risk and as the cost becomes apparent, Katherine must face up to the choices she has made.

'Katherine's search for liberation from sadness and isolation, for joy and authentic human contact, is deeply affirming.' *Guardian*

'Woof writes in simple, spare sentences, but there is poetry too in the way that she reveals the presence of the extraordinary in the everyday . . . A moving and haunting novel.' *Daily Telegraph*

'An immensely readable novel . . . that marks her as a debut novelist of the first order.' *Financial Times*

ff

Faber & Faber – a home for writers

Faber & Faber is one of the great independent publishing houses in London. We were established in 1929 by Geoffrey Faber and our first editor was T. S. Eliot. We are proud to publish prize-winning fiction and non-fiction, as well as an unrivalled list of modern poets and playwrights. Among our list of writers we have five Booker Prize winners and eleven Nobel Laureates, and we continue to seek out the most exciting and innovative writers at work today.

www.faber.co.uk – a home for readers

The Faber website is the place where you can find all the latest news on our writers and events, and browse and buy in the Faber shop. You can also join the free Faber Members programme for discounts, exclusive access to events and our range of hand-bound Collectors' Editions.